The True Memoirs of Charley Blankenship

Books by Benjamin Capps

The True Memoirs of Charley Blankenship
The White Man's Road
The Brothers of Uterica
A Woman of the People
Sam Chance
The Trail to Ogallala
Hanging at Comanche Wells

THE TRUE MEMOIRS

of Charley

Blankenship

A Novel by Benjamin Capps

J. B. LIPPINCOTT COMPANY
Philadelphia & New York

U.S. Library of Congress Cataloging in Publication Data

Capps, Benjamin, birth date
   The true memoirs of Charley Blankenship.

   I. Title.
PZ4.C247Tt [PS3553.A59] 813'.5'4 79-39637
ISBN-0-397-00760-4

To my son, Benjamin Franklin Capps, Jr.

Contents

The Manuscript

THIS TALE, Mr. Charles E. Blankenship's account of ten years in his life, was written in 1909. The paper upon which he wrote was wood pulp, quite cheap, and today brittle; the pages will invariably crack or break upon being lifted carelessly. The problem of transcription has been made still more difficult by the fact that the ink has faded to a dim sepia color, hardly distinct from the hue of the browning paper. The reader may be assured, however, that the present version is as accurate as reasonable care and patience and persistence can make it.

The title, Mr. Blankenship's own, is worth consideration. Apparently he used the word "true" to describe his "memoirs" because he was aware of accounts of cowboy life which seemed to him untrue. "Memoirs" implies material worthy of remembering. In fact, he was describing only about one fourth of his life up until the time of writing; obviously he thought of those years when he worked as a cowhand and wandered around in the West as of particular interest or significance. It is a measure of his modesty that he does not mention owning a ranch in eastern Colorado subsequent to the events of this narrative; it was a successful venture in the 1890s and he still maintained a financial interest in it at the time he wrote his "memoirs," though he had by 1909 taken on the additional task of managing his father's large farm in Missouri.

Three aspects of the young Charley Blankenship's situation and experience seem noteworthy, for they indicate that he had a valid claim to being the typical American cowboy. First, he ran away from a farm on the eastern edge of the Great Plains, which region, from Minnesota to east Texas, provided a large percentage of the skilled labor for western ranching. Second, he worked in a number of the famous old-time ranching areas: along the Powder River in Wyoming, in the Tonto Basin in Arizona, along the Pecos River in New Mexico, and for large ranches in northwest Texas such as the Matador and the XIT. Third, he ends his story not upon some climactic event in his own life but appropriately, though probably unconsciously, at the time of his first return home in 1890, which is the year symbolic of the closing of the American frontier.

I wish to express publicly my appreciation to a granddaughter, Miss Amelia Blankenship of St. Louis, and to the estate of Charles E. Blankenship for permission and cooperation in publishing this unusual story.

BENJAMIN CAPPS

Chapter 1
I See by Your Outfit...

I<small>N</small> M<small>ARCH</small>, 1880,
I turned seventeen and about two months afterwards in the
late spring finished school at Sulphur Junction, Virginia
County, Missouri. At that time I got a bad itch and could
not find the place to scratch. To see what I mean you have
to know a little about my family, especially my two
brothers.

Pa owned a good black-land farm and knew how to work
it. He was built low to the ground and walked with his
hefty arms spread out like a man guiding a Georgia stock.
He came from a line of farmers and was the kind of man
that takes seriously the saying in the good book: He that
spareth the rod hateth his son. Pa showed a lot of affection
for us boys. Ma was not so strict. She liked to feed people
and did not believe it a sin to slip a piece of pie to a growing
boy between meals. Her folks were all in the grocery and
dry goods and hardware business except for one of her
brothers, Uncle Milt, whose trade was supposed to be a
secret around our place. If they were talking about him
and one of us boys came into the room, they would go to
discussing the weather. The fact is that Uncle Milt was a

gambler on the Mississippi River and a disgrace to all his relations. Though Pa never said it, chances are he whipped us so much because he wanted to make sure none of his sons took after Uncle Milt.

My brother Ed was five years older than me. Pete was three years younger. Ed had run away from home and gone out West about four years earlier. He came home for a visit when I was fifteen and he was riding the classiest Appaloosa paint ever seen in Virginia County, with a full-stamped Texas saddle and a pair of nickel-plated spurs. Also, he had a new nickname, "Buck," which he asked me and Pete to call him. All his friends called him that, he said. And money to burn. He brought Ma a twenty-dollar brooch with a turquoise stone set in solid silver, and to me and Pete he gave eight dollars apiece. He peeled that money off of a roll of one-dollar bills big enough to choke a horse.

When Buck started back West again, I and Pete begged him to stay a little longer, but he couldn't. He said he had to go "see the elephant and listen to the hoot owl prowl." We didn't ask what that meant. It was plain that it had a powerful meaning that wasn't supposed to be explained.

We did not see hide nor hair of Buck for the next two years, but by the time I turned seventeen and finished school my memory of him had not dimmed at all. About that time I had a little run-in with Pa.

I wanted to go into the town of Glenville with some friends, and the round trip would take most of three days and two nights. "What did you lose in Glenville?" Pa asked. "Is Sulphur Junction getting too small for your style?"

What can you do with a question like that?

He went on. "Who did you aim to do your chores?"

I'd thought they would all pitch in, but I said, "Pete."

Pa said, "Young man, you're getting too big for your

britches. You and Pete are staying on this farm and working till you're twenty-one years old, and you may as well get used to the idea."

He seemed positive about it, and I was not so stupid as to put any doubt in his mind. The thing that bothered me most was being thrown in the same boat with Pete, who was some shy of fourteen and had not got much more than half his growth, especially when I'd been dreaming about riding the golden western prairies alongside of Buck.

It took me two days to get all my belongings together on the sly and hidden in a sack down in a fence row. Then I waited that night until past nine o'clock, when Pa's snores had become steady and peaceful, and slipped out, picked up my sack, and headed west. After putting some distance behind me, I slept in a ditch four or five hours and the rising sun waked me. Then I walked on.

You don't do such a thing without mulling it over, and my second thoughts were good. For one thing, as soon as I got out West, I'd look up Old Buck. Then, also, I figured I'd been around a good bit; besides Sulphur Junction and Glenville, I'd been to the towns of Blossom and Allen's Cove and Kevin. I told myself that out there in the great West where I was going I would give back as hard a blow as any given to me and would put my wits up beside any I might run into; my ma and pa didn't raise any weaklings or any fools.

I had plenty of money, seven dollars, but was not too pleased with my clothes. I wore a straw hat, bib overalls, and a pair of clodhopper shoes. In my tow sack I had some more overalls, another shirt, a brown sweater, two suits of longhandles and one suit of short drawers, my hunting knife, and a pair of work gloves. I'd forgotten to bring any socks except the ones I had on.

For food I had brought six ears of dry corn, which does not sound like much to eat but beats nothing. I had not wanted to take anything from the kitchen or pantry at home because it would give Pa a chance to say I'd swiped something and ran off. Running away was bad enough. But it did not seem too bad to take six ears of corn. During the first full day of my journey I stopped and built me up a fire and parched the corn the best I could, just enough to make the kernels swell, then shelled it off and had me two pockets full of food. It wasn't bad eating, and the only thing against it was that I didn't have any salt to go with it. That same day I went in a crossroads store and bought three cans of sardines and a loaf of bread and a nickel's worth of salt.

For a week and a half I traveled by shank's mare. Actually, during that time I didn't get homesick. Two serious ideas stayed in the back of my mind or the front of my mind all the time. First, Pa could put somebody on my trail, so I'd be smart to get some distance behind me and to stay off the main-traveled roads and sort of circle around the towns. Second, I had bit off a pretty big chew, as they say, in taking off on my own; it's one thing to be sure you can look out for yourself when it's only a kind of argument, but it's another thing when it's a fact. I felt certain I could make it if I'd keep in mind that there was nobody to fall back on and always try to look ahead and not do anything stupid, like get snake bit or break a leg. One thing that gave me a little trouble during that time was finding a place to sleep. Not that I minded sleeping on the ground. But you don't want to sleep close to somebody's house, where they might sic the dog on you, or by a snake hole, or on an ant bed, or in the road, where some fool buggy driver might run over you. So you need to choose your place in daylight. I would usually try to find me a good spot not far off the road about sundown, then get to sleep, get up two or three hours after midnight, get back on the road, and make tracks west in the darkness.

It seems like a rule of life that when a man needs a job they are scarce as hen's teeth, but if he's not looking for one it will seek him out. I had no idea that I needed a job; therefore a few miles south of Joplin one came to me out of the clear blue sky. I stopped at a spring where a man had camped with two wagons and a sickly wife and a half-dozen kids. He started pumping me for information. Did I know how to drive a team? Where was I going? Was I to be trusted? Had I stolen anything? I gave him as little information as possible.

He said he was going to Texas, but his wife had taken ill. He was trying to employ a good man to drive a wagon. It sounded favorable until he finally told me the wages—board and room. But I took him up on it. Buck could be in Texas as well as anywhere else.

We cut south across Indian Territory on a tedious journey, making fifteen miles a day. My room at night was under a tree with my head on my sack, except for one time it rained and I got to sleep under the wagon. As for the board, two meals a day, you had to be hungry to eat it. I decided that the woman was sickly on account of having to eat her own cooking. She had a bunch of green-tomato preserves put up in quart jars, and we had them every meal for dessert. I sure got burnt out on green-tomato preserves.

They lost the milk cow nearly every day. She would find a patch of grass and get behind; they would send the oldest kid back to get her; the sickly woman would go back to find the kid; finally we would stop the wagons and all go hunting the woman and kid and milk cow. Also, the kids had a bad habit of riding in the wagons a while to rest up, then jumping off to run ahead and out to the side among the trees for all the world like a flock of guinea fowls. I learned to close my eyes when one would start to jump on my wagon, because I hated to see what would happen if he fell under a wheel. But all that did not faze me as much as our infernal slowness. It did not seem we were getting anywhere. We passed through Indian towns with houses just like anybody else's houses, and the redskins looked like a bunch of Missouri farmers. Not a feather in the lot.

When we crossed Red River into Texas I was disappointed to see that the country looked just the same, but the straw that broke the camel's back was when we passed through a town called Sherman and took a road leading southeast. We'd been going away too much south for me, and the east part of it was more than I could stand. That evening I told my employer I needed to go west to look for my relations. He said for me to think it over another week or two, and if I decided I wished to leave my employment, he would release me at that time.

He released me that night. I took my sack as usual and walked out as if looking for a tree to sleep under, but soon as I got out of the firelight I circled and went west. I only went a couple of miles. I didn't want to argue with the man, but I figured as much trouble as he had keeping up with his milk cow he sure couldn't find me two miles away.

At sunup I made tracks west. Now that I didn't need to stay off the main-traveled roads, there weren't any. It was hot, but I felt good and still had plenty of money, over four dollars. I walked a week, living mostly off of crackers and cheese and horehound candy. The towns got smaller and farther apart. My socks wore out; I took them off and threw them away. At a town where there was only one store and three or four plank shacks, I gave two bits for a used army canteen. It was getting mighty dry and hot.

The next night my conscience hit me. I went to bed hungry. I hadn't found a town or seen a living soul all day. I decided to sleep on a big flat rock that was nearly level. The stars didn't look the same as they did in Missouri. Suddenly I thought about Ma. The first thing I remembered about her was the way she used to bake a big, rich dewberry cobbler. I could see her taking it out of the oven, holding it by a pot rag on each side, and setting it on the back of the stove to cool. I could see where a little purple juice had bubbled out on top and see the glaze of melted sugar Ma had sprinkled on the crossed dough strips. I could smell the steamy thing sitting there on the stove. The worst thing about it really was not the hunger. It was that if she had known I was hungry she would have done anything under the sun to get me some dewberry cobbler with thick cream on it, and I'd spent the past month getting hundreds of miles away from her. I couldn't stand to think about Ma, so I thought about Pete, how good-natured he was and how he always grinned when I would tease him. I thought about Pa and how he was not so bad and had probably never whipped me except for the good of my own soul and to keep me from turning out like Uncle Milt. I even thought about that black-land farm and how good it would be to feast my eyes on the back yard and the chicken pen and spring house and toilet and barn. But my mind kept coming back to Ma.

Finally an owl or a mourning dove or something hooted out in the darkness, and an idea came to me that drove away the homesickness. Buck had said he had to go see the elephant and listen to the hoot owl prowl. I got the crazy feeling that I wanted to stand up and yell to the west: "Buck! Are you out there? Hey, Buck! Wait for me!"

Next morning I walked away from the sunrise watching my long shadow. Something began to dawn on me about this country. I'd come into it so gradually that I hadn't noticed the change. Not a tree could be seen, only some scattered cactus and some dusty-green thorny brush that I would later learn was chaparral. The bunches of grass were farther apart. Patches of alkali ground and breaks grew hardly any grass at all. It seemed like you could see forty miles.

About noon I came upon a broad mark across the land that had me stumped for a while. It looked like a shallow riverbed a hundred yards wide, maybe a foot deep, stretching away to the north and south, running like no river ever did before. It came over a rise in one direction, crossed a small gully, breaking down the banks, and disappeared over a rise in the other direction. There was no river gravel in the bed, only dust. And cow droppings. I picked up some of the dust and saw that it was half manure.

I stood there with that dirt on my sweaty hands, and a thrill crawled up my back like cool water. "That's the Chisholm Trail!" I whispered. I'd heard of it away up in Missouri since I was a little kid, the route over which they drove the Texas longhorns to the railroads in Kansas.

My geography was off. In fact I had crossed the Chisholm Trail five or six days before without knowing it and was lucky to have cut the Western Cattle Trail at a place where the lay of the land caused most herds to follow the exact same path. But my confusion was no more than that of most cattle workers of the time, as I would come to know later, for nearly every cowhand who drove cattle out of Texas claimed he was driving on the Chisholm Trail.

Now that I had got into the West, I did not know my next move. The sun burned down hot as a depot stove. It didn't look like it ever rained in this country, and I had maybe three swallows of water in my canteen. My stomach felt like it was stuck to my backbone. I started ambling north alongside that river of dust.

They say the Lord looks out for fools and drunkards. I had not walked an hour before I saw, a mile ahead, a string of trees with green leaves. Could be some water there. I turned up my canteen and drank the last drops. About that time I heard a racket and looked back. A big wagon was coming fast, over on the west side of the trail. It was loaded to the bare bows with a pile of gear, had wooden water barrels hanging out on each side, and had a high box sticking up at the rear. On the spring seat at the front an old man crouched, often flailing at the lines and shouting "Hyah! Hyah!" at the galloping four-mule team. They were really traveling, for such a heavy rig on the rough ground. He seemed to be balled up, resting on his seat, until he would suspect some laziness in the mules; then he would half raise up, as if he were going to spring on their rumps, yell "Hyah! Hyah!" and whack the lines against them.

He passed maybe a hundred yards from where I stood. I raised my hand at him. He looked at me two or three times as if I were a stump, yelled at his team, and rattled on past. It seemed like a steam gristmill passing. I watched him a minute until he veered off toward a clump of trees in the greenery ahead.

About a mile behind the wagon came a band of horses,

trotting along in less of a hurry. There were maybe fifty, mostly scrawny and scraggledy bays, duns, roans, sorrels, paints. The rider with them didn't look a day older than I was. He waved back at me. I guessed that the strange wagon and the band of horses belonged together, and I would learn in the days ahead that a big cow outfit can hardly get along without the two things I'd just seen: a chuck wagon, which may be the only home a cowhand has for months at a time, and a remuda, which is made up of the strings of horses used by the men of the outfit.

I walked north at a good clip, heading for the spot the wagon had seemed to be moving toward. In a quarter of an hour I found it. The wagon was parked under a cottonwood tree, the team still to it. A few feet away a fire blazed. The old man who had driven it had let down a table at the back of the wagon and was hunched over it with his bare elbows jerking up and down. He looked up shortly several times as I walked toward him but did not slacken his work.

He wore a floppy black hat, a white shirt buttoned up tight to his neck, a pair of black trousers, and a pair of suspenders that seemed to cut into his hunched shoulders. His sleeves were pushed up and he had flour on his arms almost to his sharp elbows. His face was red, speckled with white beard stubble. I walked up to him.

"Hello, son," he said. "You live around here?"

"No, sir, I'm just passing through."

"Whereabouts you going?" His eyes darted up every few seconds to look this way and that.

"Actually," I said, "I'm sort of looking for my brother."

"What's his name, son?"

"Buck Blankenship. Sometimes he goes by the name of Ed."

"Never heard of him. This bread ain't going to rise. I can see that. It won't be fit to eat. What's your name, son?"

"Charles Blankenship."

"My name's Mr. Dunlap. I'm in charge of this outfit. That fire's so hot you can't get close enough to do no cooking. I ain't going to get the meat done, I can see that. Buck Blankenship, hey?"

"That's my brother."

"He ain't with this outfit, son."

The water barrel on the near side of the wagon looked cool and inviting because the wood was damp where the water had seeped out between the staves. A drop hung from the spigot.

I ask if I can have a canteen of water.

"Hep yourself," he says. "Don't drip no water around the wagon. One of the worst things you can do is throw water around the wagon and make a hog pen to walk in. I'm in charge of this outfit. I tell them and tell them about the water, but you can't get it through a bunch of cow-hands' thick heads."

While I'm filling my belly and canteen with water, a young man rides up, the one who had driven the horses. Evidently he's left the horses grazing not far away. He's about my age, but I feel like a kid when he says "Hi," because he's dressed like a cowboy, high-top boots, felt hat, spurs, and all.

Mr. Dunlap says, "Hobble out the team, Dub. Hump it! I want you to hep me. We ain't going to get no groceries ready to eat around here tonight. I can see that." Every so often he pushes up his sleeves and gets more flour on his arms. "My sourdough has gone bad on me," he says. "These biscuits won't be fit to eat."

It has come to me that he's looking on the dark side of things. How can he tell they won't have any grub before dark? But I've guessed that coming up from the south is a big herd of cattle, and since Mr. Dunlap is in charge of everything he probably has many worries on his mind. The young man called Dub unharnesses the team and hangs the gear on the front of the wagon, then leads the four mules toward the creek. Mr. Dunlap grabs a long-handle shovel and walks over and begins poking the fire. I notice that he has a bad limp. I'd been wondering why the boss is cooking instead of out telling the cowboys what to do and now I know—he's got a bad leg.

What I want to do is sit down in the shade of the wagon, but I don't have that much gall. I pick up my sack and say, "Thanks for the water, Mr. Dunlap. I guess I better be moving on."

He stops arranging the fire and stares at me for a long two seconds. "Where you going? Ain't no place to go out here! How come you don't want to take supper with us? I guess if we can eat it, you can."

I grin like a fool and say, "I sure appreciate it, Mr. Dunlap."

He snorts and goes back to his dough. He pinches off balls the size of a turkey egg, flops them over a couple of times in a plate of grease, and arranges them in two large Dutch ovens.

"Son," he says, "I'll tell you a few things about trailing cattle. It takes some fellers a lifetime to learn, seems like. You can boil it all down to three rules. First, don't throw out water around the wagon. Don't do things like that. What I mean is use your head. When you need to go to the bushes, where do you go? To the bushes. Second, listen to common sense. If somebody knows more than you do, don't be so high and mighty and smart. Pay a little attention. Then, number three, always keep some dry matches on hand. You might not think that's important, but it is. Why? For the simple reason, everything can be soaking wet, but you can dry it out around the fire, but how can you start a fire with wet matches? You think about that."

I nodded and thought about it and didn't know what to make of it. The only thing that came to me was that if I had not been wearing the straw hat, bib overalls, and clod-hopper shoes, he would not have made the three points with me.

Dub came back and Mr. Dunlap told him to wash his hands. The young man took from the wagon an apple crate, tin washbasin, chunk of lye soap, and a large towel. He filled the basin, set it on the apple crate, and washed his face and hands. I saw that he carried the dirty water several steps from the wagon before he threw it out.

"Put on the big pot," Mr. Dunlap said. "We got to boil up some things. We ain't got time to get the meat done. I see that. If there's anything I hate it's meat that ain't done, especially fat meat. Put in water, Dub. More water. More. More. That pot will crack right in two if you pour cold water in a hot pot. Bank up the coals around it. I'll tell you young fellers something you ought to remember. Most of the sickness in this country comes from eating meat that ain't done. It's unhealthy.

"Cut up some sowbelly and throw in there, Dub. Small chunks. Not too small. This is the skinniest beef I ever saw. Ain't hardly fit to eat. It's going to spoil before we get it used."

He slashed at a quarter of beef with a meat cleaver and began to throw away bones and pieces of gristle. He chunked up about a peck of it and carried it by the double handfuls to plop it into the boiling pot, where Dub was chipping up a half a pound of sowbelly. It was already beginning to smell interesting.

He said, "Dub, get you the long spoon and souse that around a little bit. It's going to stick. I can see that. We won't never get that pot clean. You better open a half gallon of tomaters and throw in there."

The old man began peeling potatoes, quartering them, and plunking them into the pot. He lifted up the cloth which he had spread over the Dutch ovens, peered inside, and said, "Well, I reckon they're going to rise. It's a wonder. My starter has gone bad on me." He moved around surprisingly fast to have a game leg.

He began peeling onions, glancing up quickly now and then in every direction. Finally he said to Dub, "Down yonder on that elm tree is a dead limb you can reach. That tall one with the vines on it. See that dead limb? Take the ax and get it and drag it up here and put it in the possum belly. I don't want no green wood and I don't want no rotten wood. The wood hogs has been through this country and got nearly every stick fit to use. We'll be cooking on cow chips inside of a week. I can see that."

I went with Dub after the wood. He turned out to be a friendly young man. One thing he said, "Old Limpy ain't too bad when you get used to him," struck me as strange. Mr. Dunlap might have his own ways about him, but to call the boss "Old Limpy" did not seem respectful. We got the limb down, drug it back to the wagon, chopped it up, and threw the pieces into the place called the "possum belly," made by tying a big cowhide under the wagon box.

The old man had set the Dutch ovens on the fire and put some coals on top of their lids. He was filling up a coffeepot that held about three gallons. The food had started to smell so good I could just barely stand it.

Around an hour before sunset the herd passed us, more cows than I had seen in all my life put together. They

were big rangy steers with ridiculous horns and every color
and marking, roan and brindle and brockle. They had saggy
backs and knobby knees and their dewlaps swayed as they
plodded north. I counted ten riders around the strung-out
herd. The dust they raised drifted in the other direction
from us, and I thought we were lucky that it would not
settle in the open pot of stew. Of course there was no luck
to it.

At sundown seven of the riders came to the wagon. Two
of them were colored men. They all wore big hats and
dusty clothes and bandanna handkerchiefs around their
necks. They all grinned and said things like, "Limpy, you
got anything good to eat around here?" "Get hot enough
for you today, Dub?" "That smells good." "Keep old
Shorty out of that grub until he washes." "Lord-a-mercy;
it was hot as a two-dollar pistol out there today." It seemed
like every one of them belonged exactly where he was and
knew exactly what he was doing, the way they walked and
stood around and laughed and talked to each other. They
called Mr. Dunlap "Limpy" to his face; every last one of
them threw out his wash water right by the wagon. I was
afraid it would make a mudhole, but the dry ground soaked
it up as fast as it hit. A time or two Mr. Dunlap said,
"Don't throw out no water where we got to walk in it."
They did not seem to hear him. I'd already started wondering about the man when he gave me the three rules for
trailing cattle, which amounted to where to throw out water
and listening to advice and keeping dry matches. Now it
was getting to be plain as the nose on your face that somebody was driving that big herd to market, and it was not
Mr. Dunlap.

I cannot describe the stew. When the cowhands started
dipping it out into tin plates with the long spoon and the

steam from it began floating in the air, you could not have run me off with a bull whip. I tried to be calm and not do anything to draw attention and do the same as everybody else, except for throwing out my wash water farther away. I found the food to be the best I'd ever sunk a tooth in. You could cut those big chunks of beef with a fork. The biscuits were light and crusty and tasted like the smell that comes out of a bakery in town. I saw some of the hands go back for seconds, so I got me another plateful.

Some of them sat on a rolled-up tarpaulin, others on the grass with their legs folded in front of them. They must have heard something about me from Mr. Dunlap or Dub, because one of them asked, "Looking for your brother, are you?"

"Yes, sir."

"What's his name again?"

"Ed Blankenship. They call him Buck."

"What outfit's he supposed to be with?"

"I can't remember," I said.

I wished they would not ask me about it because it didn't leave me much choice but to lie or look like an idiot. My geography might be off a hundred miles one way or another, but when I was forced to get down to cases I knew how big the West is, and Buck could be any place from North Dakota to Texas to Arizona to Oregon. If I admitted that, the next question would be, Then what are you doing wandering around afoot in this particular wilderness with a tow sack on your back? I was feeling uncomfortable enough dressed the way I was without making them think I was simpleminded.

One of them says, "Blankenship. Blankenship. Is he a fat man with red hair?"

"No, sir. About average with kind of brown hair."

"Did he used to work for Blocker?"

"No, sir. I don't believe so. He might have, I guess."

One of the colored cowhands asks, "You say he's sup-posed to be trailing to Dodge City?"

It sounds like a lie that might stand up. I say, "Yes, sir, I think so."

"Was he supposed to be going up early in the year, or late?"

"Sort of in between, I think."

One of the men who looks like the other hands and acts like them but is a little older says, "You don't stand much chance to catch him. Most everything has already gone north. Your best bet is to write him General Delivery at Dodge." That seems to settle it with the others; they stop asking questions. It turns out that the one who has settled it is the only cowhand everyone calls "Mister." His name is Mr. Garrison.

I slept there that night. Give some people an inch and they will take a mile, they say. I'd come up to get a drink of water. Then I ate supper. Then I stayed all night. I slept on the ground with my head on my tow sack and enjoyed hearing the snores of the cowhands around me.

Next morning the place was bustling before good day-light. Men rode up to the wagon and others rode away. A couple of them said to me as they left, "So long, kid. Hope you find your brother." I thought I would hang around until I saw Mr. Garrison, not to say "Thanks" to him, nor "I enjoyed the visit," because that didn't sound right, but maybe "So long, Mr. Garrison; I guess I better be going."

Mr. Dunlap was cooking flapjacks, eight at a time in two frying pans. Dub was harnessing the mules, throwing bed-rolls in the wagon, and washing dishes. Only two or three hands ate at one time. Suddenly Mr. Dunlap said to me, "You're next, son. Where's your plate? These are going to be burnt to a cinder." I grabbed a tin plate off the drop table and he filled it up. He had put a little cornmeal in his batter. The flapjacks were brown and crisp. I covered them up with sorghum and lit in.

Mr. Dunlap said, "Dub, I want you to pack some of that gear down better in the wagon. We'll hit a bump and bounce half of it out one of these days. We ain't got no decent storage space. One of these days it's going to come a big rain and get the rice wet and the beans wet and the apricots wet and we won't have a thing left to eat.

"We got to get some water. I guess the water hole is all trampled up by now. I tell them and tell them I got to have a good clean place to dip water, but you can't tell a bunch of thick-headed cowhands anything."

Dub said, "There's a good pool up above where they watered. Maybe half a mile."

Mr. Dunlap said, "We'll probably have mud three inches thick settle in the bottom of those barrels. I can see that." He carefully wiped out the skillets with a rag. He took a long-handled shovel out of the wagon and began to throw dirt over the fire coals. As he limped around working at it, he said, "I wish you'd look at the handle of this shovel. Look at the grain of that wood, the way it anti-goggles. That handle's going to break right out of this shovel some day. They don't make things the way they used to. I want to tell you young fellers about making things. You can boil it down to three rules. Number one, take pride in your work. What's the use to do anything if you don't take pride in it? Second, listen to common sense. If somebody knows more than you do, don't be so high and mighty and smart. Pay a little attention. Then, number three, do it right the first time and you won't have to do it over. That's where most time is wasted, doing things over, and there ain't no sense to it. Why not do it right in the first place?

"Dub, we got to get out of here. We're running late. Mount up and show me where that pool of water is at."

I thought the least I could do was go down to the water hole with them and help fill up their barrels, which I did. Mr. Dunlap limped back and forth from the water to the wagon, warning us not to dip up any tadpoles or water spiders, while Dub and I filled the barrels. Then Dub rode away on his horse and I, having nothing else to do, walked north behind the chuck wagon.

We passed the herd, which was spread out, grazing. At first I did not mean to walk close to the wagon longer than an hour; then I began to argue with myself about it. I knew I ought to go on about my business and not make a nuisance of myself. On the other hand I had as much right to walk along here as this herd of cattle did, and what could they do to me if they didn't like it? I supposed they could break both of my legs if they were a mind to. Of course, they wouldn't. What they could do that would be worse was laugh at me and ask what in the Sam Hill I thought I was doing. I was like a pup told "Go back! You can't go!" and he looks at you and puts his tail between his legs; he's got to go and got to stay at the same time. It seemed to me that this outfit was going exactly where I wanted to go, and I couldn't stand the idea of losing sight of them. Along toward midday we were away past the herd and the remuda. Mr. Dunlap began to whip up the team and yell "Hyah! Hyah!"

I knew he must be thinking about stopping for dinner. I angled away from the trail and went about a mile out to a hill. I didn't have the gall to show up for another meal, especially since some of the hands had told me good-by hours before. I sat there and watched Mr. Dunlap limping around his parked wagon, watched them fan out the steers and the horse band, watched the hands go to the wagon two or three at a time. Mr. Dunlap had not built a fire. I figured they were having the leftover stew.

That afternoon I kept the wagon in sight. Whenever I saw Mr. Dunlap dart a look at me, I would wave to show that I was not sneaky.

Late in the day I found a limb of wood in a dry wash, a good solid piece, but heavy. I began dragging it, thinking I would catch Mr. Dunlap after he had camped and tell him I happened on it and knew he was short on wood. At first I meant to drag the wood purely out of friendship. It turned out to be a job. I decided I would deserve my supper after all that work. Sweat poured down my skin underneath my clothes. It was just too confound clumsy. I laid down my sack and dragged the limb a ways, then went back after the sack. Finally, I came on a rise and saw the wagon bouncing over a rise a mile ahead. I dropped the limb and let it lay.

Unfortunately I chose a place to spend that night down-wind from the cow camp. I could smell Mr. Dunlap's cooking. It like to have drove me crazy.

Next day I kept them in sight and made up a plan. After they camped for the evening, I would find a piece of wood somewhere and tug it in, even if it took me all night working at it. But in the middle of the afternoon I saw Mr. Garrison loping his horse out toward me. I had no place to hide so I grinned and said, "Hi, Mr. Garrison. I just decided to move on north."

He says, "What are you eating these days, Blankenship?"

Thinking quickly, I say, "I have food in my sack."

"If you want to, you can take chow with us till we get to Doan's."

Like a nut, I say, "Oh, I'm not hungry, Mr. Garrison. I have plenty of food in my sack here."

"Suit yourself," he says and reins away.

"I might come in for supper," I say. "I sure appreciate it, Mr. Garrison."

I caught the wagon as quick as I could, and when Mr. Dunlap whipped up his mules I ran and stayed right behind him. He did not seem surprised when he parked and got down and saw me. "Son," he said, "this heat ain't fit for dumb critters to be out in, much less a human. I tried to tell them you can't drive no cattle this time of year. If they had to work around a cook fire, they'd get a little sense in their head. We won't never make it to Dodge City. I can see that."

It turned out that he had simmered a pot of beans all night the night before, and they only needed warming. But when Dub showed up, Mr. Dunlap said, "Hobble out the team, Dub. Hump it! Then come back and grind some coffee. They're going to be in here on us the first thing we know and we won't have a thing to eat."

Later he was mixing up a batch of cornbread, saying now and then that it wouldn't be fit to eat because the baking powders had caked up and gone bad. He told Dub to put on the round-bottom pot and put water in it. "More water," he said. "More. More. We're going to make some Spotted Pup. You got to have the right amount of water. More. No, that's too much. Take some of that out. Put in a good big pinch of salt before you forget it. There's some damned fools that don't know you've got to have salt in sweet things. Get you a big scoop of brown sugar out of that round tin on the right and throw it in the water. Souse it around till it dissolves. More sugar. Heap it up.

"The hardest thing in the world to cook is rice. You

can't make Spotted Pup at all unless you know how to cook rice. It will gob up on you if you don't watch out. This cornbread won't be fit to eat. I can see that.

"Dub, that's boiling good. Now I'm going to put in the rice while you souse it around. But listen first. Don't quit sousing till I say so. I'll put in rice till it's just right. Then in a minute I'll put in the raisins. When I say 'jerk it!' you be ready and get it out of that fire. You let that stuff gob up on you and it's just too bad."

He throws in handful after handful of rice while Dub stirs the pot with the long spoon. The way Mr. Dunlap looks in the pot you would think he had the grains counted and it will be spoiled if he throws in one too many. In a few minutes he tosses in raisins, carefully separating them. Then, in one of the few times I ever saw him doing nothing, he stands with his hunched shoulders sticking up and his sharp elbows out to the side, looking, waiting. "Be ready, boys," he says. "Souse it, Dub! Have your rag ready and your hook. Don't waste no time."

I'm on my toes, ready to help. It's not clear what will happen if we don't jerk the pot off fast enough, whether something would explode or what; it will just be too bad.

He gets tense. Then he yells, "Jerk it! Hurry! Get it out! Get it clean away from that fire. Don't mess around and turn it over. Watch it! Dub, get you the flat lid and put over there. Let it set and stew in its own juice a while. It won't be fit to eat. I can see that."

All we had for supper was red beans with bacon in it, cornbread, sliced onions, chowchow out of a jar, Spotted Pup, and coffee. I was embarrassed going back for the third helping.

In two days we got to Doan's Store, a picket house with a roof of grass and mud, sitting in a sea of sand and cow

tracks. I had been walking beside the wagon, sometimes
throwing wood in the possum belly and helping Mr. Dunlap and Dub in any small way I could. I went with Mr.
Dunlap to the store while the herd grazed a couple of miles
to the south. We bought a lot of things like flour in cloth
sacks, dried fruit, and coffee berries in tins. Mr. Doan gave
Mr. Dunlap the hindquarter of a deer and two wild turkeys
shot that morning.

In my mind was Mr. Garrison's words: You can take
chow with us till we get to Doan's. I asked Mr. Doan if
he had some kind of food that was not too heavy to
carry and would keep. He produced some packages of
hardtack wrapped in paper. It seemed like it might be just
what I needed to get by on, but Mr. Dunlap said, "Is that
army stuff?"

Mr. Doan said, "Yes, it's guaranteed army stuff. It will
keep forever."

Mr. Dunlap said, "Son, you don't want nothing like that.
That is left over from the War for Southern Independence.
What do you want with that kind of doin's? How come
you can't eat what the rest of us eat?"

I didn't know what to do. The stuff would probably keep
a person alive while he followed a trail herd, even if it
was fifteen years old, and this was my chance to get some
food in my sack. Plainly Mr. Dunlap was ready for me to
go on as I had been doing, but Mr. Garrison had said: till
we get to Doan's.

My problem got harder on account of a gal who stood
over behind a pickle barrel watching me. The front of this
picket house had stiff buffalo hides to cover the door and
windows; they were folded back to give a dim light inside. I could not see the gal clearly, but she had long black
curly hair and brown eyes and was probably exactly my

age. I couldn't stare at her, but I sure couldn't pay no attention to her. With those brown eyes looking at me I could feel every straw in my straw hat, every thread in my bib overalls, every place my clodhopper shoes touched my bare feet. A gal like that doesn't guess what she does to you. It was bad enough at best and I sure didn't want her to think I lived on hardtack, so I didn't buy any.

We crossed the broad sandy bottoms of Red River and pulled up onto higher ground. I didn't know whether we were in Texas or Indian Territory. The main thing in my mind was what does Mr. Garrison think I'm doing around here, so I tried not to get right straight in front of him. I knew he saw me, but there was no point in making him admit he saw me. Many times I went to the other side of the wagon with my loaded plate and sat down on the grass, leaning against a wagon wheel.

Somewhere in the middle of the Territory three soldiers, one with sergeant's stripes, rode into our night camp. The sergeant talked to Mr. Garrison, then to the hand called "Shorty." I believe he gave a letter to Shorty. After the soldiers left, Mr. Garrison and Shorty talked by themselves a while. I heard Mr. Garrison say, "You better go back and give yourself up. They'll say you ran off. The quicker you show up, the better."

"I hate to leave you shorthanded," Shorty said.

"We'll make do," Mr. Garrison said.

I never did find out what the trouble was, but Mr. Garrison paid him off in cash, and Shorty rode away south that night.

The next morning I went with Dub to catch the mules. Mr. Garrison rode from the place where the herd was bedded down out toward us. I thought I was going to catch it at last.

He asks me, "Blankenship, can you ride a horse?"

"Yes, sir."

"Were you raised on a farm?"

"Yes, sir."

"Do you think you could wrangle the horses and give Limpy a hand?"

"Yes, sir. I'm sure I could."

"The pay is a dollar a day," he says, "if you want to give it a whirl. Dub, you'll ride on the drag and take Shorty's night guard."

I was tickled enough to throw my hat in the air and yell, but it did not seem the right thing for a trail driver like me to do. Dub also was pleased as punch. He celebrated his promotion that day at dinner by washing his hands and throwing out the water right by the wagon.

I rode a lazy gray horse with a saddle of Mr. Dunlap's that he had been carrying in the wagon. The leather had turned nearly black. Wrangling the horses was not hard. Helping Mr. Dunlap kept me hopping twenty hours a day. Out on those broad plains where the cows cut the wood, as they say, I had to carry a tow sack on my saddle and when I found a place where the chips grew thickly, where a herd had bedded months before, let the remuda drift while I gathered a load. When I took the sack to the wagon and dumped it in the possum belly, Mr. Dunlap would say, "That stuff won't burn. I don't know how we'll ever get any cooking done. The wood hogs has stripped this country clean from one end to the other. Son, shake that back wheel a little and see if it's got any play on the axle. I thought I heard it squeaking. That wheel will come off one of these days and fall down and this wagon will break all to pieces. We won't never get to Dodge City. I can see that."

At a place called Camp Supply on the North Canadian

River we pulled out west of the trail and laid over a day. The hands stretched up a tarp for shade and several of them lolled under it, catching up on sleep. Mr. Dunlap saw that I had plenty to do, including boiling all the dirty towels and greasy cooking rags in a pot of soapy water. The hands called it "rag soup" and kept telling Mr. Dunlap they wanted to add some underclothes and socks. He says, "Take your filthy underriggings down to the river. I ain't got time to put up with your horseplay."

Dub is resting in the shade with four or five of them, and one says, "Boys, we ought to give Dub a bath, don't you think? He's pretty rank. Let's carry him down and throw him in the river." Before you can blink an eye, four of them grab him, one on each arm and leg, and go carrying him down the hill, bumping him a little on the ground now and then. Dub is laughing and shouting, "Hey! Let me loose! Hey! Hey!"

In a minute they come back and one of them says, "While we're cleaning up this crew we better get Blankenship. He sure needs a bath."

I say, "I'm willing to go! I'll go."

One of them says, "It's too late to go on your own, boy. We're going to take you down there and scour you good with sand. Your nasty days are over."

I drop my clothes-punching stick and back away. They start surrounding me. Mr. Dunlap swings around from the back side of the wagon with the long-handled shovel raised over his head. He says, "You put a hand on that boy and I'm going to lay you low! I ain't fooling!"

One of them says, "We ought to get Limpy. He's the one we ought to get."

"You try it," Mr. Dunlap says. "You'll get a knot on your head!"

They back off, laughing. Two of them take a rifle and go up the river hunting, and the others go back to sleep in the shade.

I got a chance to take a short bath in the river late that afternoon and wash out my extra clothes. I thought about it that night laying there looking up at the sky. It came to me that people know things they don't understand. There was sort of two bunches of men here. One was Mr. Garrison's and one Mr. Dunlap's. Mr. Dunlap had already lost Dub and not a thing to be done about it. But when he warned them not to put a hand on me, they knew he had a right to, and they had to back off.

I'd envied Dub before on account of his clothes, but never as much as that night. In fact, I'd have given every cent I had, over four dollars, to have had those cowhands carry me down and throw me in the river. You can't please some people; there I had a steady job making big money, but I wanted to be thrown in the river.

In southern Kansas we bought a half-Jersey calf and butchered it. The steers in the herd were too big and too near market to eat. Mr. Dunlap started making son-of-a-bitch stew. You have got to get the right parts, the marrow gut, liver, kidneys, and such, cut them up right, and cook them right. It is almost a sin how good it tastes.

I had guessed we were coming toward the end of the trail, because Mr. Dunlap gave me more advice daily about how to get along in Dodge City. First, stay away from gamblers and loose women. There is nothing but grief in them and they look on every man from Texas as a sucker. Number two, listen to common sense. If somebody knows more than you do, don't be so high and mighty and smart. Pay a little attention. Third, don't drink because it will get you in trouble sooner or later.

"Son," he said to me, "son-of-a-bitch stew is about the richest food to eat there is, but some thick-headed cowboys turn their nose up at it. We better slice up some steak. It probably won't none of it be fit to eat. These biscuits are going to stick in the pan."

All we had to eat that night was son-of-a-bitch stew, fresh steak smothered with onions, lima beans, peach jam, light biscuits, and coffee.

We forded the Arkansas River in sight of Dodge City, just upstream. We did not take the herd to the stockyards but delivered them to a buyer out on Sawlog Creek. Mr. Garrison sold remuda and all, even the lazy gray I'd been riding. Everybody got paid off, though I believe most of the men meant to go back south with Mr. Garrison. I drew nineteen dollars.

The last I saw of Mr. Dunlap was when I helped him harness and hook up to the wagon. He climbed to the spring seat and sat there with his shoulders hunched up and his sharp elbows sticking out. "Son," he said, "I've tried to learn you a few things and I hope you keep it in mind, because I've taken a liking to you. I'll tell you one thing. That red mule will go lame one of these days. Then I won't have no team. We won't never get this rig back to Texas. I can see that." He got them moving and headed down toward the bridge on the Arkansas River in the edge of town. I believe he meant to camp beyond the river, and several of the men would head south together.

Reader, that old man's name is Limpy Dunlap. If you ever run into him don't believe a word he says, but if you get a chance to eat at his wagon don't miss it. About his lying, when he said he was in charge of the outfit, remember the saying: an army travels on its stomach. About the hands not paying attention to what he said, when it was chow time and he beat on an iron pot with the long spoon you never saw anybody pay closer attention to anything. The fact is that I hardly remember Mr. Garrison and can only think of one real fine thing to say about him. He had sense enough to put up with Limpy Dunlap.

I walked into the big city of Dodge. My tow sack I had rolled up and tied with a cord so I could carry it under my arm instead of over my back. It looked better. But my hick clothes had not changed a whit.

It was the biggest town I'd ever seen and the busiest. The towns I'd known in southern Missouri were quiet and had trees growing in them; about the loudest sound you'd ever hear would be a blacksmith pounding a piece of iron; you might see a merchant sitting in a wickerwork chair on the porch of his store, snoozing or whittling on a stick. Here in Dodge no merchant was whittling.

The wide main street had the Santa Fe railroad tracks running down the middle; then there were side streets and cross streets. People were going every which way on foot and on horseback, in buggies and wagons. Seemed like they all had some place to go. As I walked along looking at the sights, I could hear a dozen different noises. Down in the pens cows were bawling, high and low, long mournful bawls and short ones. I could hear men sawing and hammering down a side street where a pile of new lumber was stacked. Music of pianos and fiddles and horns came out of some of the doors. You never saw the like of freight wagons backed up to the fronts of buildings or the sides or rears. One came down the main street heavy loaded and pulled by eight fat dun steers. One wheel was screeching from lack of grease. The driver walked beside the team, cussing a blue streak, but you couldn't hardly make out his words. Every dozen steps he would raise up a long whip and whack it over the back of the oxen with a crack like a pistol going off.

I saw three men unloading heavy barrels out of a railroad freight car, trying to ease them down a plank ramp, yelling to each other, "Watch it! Catch it! Have you got it? Careful! Look out!"

It seemed like they had stores where you could buy nearly anything from hardware and groceries to ammunition and fine wines. Some of the buildings were large two-story hotels, painted white, some just pine shacks. The places like the Comique, the Green Front, the Western, the Lady Gay had swinging doors.

It was exciting to me just to be in that town. I didn't see anybody dressed like I was. I did see a Chinaman trotting along with a tow sack over his shoulder. I saw three soldiers coming down the boardwalk arm in arm; they had been drinking. I saw two Mexicans riding by on classy horses and dressed in fancy clothes. You could see a few women here and there, holding up their skirts slightly to stay out of the dust. But plainly more than half the people in town were cattle people, a few rich and dignified, evidently in Dodge on business deals, the others cowhands, bent on fun, laughing, calling to each other in loud voices, going in and out of the swinging doors.

In the eastern edge of town stood a building with a neat front and this lettering on the window: N. L. Pebbles, Undertaker, Complete Arrangements. What caught my eye was a cardboard sign with crude writing tacked on the door: Good Horse And Saddle For Sale. I was not especially hopeful but had a hankering to talk to somebody. Here was a good excuse.

I pull on the door and it rings a bell as I open it. Through the partition comes a tall, pale man, who eyes me a while, then says, "Yes?"

The place has a strong medicine smell about it. The man looks so serious that I "inquire" instead of "asking." I say, "I am here to inquire about the horse and saddle which are for sale."

He says, "The horse is twenty dollars. The saddle is forty dollars. If you wish to view these items, please step around to the rear."

I don't like the idea of spending most of my twenty-three dollars on a horse, but I ask, "Does a bridle go with the horse?"

"The bridle is two dollars," he says. He's measuring me up and down with his eyes till it makes chills go up my spine. Then he says, "I have some good clothing that will fit you exactly. I'm letting it go for half price."

I'm insulted and interested and don't know what to say.

"Please be seated," he says.

In a minute he comes from the rear with an armload of clothing, topped off by a big gray felt hat. "This is very high-class clothing," he says. "How much money do you have?"

That's a little too blunt for me and starts my Missouri brain going. I say to myself that I was not born yesterday, but as I look at the stuff I get more and more interested. The Justin boots only need polishing to be like new. The hat is a good one made by John B. Stetson. The blue denim pants and jacket, made by Levi's, only need washing. I say, "I might be able to raise fifteen dollars."

He says, "The boots alone are worth fifty. I might consider letting them go for half price. You see, there is money against this clothing, which must be realized. You are very lucky that it fits you exactly."

I figure that I might be lucky, but he's not. A horse and saddle will fit nearly anybody; clothes won't. He had not even put the clothes on his sign. The Stetson is slightly large.

He says, "You have to put a little paper inside the sweatband. That's the way they buy these hats, slightly large, then insert paper. Any type of paper."

I take off my right shoe. His pale face seems to show pain as he looks at my bare dirty foot. When I pick up the right boot he says, "Wait! Wait!"

In a minute he brings from the rear a box of powder, which he sprinkles over every inch of my foot. The boot slips on. It feels good. I measure the Levi's against myself and they seem right. I say, "I like to buy things new and break them in myself, so they will fit."

"I will sacrifice them all for forty dollars," he says.

I say, "I'm sorry, sir. Fifteen would be the highest I could go."

My dirty foot has evidently shocked him out of all his trading powers. "Sixteen," he says.

I buy them on the spot.

I go down in the river bottoms, get behind a clump of willows, and put on my new clothes. The only thing I can see wrong with them is two small holes in the jacket, one in the front and one in the back. I wrap the denim jacket around my tow-sack bundle, so it will look better. I'm feeling so good about my new outfit that I leave the straw hat and bib overalls and clodhopper shoes right there in the weeds behind the willows; they're nearly worn out anyway.

Then I march up Front Street in Dodge City, looking as good as most of the men in town and better than some.

Chapter 2
A Dear Teacher

I HUNG AROUND TOWN about five days, mostly looking at the outside of the stores, saloons, gambling dens, hotels, cathouses. It was costing me four bits a night for a cot in the hallway of a crowded rooming house, and I could see my money supply sinking fast. Once a day I went into the Dixie Lee Restaurant to eat. A few times I asked about my brother, but no one had heard of him.

At a livery stable I told the man that I was looking for work. He knew about a job as a swamper at a dance hall; then, when I didn't act too eager, he said to come around tomorrow and he thought a cattle buyer named Wright would consider hiring me. I met Mr. Wright there the next day and told him that I was a cowhand looking for work.

"Whereabouts you from?" he asked.

"Texas," I said. "I came up here with a trail herd." I was hoping he didn't go into the matter too far, because I didn't have a long story made up and did not believe in lying anyway if I could get by on the truth.

"You got a horse and gear?" he asked.

I'd thought of that question. "No, sir. I owed a debt and had to let my horse and saddle go." I'd owed the saddle to Limpy Dunlap and the horse to Mr. Garrison. For a minute it seemed like I could read Mr. Wright's mind and he was thinking, Yes, you gambled away your wages and sold your horse and saddle and gambled that away.

He asked, "From Texas, are you?"

"Yes, sir."

"I've got two or three extra horses out there, but I'd have to advance you the money for a saddle and take it out of your wages."

"That would be all right," I said.

The livery stable man had an old saddle with a broken girt, which we bought for ten dollars. Mr. Wright also bought a new bridle and a new girt uptown and marked them against my wages. That afternoon we drove in his buggy eighteen miles north to Buckner Creek, where he had a cow camp and nine-hundred-some-odd steers, which for reasons of his own he was not ready to ship. Evidently he stayed in Dodge City and only came out to camp once a week. He had four men already working for him watching the cattle. They lived in a big tent.

There on the hot grassy hills in the middle of western Kansas I began to try to pass for a cowboy. My scheme was to keep my eyes open and my mouth shut and grin a lot.

The main job was to keep the herd spread out and grazing within two or three miles of camp and keep outside cattle driven away. Wright's stuff had a WJ brand on the left hip. A few of the steers would get frisky and run now and then on account of heel flies; you had to keep an eye on them. If the whole bunch was grazing slowly toward the water hole or toward camp it was all right to find a shade tree and dismount and rest, only shade trees were about as scarce as hen's teeth on the ridges and hills where you could see what was going on.

We guarded in pairs and rotated from days to nights each week. The day men tried to stay on opposite sides of the herd, but the night men rode together. The spare men watched the horses or toted water and wood or patched the tent or cooked, such as our cooking was, or tried to catch up on sleep.

Jake, a big rawboned fellow, was not the boss but he was a little older than the others, and we usually followed his ideas. He seemed to know that I was green as a gourd, but he had a live-and-let-live way about him. It was an advantage to me that I had grown up on a farm and had been around work stock and saddle horses and a few cows; still, I had plenty to learn. One good thing, there was plenty of time to watch how cows act in a big herd. It didn't take me long to see that some of the critters are leaders, some followers, some loners; if a dozen of them head off in a direction you don't want them to go, the problem of turning them back may be taken care of just by turning back one or two and the others will come back by themselves.

Blowflies were bad. Mr. Wright always told us to be on the lookout for screwworms, though there was not much reason for the steers to get any kind of wounds. We found a case about a month after I hit camp. Jake and I were on nights. One of the day men came in and rousted us out in the middle of the afternoon. We saddled up and rode to the herd. A lanky spotted steer had a dark wound in his flank and fresh blood on his leg below it. He had probably run against a broken limb or got a horn in him. We cut him out. He was so contrary that it was all we could do to drive him. We hazed him down into a flat where a grove of cottonwoods grew.

There I learned what they had meant when they said that Jake's and another horse were roping horses. The only thing I'd ever roped was a Jersey cow and a milk-pen calf and a donkey our neighbors used to have when I was a kid. Jake and the other fellow also rode roping rigs with a back girt to keep the saddle from kicking up. They unlimbered their lariat ropes, trailing big loops behind them almost to the ground. On the first throw they put them on the big scared booger, one on his neck and one on his horns, and those horses brought him to a plunging, jerky halt in the edge of the trees.

They dismounted and let the horses hold him. He was choking himself, moving back and forth, head down, tongue out. One of the men got him to step into a loop with his back feet. We rushed it tight around a tree trunk, heaving and taking up slack, stretching him out. A pull on his tail laid him on his right side. He was as unhappy as a sore-footed bear, about a thousand pounds of horn and hide and sinew and muscle. The wound had not helped his disposition and now, whatever was happening to him, he didn't go along. He breathed hoarsely and rolled his big white eyeballs. Suddenly he hunched up. The half-inch rope on his feet said "whack!" Its frayed hemp ends sprang back toward the tree and the steer. Up he came.

The men laughed. A lariat rope with a knot in it is no good. Of course it belonged to Mr. Wright, but I think they would have laughed anyway. That's something strange about cowhands. They do their share of cussing and griping, but they laugh more than their share. Reader, later on I saw a cowhand get his feet frozen so bad he lost three toes, and it was so funny he could not mention it without laughing.

When the steer found he was still held by the ropes on his head, he quit sashaying around and sulled like a possum. We tossed a rope under his belly, brought it up in a loop on his legs, and jerked him down again. We put a couple of half hitches on his legs and went back around the tree, but one of the hands held the rope instead of tying it, so the steer wouldn't have anything solid to pull against. He quit fighting and only lay there with his nose in the dirt, moaning.

Jake cut a tree branch and whittled out a small flat stick. He dug a half a cupful of screwworms out of the hole in the critter's hide. He probed down into the live meat, flipping out the small wiggling white grubs. Then he sent me to get the can of creosote in his saddlebags and poured some in the hole, swabbing it around, even covering up all the blood in the hair down on the steer's hind leg. The acrid smell of creosote covered up the stink of the wound.

Two of us sat on the steer's head while we took the ropes off over his horns. When he backed away it came to me that here was a thing I knew about cattle from growing up on a farm: they get up back end first. It's a good idea to take your ropes off front end first if you ever want to see them again. The old boy kicked his back legs free, staggered up, and took off for the herd running with his head high, looking to be sure he didn't get into any more trouble.

In the weeks following that, I used to practice roping on the sly out of sight of the others. I'd chase out after one of those big steers, kick my horse up to about fifteen feet of him, unlimber my rope and throw out a small loop, trying to catch one horn, then dally my rope fast around the saddle horn. Sometimes I'd make a good throw and jerk the critter good before the rope came off. But I never did get unlucky and really miss big, by which I mean catch two horns or a horn and a nose. If I'd done that, good-by rope, because I couldn't have got it off by myself. Probably my horse thought I was the sorriest roper he'd ever seen, not knowing the crazy things a young man will do trying to learn to be a cowhand.

Jake and the rest of us doctored three or four more steers that fall before the weather cooled enough to stop the blowflies. The heel flies let up too.

One day I was putting more paper in the sweatband of my hat and noticed a thing I had not seen before. Printed in ink on the back of the leather it said: Property of Duke Green. I scratched it out as well as I could with a pencil, then got to thinking. The fellow did not need his nickname any more, and it had a good sound to it. When I found Buck we would probably run together a lot. People would say: There goes those Blankenship boys, Buck and Duke.

In November I borrowed some paper and an envelope and wrote a letter to Ma and Pa. It was hard to figure out exactly what Pa might do if he knew where I was, so I said I was passing through Dodge City, Kansas, and thought I would drop them a line before I continued on my travels. I told them I was feeling very well and working in the cattle trade. For the sake of Ma, I said that I'd been lucky enough to find good people everywhere I went. I mentioned searching for Buck. For the sake of Pete, I mentioned that I had a new nickname—Duke. Mr. Wright mailed the letter for me.

When winter hits in western Kansas, you know it. We'd been having chilly nights and we staked down the flaps on the tent. But one day it seemed like the North Pole ice fields blew right in on top of us. The wind was so hard that the sleet and snow did not fall out of the sky but bounced along the ground going south. I put on every stitch of clothes I had, including two pairs of longhandles and two pairs of pants, and still got cold. I wrapped a wool blanket around me the first day the blizzard hit. The bony black horse, Cricket, that I usually rode, didn't know me bundled up that way and wouldn't hardly let me mount up.

When Mr. Wright came out I asked him to buy me a coat like Jake's, which was good canvas and a belt and heavy sheepskin lining. He did so a week later and marked it up in the books. I was away ahead in the books but had no need for any money. We played Whist and Old Maid in camp but did not gamble.

During a clear warm spell late in January we drove the herd to the stockyards in Dodge with the help of four more hands Mr. Wright had borrowed for the day from another owner. My job with him was over. I'd ridden Cricket that day and when he started to settle up with me down at the livery stable, he said he was going to sell the horse for eighteen dollars. That's what he had paid a year ago, and the horse was worth every cent of it. I bought me a horse. He showed me the books, every cent I'd earned and every cent I'd spent. I had one hundred and one dollars due me, which he paid spot cash. He said he appreciated my good work; evidently the other hands had not told him a thing about my ignorance.

Jake and I went uptown and got us a hot bath and a haircut. I also bought me a new checkered wool shirt. Jake was going to ride east on the cattle train with Mr. Wright, but he had a while to fool around. Dodge did not look the same. It had fewer cowboys this time of year, but plenty of bullwhackers and teamsters and soldiers from the fort. Also, it looked different to me because I had cowhand experience and money in my pocket.

Now, to get along as a cowhand you need to know a lot of things that have nothing to do with cows. I didn't know this at the time, but I was fixing to find out. I'd been getting along by keeping my eyes open and my mouth shut and grinning. Of course, I hadn't tried my system on any city slickers. They say that experience is a dear teacher, but a fool will learn from no other. Reader, I don't think you've even got to be a fool, though it helps.

I and Jake started looking for a place to have a drink. Jake was choosey but finally led me into a joint called the Blue Palace down on the south side. The bar and the tables were made of plain lumber, painted blue, the same color as the metal shades on the lamps that swung from the ceiling. We took our drinks to a table against the back wall.

"I like a place with class," Jake says, "but not too classy. Who pays for all that polished stuff and mirrors and paintings up yonder at the Long Branch? You and me do if we go in there. On the other hand if you go into one of these low-class dives the glasses are dirty and you may get rolled."

We talk about it and he says he's willing to pay for a little class on the one hand or to be cheated a little on the other hand, but neither one should be run into the ground. I expect to hang around the town a couple of days on my own and, not wanting to be taken, think I should get any gems of advice he can give. Forewarned is forearmed, they say. I ask him, "You've been around quite a few wild cow towns, haven't you?"

"More than my share, Charley."

"How many dishonest people do you reckon are in this town?"

"It ain't that simple. How many people in this town do you reckon are in cattle buying and shipping and freighting business and such?"

"I don't know. Maybe a quarter of the whole bunch."

"Well, Charley, the other three quarters are after your

money. If you've got twenty dollars they want it. If you've got three hundred they want it. If you go out of this town with money in your pocket they slipped up somewhere."

"Come on, Jake. You trying to tell me a man can't get out of this town with money in his pocket?"

"Never said that. You can go out that door right now, go up the street, get your stuff at the livery stable, and ride right off."

"That's what I thought. And my money right in my pocket."

"You *can*, Charley. That's what makes it sad. A man *can* do it. But you ain't going out that door right now, are you? You're setting here with me drinking good bourbon. If you drink a dollar's worth, you won't know what's good and what's not. Then they'll serve you moonshine cut with water and colored with tobacco juice. Then you'll give them a ten, and they'll give you change for a one."

"I might just start raising hell about that time."

"Well, if you've got two friends with you and they saw the ten, then the man will say, 'I guess maybe that was a ten; excuse me.' But if you're alone he'll say, 'You never give me no ten; you must have lost it some place else.' About the time you start raising hell a big ugly bastard with a star is there. You look up and there he stands frowning at you and he says, 'Is this cowboy trying to cause trouble?' "

"Jake," I say, "I don't dispute your word. It could happen if a man don't keep his wits about him, but if this whole town was as crooked as you say the cattle people wouldn't come here at all."

He buys a bottle, a quart about half full, and brings it and sets it on the table. "You don't get me," he says. "When you say 'dishonest' and 'crooked' I say it ain't that simple. Charley, they don't jump you on Front Street and grab your money and run. The fact is, most of the time you've got to agree to it. See?"

"Agree to what?"

"Agree to them taking you."

I know he hasn't drunk enough to be silly, only enough to state things in his own way and explain later.

"Give you a case," he says. "One of these B-gals says, 'How about buying a lady a drink?' You're a gentleman, see? You buy her drinks all night and she stays sober as a judge. You're paying two bits a whack for weak tea. Do you agree to it? Why should the lady drink whiskey all night if it suits her to drink weak tea? Right?

"Give you another case. Keno. Roulette. Poker. There are straight games and crooked games. You can't tell which is which, but say it's on the up and up. You come back and come back to that straight game and bring every cent you earn. Will you win in the long run? No. They are not running that straight game for their health or because they get a kick out of entertaining cowboys."

"But," I tell him, "you do have a chance."

"See?" he says. "There you are. You agree to it."

I was of two minds about it. For one thing, I figured Jake must have learned his lessons the hard way; it didn't sound like something he'd learned from thinking or from being told. Also, as far as agreeing to let somebody take your hard-earned money, I figured the thing to do was to look at yourself every so often, drunk or sober, and remember to keep your wits about you.

The hands on the clock move fast when you drink and talk. The clock behind the bar said it was time for Jake to get back to the stockyards. I had intended to go with him, but he said that he had already paid for the bottle, in which a couple of drinks remained, and I should drink it to get our money's worth. We told each other that it had been good working together, that we would meet again sometime, and not to take any wooden nickels. The last thing he said was this: "You drink those two drinks and walk straight out of here." He left.

I felt good. Only a half-dozen men were scattered around the bar and room. Jake had not been gone two minutes when a woman came up to me. "You need a clean glass or some ice?" she asks.

"No, thanks."

She smiles real big and asks, "How about buying a gal a drink?"

I notice that she says "gal" instead of "lady," and it sounds more friendly than the way Jake said it. A thought strikes me to get up and run for the door, but, as Jake said, they don't jump you and grab your money and run. You've got to agree to it. My shrewd brain is running and I figure she can drink one of the drinks in the bottle and I can drink one and I'll be better off than if I drink both myself. I say, "Sure," and grin back at her.

Right away my bum thinking shows up, because she turns toward the bar and yells for a Tom and Jerry. She brings the drink and sits down. Her name is Lillian. She has real blond hair and black eyebrows and something on the skin around her eyes to make it dark. I think about the warning in the Good Book not to let a strange woman take thee in with her eyelids. She has rouge on her face, and from the little wrinkles at the outside of her eyes when she smiles I figure she's on the wrong side of thirty. But what impresses me most is how easy to talk to and ordinary and friendly she is. She's from Ohio.

We talk about the cow business and what a busy town Dodge is, always something going on, and how cold it gets out on the prairie when a norther hits. She has another Tom and Jerry. We talk about how it's colder in Ohio but doesn't seem so raw on account of the wind and how blue is her favorite color and the Blue Palace is quite a classy place, also about her ma and pa and brothers and sisters back home and how she would love to see them. She says that she has never happened to meet my brother Buck Blankenship.

I see that her drink is low and my bottle's gone and suddenly I say to myself, Charles Elijah Blankenship, your mind is getting foggy and you have been walking on thin ice. I look at the clock and tell her I've got to go take care of some business.

The man at the bar says the Tom and Jerrys come to fifty cents. I give him exactly fifty cents. Lillian says, "It was real nice talking to you, Charley. Please come back some time."

No sooner did I get out the door than I felt ashamed of myself. Maybe she was paid to be friendly, but you can't hardly pay anybody to be so simple and easy. She had really liked me. She really had. And she was not bad looking when you got to talking to her. It's getting bad when you have such a suspicious mind that you can't even make friends without holding your hand on your pocketbook.

I walked the streets, had a cup of coffee at the Dixie Lee Restaurant, walked the streets, went back and had their Special Plate Dinner, walked the streets. It got dark. The town was lit up from one end to the other. You could hear a lot of music and laughter. The weather was not cold. I thought about sleeping at the stable where Cricket was, then about sleeping at a place which offered separate cots with clean sheets for twenty-five cents. My money, nearly a hundred dollars, seemed to be burning a hole in my pocket, and once I thought about taking it a mile out on the prairie and hiding it under a rock or in some grass. Then I thought, What if it snowed and I couldn't find where I hid it? What I really wanted was some way to waste two or three dollars having a hot time without throwing my whole wad in danger. I went back to the Dixie Lee Restaurant and drank a cup of coffee and thought about it.

I had a hot time, all right. That was the night the town caught on fire. I was walking along sometime past midnight and saw people running this way and that, most of them going the same direction. Actually, I thought a big fight had started somewhere.

When I get there, a two-story building that looks like a hotel is burning. Flames lick out of three top windows. On one side of it is a blacksmith shop and on the other a large store, which according to its sign sells provisions, supplies, equipment, hardware, and general merchandise. People yell and run in and out of the doors. A heavy man in a nightgown is handing out buckets. I take one. We run, carrying water from a horse trough about a block away and also from some wooden barrels that line the board-walk. Several men shout orders around the fire. At first they grab the water and carry it into the hotel; then they begin passing it up a ladder to pour on the roof of the long store building.

When the whole top of the hotel is blazing, making the street as light as day, a fire bell starts clanging somewhere. Here comes a fire wagon pulled by eight or ten men. They park it, madly work the pump, and squirt the three buildings.

The heavy man in the nightgown shouts, "Let's help carry these goods to safety! Everybody pitch in! Pitch in, boys! Let's go!" I begin to help carry things out of the general merchandise store, boxes, crates, tins, kegs. We stack them in the street. The hotel fire makes it hot and I sweat like a horse. The man in the nightgown runs in and out with us, telling us what to carry and where to put it. He doesn't glance at the blacksmith shop when it starts burning but seems desperate about the goods. It's plain that he has some personal interest. Like they say, it makes a difference whose ox is gored. I snigger about it to myself a little, but about that time the man says, "Let's carry these kegs of powder farther down the street, boys, where they won't get so hot." I stop sniggering and take my work carrying kegs more seriously.

The hotel and blacksmith shop burn to the ground. Faint daylight is showing when the man in the nightgown says, "Let's help carry these goods back into the store, boys! Everybody pitch in! Let's go!" A half dozen of us start packing it in. Most of the fire fighters and onlookers leave. It gets broad daylight. I'm worn to a frazzle by the time we get the last box in off the street.

The man says, "I don't know how to thank you boys. I'd offer to pay you if I didn't know it would insult you." His flannel nightgown has become filthy. We tell him we were glad to help.

I was surprised at how quiet the streets of Dodge seemed that early in the morning. I walked toward the livery stable a couple of blocks, then turned around and started back, trying to make up my mind whether to sleep at the stable or try to find the place where you could get a separate cot with clean sheets for twenty-five cents. I was not real sleepy for some reason, maybe the excitement. I had turned around again, meaning to go down to the stable after all, when I noticed a strange thing.

On the steps at a side door of Madam Josephine's Boarding House sat a woman in a frilly dress with her head down on her arms. Not a soul was on the streets. You could hear a pin drop. I heard her sniff like she had a bad cold. I turned and strolled back by. I couldn't make it out.

Then she glances up at me and puts her head back down in her hands. It's Lillian.

I walk toward her and ask, "Could I help you, Miss Lillian?"

"Nobody can help me," she says. Her throat sounds hoarse, like she's been crying.

I stand there a minute and say, "I'm Charley Blankenship. I don't know if you remember me, but we had a long talk yesterday."

She says, "Remember you? You're the only person that's been decent to me in this town in a long time."

"Maybe if you'd tell me what they've been doing I could help you."

"You don't understand." She raises her head and shakes it slowly. "I lost everything I had in the fire. Two trunks, all my clothes. . . ."

She seems so helpless that I feel big enough to give her advice. "You'll get more things, Lillian. Don't take it so hard. You'll get more things."

"You don't understand. It's worse. . . . Nobody can help me."

My suspicious mind turns back to what Jake and I had talked about, and I immediately feel ashamed of myself. I say, "I want to help you if you'll tell me."

"You can't. My father is a deacon. . . . I don't know how to tell you. I'm so ashamed. I lost my money in the fire. I was saving to go back to Ohio and leave my life of sin and shame. To my folks. They will forgive me. I've been trying to live better and decent enough to go home. Now I've lost all my money to go on and I don't even want to live if I can't go home."

I can't hardly stand to hear her talk that way. In fact, I feel peculiar. Maybe if you work like a dog half the night saving a man's goods and he says thanks and you say you were glad to help, maybe it makes you generous and helpful, even more than it does the man you helped. Who knows? I say, "If you could borrow the money you could go on home."

She says, "You couldn't do that, Charley. You don't hardly know me. You work hard for your money. I'm not worth it. It might take my father two weeks to send you the money back. I don't know what I'll do."

Suddenly, casual as strolling down the garden path, she pulls up her dress away past her knees. "I hurt my leg too," she says. On one of her snow-white legs I see a bruise the size of a quarter. It doesn't look serious, but how do I know? Maybe a thing like that hurts a girl more. "I think it's getting feverish," she says. She takes my hand and holds it against her leg a minute. Her leg sure feels hot all right.

Across my lustful mind comes this idea: she's a fallen woman; she admits it. If I loan her the money, she'll be grateful and probably willing to do anything to show her thanks. After all, what does she have to lose? If she thinks she's already got as low as she can, what does it matter? She can start back on her decent life later.

She's put her dress down and her face is buried in her arms. She says, "I don't know where to turn. It seems that all men are alike. They take advantage of a girl, then leave her to her shame and disgrace. It's going to break my father's and mother's heart."

I think about Uncle Milt. He's probably going from one

end of the Mississippi River to the other, taking advantage
of girls. If I don't control myself I'll turn out exactly the
same. I jerk out my pocketbook and take out eight ten-
dollar bills. "Lillian, can you get home on eighty dollars?"

"I can try." She tucks it down the front of her frilly
dress. "You have saved my life, Charley."

"I'm glad to help. You get on that train and go to your
father and mother." I walk toward the street, stop, and say,
"Just have him send it to Charles Blankenship, General Delivery, Dodge City, Kansas. And good luck to you."

"I will. Good luck to you, Charley. I have not met anybody like you in a long time."

I'm so tired my rear end is dragging my tracks out.
Down at the stables I fall into a pile of hay without even
taking my hat off. The last thing that blunders across my
mind before I fall asleep is this: If she lost all her stuff in the
hotel that burned up, what was she doing sitting on the
side steps over at Madam Josephine's Boarding House?

It was dark again when I woke up. I got the hay off of
me, talked to the livery stable man a while, then went back
up to the Dixie Lee Restaurant and had a Special Dinner.
The deal with Lillian bothered me. When did she mean to
leave or had she already gone? Or . . . I couldn't possibly
be as big a simpleton as it seemed I might be. Could I?

I went to the Blue Palace, got me a drink, and sat down
at the back. Somebody broke a glass on the floor near the
bar. An old man who must have been the swamper around
the place swept up the glass pieces, then scattered sawdust
on the wet spot. Half an hour later he brought in a plate
of food, mostly fried potatoes, and sat down close to me.
He didn't pay much attention to anything but his food.

I moved over in front of him, grinned, and said, "I don't
see Lillian around tonight."

"She quit," he said.

After a minute I said, "I guess she's from Ohio, isn't she?"

"Lil is from any place she wants to be from," he said. "She came from New Orleans before she started making these Kansas cow towns."

I mulled it over a while and said, "She seems to be a real friendly gal."

"She's about as friendly as she gets ready to be. Over in Ellsworth they give her the name of Weeping Lil. They had a big Injun scare, so she told some old boy she lost everything she had in an Indian attack. She took him for a hundred dollars.

"Right here last spring we had the river flood out of the banks a little. Four or five cowboys came in off of a trail herd, and she told them she lost her trunks in the Arkansas River. They taken up a pot among themselves, about eighty dollars, and give it to her."

He finished eating and picked up his plate, shaking his head. "Weeping Lil," he said, then went out the rear door.

I sat there and lost track of time, watching the bull-whackers, soldiers, mule skinners, cowhands, and goodness knows who. Whether the bartender started giving me moonshine cut with water and colored with tobacco juice, I don't know. Part of the time I felt like I could whip any man in the house, and might; part of the time I felt twelve years old. The days and nights get mixed up in Dodge. When I went outside it was coming light again.

Madam Josephine's Boarding House seems to have moved. I have trouble finding it, also some trouble staying on my feet. I climb the steps to the side door and begin knocking, calling out, "Lillian! Lillian!"

No answer. I beat loud and long with both fists. "Lillian!" Even if they're asleep, I mean for them to get up and talk to me. "Lillian! Lillian!"

I don't know how the man with the star gets there. He's just there. I hear him say, "What are you doing? What do you think you're doing?"

It's not clear whether he's talking to me or not, but I more or less figure to do again what I been doing, and then he can see. I yell "Lillian!" and knock. I see the gun barrel raise up, only I don't know what it is. It looks like a long black finger pointing at the morning sky. When I see it coming down at me it's too late to dodge. He buffaloes me. I feel the crackling clear down to my toes and go blank.

You can do nearly anything to a man who drinks too much; then when he wakes up, he is apt to take most of the blame on himself. I remember laying on an iron cot with a thin bare mattress a long time feeling like a poisoned pup. Some of the men in the jail ate, but it seemed like a real bad idea to me, especially the way the place smelled. A marshal asked me, "You ready to go before the judge?"

I was as ready as I would ever be. I had no idea whether this marshal was the galoot who had whacked me.

The judge was a small fellow with a potbelly and he wore brass spectacles. He got himself set behind the desk, ready for business, and asked, "What did he do?"

"Disturbing the peace," the marshal says.

"Firing off his gun on the city streets?"

"Naw. Banging on a door and yelling. I told him to quit and he didn't."

"What time of night did he do it?"

"Eight o'clock in the morning. Right when everybody's trying to sleep."

"Whereabouts at?"

"Josephine's."

"Young man," the judge says, "do you live at Josephine's rooming house?"

"No, sir, I was trying to get in touch with a woman named Lillian."

"Is that the way you get in touch with people? Yelling your head off and beating on the door? Scaring people? Disturbing the peace?"

The marshal says, "Lillian don't live there, Judge, and besides that she took the stage north the day before. I seen her go."

I don't want to admit anything about my financial dealings with Weeping Lil.

"Young man, who's your employer?"

He catches me off guard and I tell the truth. "I did work for Mr. Wright, but he let me go. He sold his cattle or something." Right away I wish that I'd said I worked for a big outfit.

"Young man, I'm going to tell you something you don't know. Rowdies and transients think they can come into this town and do anything they get ready and get away with it. Well, the citizens are getting sick and tired of it. They live here. They don't come in here to raise hell and disturb the peace. They live here. They've got their women and children here. If you rowdies and transients think you can do anything you want to any time of the day or night and pick fights and disturb the peace, you've got another think coming.

"I'm going to let you off easy this time, because maybe you fell in with bad companions and got your head full of wrong ideas. You can go. But don't ever forget that we don't put up with rowdy ways in this town. Do you have any visible means of support?"

"I'm looking for a job," I say.

"That's a fine way to look for a job," he says. "Yelling. Fighting. Firing off your gun on the city streets. Disturbing the peace. No telling what all. You'd better get out of town. Marshal, I want you to keep an eye on this man and see that he leaves town. Because if he ever comes before me again I'm going to throw the book at him."

I thought of telling him that I didn't have a gun to fire off on the city streets, but it seemed like a good time to keep quiet.

I headed straight for the livery stable, stopping only once at a grocery store to lay in a supply of crackers and cheese. When I got to the livery stable and asked the man what was the bill on Cricket, he said it was taken care of, that Mr. Wright had said to put it to his account. He smiled at me and said, "Come again." The smile went a long ways with me, because I wasn't feeling good about Dodge City.

On the top of my head I had a knot, a touchy ridge two or three inches long. When I felt of it, little pieces of crumbly dried blood were scattering around in my hair. Good thing, I thought, that I had my hat on at the time and have thick hair on top and have a naturally hard head.

I rode west. When I got out of sight of town, to cheer myself up I sort of counted my blessings. I had an eighteen-dollar horse named Cricket, a black saddle, some of it held together with wire, a good hat and boots and other clothes, a canvas coat with heavy sheepskin lining, four dollars cash money in my pocket. A man could be in worse shape.

About my eighty dollars, which added up to nearly three months' hard work, I think Jake said the facts when he said you've got to agree to it, but that didn't put it plain enough. Sometimes it may be that you *must* agree to it and that's that. First, like Lil said, she had not seen anybody like me in a long time. All right. Then, the fire. It's an accident. We're all human beings trying to get along; we pitch in. It puts you in a mood. Then the white, hot leg of Weeping Lil. Then conscience, a tricky thing at best. Then eighty dollars. It's a high price, but maybe not too much, because it won't happen to me again.

The weather held warm for several days. Like they say, God tempers the wind to the shorn lamb.

Chapter 3
Four Horsemen Named Smith

ABOUT FIVE DAYS WEST OF DODGE I ran into a bone-picking crew, a man named Hightower, his Indian helper, who Mr. Hightower called "Chief," and an Indian woman, the helper's wife. They had a heavy wagon with high sideboards, six work oxen, a tent, and camping gear. I was lucky to find them to camp with because it was turning cold again.

The night I stopped there a blowing snow came, and the next day it was a first-class blizzard. I helped them move camp to a low place and set up the tent in the lee of a clay bank. That night snow covered the tent so that we had to dig out, and it looked like we had spent the night in a cave in the side of a hill.

Mr. Hightower told me he had to have a little gab session with me and no beating around the bush. He hated to run me off, especially in weather like this, and he didn't know where I could go, but he was in debt and trying to run his bone-picking business on a small margin and having bad luck because all the bones were covered with snow. I'd have to move on. He was a family man just trying to support his wife and kids and he was paying that chief's wages and getting no good out of him with the snow on the ground. The only way I could stay was if I was willing to work it out when the weather warmed up a little.

He would not tell me how much I had to work for him for how many days of grub and sleeping in his tent, but I agreed to work it out. It had become plain to me that I had no business wandering around in this country alone with no camping equipment and no food. I supposed that if he could trust me I could trust him.

We stayed snowed in about two weeks with little to do but cook, drag up wood, and take care of the oxen and Cricket. I never heard the Indians utter a word of English, only a kind of fast, catchy gibberish to each other in low voices. Mr. Hightower said they were maverick Cheyennes. They dressed in white man's clothing, but it did not seem to fit them, and the chief's black hair was plaited in long braids the same as his wife's. Mr. Hightower talked to him by saying words in slow simple English, if you could call it that, such as "You . . . go . . . getum . . . water," and making wild signs and pointing at things. I could not keep from envying the chief on those cold nights, for the woman looked warm to sleep against, and they would pile up inside about a half dozen buffalo robes they had. I slept in Mr. Hightower's blankets with him, and his skinny back was about as warm as a picket fence, besides him having a rancid smell. Sometimes as late as midnight you might hear that low gibberish in their own talk coming out of the pile of robes, and Mr. Hightower would yell, "Chief! stop that and go to sleep! It might fair off tomorrow and we'll have to work. Go . . . um . . . sleep! Go . . . um . . . sleep!"

Mr. Hightower explained to me some of the troubles of the bone business. As time went by the bones near the railroads were all gathered, and the haul got longer and longer.

He could only get four dollars a ton. In the coming summer he expected the prairie to be swarming with fools driving bone wagons, and he wanted to get ahead of them if he could and try to get out of debt.

When the snow was gone we still had to wait three days because it was too muddy to move the wagon. Then we went on a great search, Mr. Hightower leading the oxen, Cricket tied behind the wagon, the woman following Cricket, and the chief and I carrying and loading bones. Where a single buffalo had been killed, two armloads would clean up the scattered gray-white remains. If the wagon was some distance away we left the small ones. Sometimes we found a place where a dozen or even twice that many had been shot in an acre or two, and then Mr. Hightower would help us load. Some of the buffalo skulls still had patches of hide and stringy hair remaining; they had a fragrance about them that made you want to stay upwind from the wagon.

Some places you would find the bones of loafer wolves scattered around the bigger buffalo bones, and you had to use your head to figure out what had happened. These wolves had always followed the herds, catching the old cripples and the new calves. They were in hog heaven when the hunters and skinners started leaving all that bare meat lying around. Then some smart hunter had started doping his carcasses with strychnine and coming back the next day to collect some good wolf pelts. If the wagon was close we threw the little skulls and bones in with the big ones; a bone is a bone.

When we had a load it took us three days to get it to the railroad. On the bare prairie at a rail siding a bone-pickers' town had sprung up, a few tents here and there and long stacks of bones twice as high as a man's head. Evidently each man who was hauling had someone to guard his stack while he was away, in some cases his wife and children.

It seems there is always a joker around, and others ready to follow the leader. On the tip top of three different bone stacks I saw human skulls, sitting up there grinning and staring out of their big eye holes. You wondered what they had been, soldiers, Indians, trappers, travelers; it probably didn't matter to them now. A bone is a bone. I thought about a story it tells in the Good Book. This fellow Ezekiel saw a valley with dry bones scattered everywhere; somehow they were all going to be gathered together and hook up the way they belonged. I could just see one of our bone piles trying to straighten itself out after us scavengers had mixed them up that way.

I'd been thinking they used the bones to make buttons and knife handles and such, but seeing those big piles, it was plain there were just too many. I asked around and most of the people didn't know what bones are good for, only that you can sell them. Finally a man told me that they make fertilizer out of them and also use them burnt some way to help turn brown sugar into white sugar.

Mr. Hightower took it for granted that I would go after another load with him, so I did. It took about a week. When we had unloaded the second time, I told him I had enjoyed working for him and it was about time for me to move on. He said he needed me real bad and explained again about his debts and supporting his family and I could go on helping him on the same arrangement as before, by which I guess he meant I could eat his food and in case of a blizzard sleep against his skinny back.

I said I couldn't stay unless I could draw wages, and he said he was already paying the chief eight dollars a month, besides all that free food the Indian woman was eating.

After considerable complaining about the bone business, he agreed to pay me eight dollars a month. Actually I was not sure where I wanted to go anyway. The thought had been in my mind that during cold weather my brother Buck would probably be working in a warmer place like Arizona Territory, which was wishful thinking on my part; then also I'd heard some of the bone men say that the great buffalo herd was still running up in Dakota Territory and a fortune could be made in buffalo hides. In any case, it was not certain that winter was done, so I said I'd work one month.

To hear him tell it, Mr. Hightower was going broke. At the end of the month I asked for my pay. He said he would have to wait till his partner came. Of course I asked when that would be. He didn't know. He was in partnership with a fellow who handled all the business and I would have to wait till he came.

It wasn't the eight dollars so much, but I had got my pride up. The next day when Mr. Hightower set out for the wilds with his bone wagon, he was leading the oxen, the chief walked on one side, the woman walked behind, and I rode Cricket on the other side. When we got to the bone fields, I stayed on my horse and did not pick up a single rib. All I did was eat with them and discuss when the partner would come so I could get my money. After four days of eating and discussing, Mr. Hightower asked if I would be willing to take a little equipment or something instead of the eight dollars. I agreed.

He was hard to trade with. I got a skillet and small cast-iron pot, a lariat rope, a can of sulphur matches, a blue wool blanket with a hole in it, a spoon, about six pounds of red beans, and a piece of hog jowl.

I headed west, glad to ride away from that man. I've

wondered later how the chief ever got his pay from Mr. Hightower and would not be surprised to learn that he had to take it out in hair.

My idea was to drift west a ways and then maybe north. Surely winter was over. It seemed to me that Buck, even though he would rather work cattle, would probably be where the money is. I wanted to find out more about the great buffalo herd up north and whether there was big money in skinning the critters.

On the twenty-ninth of March it was not certain whether I was in Colorado or Kansas. It was not even the twenty-ninth for sure, but I felt in my bones that it was. It seems like you know it when it's your birthday and you turn eighteen. The look and feel of the lonesome land on that day is burned into my mind. The soil was grayish or pinkish or yellowish, with long sweeping ridges and bare gullies and some sand hills. You could see a tinge of tender green from the spring grass. Cloud shadows lay spotted around out there on the rough ground. Up through the clouds the sky looked deep blue, paler down near the horizon, and where the hills opened out so you could see past, there was nothing; like not a thing was out there. It seemed to me there must be thousands of miles of this same country, and it was a relief to see green Spanish dagger plants, huddled together as if for company on account of the size of the land and its emptiness.

My thoughts turned back to past birthdays. It seemed like I'd been gone from home for years. My ma always noticed birthdays; maybe she wanted everybody to know she was glad they were born. She would cook something good like fried chicken or baked ham with fruit sauce and usually, whoever had the birthday, she would sew him up a new shirt or knit him a sweater or a toboggan cap.

Being eighteen, I felt a lot older and did not really want

to be at home, but imagined how good it would be to see them. Someday I would have a first-class horse and saddle, good clothes, and about a thousand dollars, and I would go back. At first that thought was only a daydream, but why not? I made myself a promise; I'd do it. As for the thousand dollars, a small fortune in anybody's books, a man could do it if he would steer clear of Weeping Lils and Mr. Hightowers.

The next day I learned that I was not alone in that wilderness but shared it with four unusual men, every one of them named Smith. Our meeting was peculiar.

It was horse-killing country, no road, up and down hill, sandy footing. Cricket had a good load with me and my pack, so I had got off to walk a ways and rest him. I'd been watching where I walked, then happened to look up ahead. On a rise nearly a mile away sat four horsemen with four extra horses on lead ropes. They seemed to be watching me. In fact, one of them seemed to be looking at me with a telescope, which gives you an uneasy feeling. I waved toward them. In a minute they turned and rode away over the hill.

A quarter of an hour later there they were again up ahead, sitting looking at me. I was half a mind to stop or turn. Then two of them rode toward me. It seemed more friendly than to just sit a mile away and look. But when the two got within a couple of hundred yards they split and went circling out to come at me from opposite sides, like I was a dangerous animal. They both rode long-legged bays and both wore six-shooters and belts of ammunition, as well as carrying carbines stuck in a boot hung from their saddles. I stood there looking from one to the other.

The one on my left was squat and red-faced, maybe fifty. He was grinning.

The one on my right, maybe thirty, had his hat pushed

back on his head and his hair was sun-bleached yellow. He asked, "What are you doing?"

The question seemed pretty silly. I was standing there holding my horse Cricket, but I grinned from one to the other and said, "Just traveling."

The squat one asked, "Whereabouts you headed?"

"I was thinking about going up to Dakota Territory. Whereabouts you headed?"

The squat one laughed. "Ain't you got airy gun about you?"

I didn't know whether to wish I had a gun or be glad I didn't have. I said, "Why do you ask? I don't figure on shooting anybody."

The yellow-headed one asked, "Why have you been following us?"

"I haven't been following anybody. I noticed you a while ago; that's all. I was already going this way."

"My name is Sam Smith. That grinning runt there is named Carolina Smith. What's your name?"

"Charley Blankenship."

"What business you in, Charley?"

"I'm a cowhand."

"You're just a cowhand out here wandering around by yourself, are you?"

"That's about the size of it."

The one he called Carolina began laughing more and slapping his leg. "Damned iffen I don't believe he's telling the truth, Sam, but Bo won't believe it."

"Mount up, Charley, and let's go talk to Bo."

Something not quite on the up and up was going on. These two were not unfriendly, but they were not saying "please" about going to talk to Bo, whoever he was. I figured it was just as well not to cross them and bring it out in the open that they were ordering me around. No use in fishing in troubled waters, as they say.

Carolina Smith chattered as we rode, asking such as, "Where did you get that air horse, Charley? Is he fast? What would you take fer him?" He was making fun of my mount, but he had something about him more like a kid than a fifty-year-old man, and it made you laugh with him instead of get sore. What I did not like was seeing one of the men up ahead watching us with a telescope. I knew he was looking at me and it made me want to hold my hand up in front of my face.

He did not lower the telescope until we came about a hundred yards from him. Then he turned the telescope back up and slowly looked all around at the horizon. He was huge and had a great black mustache and curly black eyebrows, also a mat of chest hair sticking out of his shirt collar. He looked like he could fight a bear with a switch. No doubt he was Bo. The telescope was a long one that slid together. He slapped it with the palm of his hand on the end so that it went together—*click, click, click*—and glared at me.

Sam Smith said, "This here is Bo Smith and Elmo Smith. This here is Charley Blankenship, and he's just a cowhand riding around and thinking about going up to Dakota Territory."

Bo said, "What you doing following us?"

"I haven't been following anybody. I was already going this way before I ever saw you."

Elmo Smith, who was holding the horses, said, "He don't look like no law to me, ner no Pinkerton neither."

Bo glared at him and said, "You don't watch what you're talking about, you ain't going to look like nothing yourself but a greasy spot."

Elmo was the youngest, twenty or so, and he had a big downy mustache, which he was probably trying to grow to look like Bo's. None of them looked like they were kin to each other. They had a regular arsenal of guns. Elmo wore two at his waist, and Bo had a double-barreled shotgun in a boot on one side, a rifle in a boot on the other. Their eight horses looked like fast blooded horses. Three of those not carrying saddles were loaded with light packs. I felt less easy with Bo and Elmo than I had with Sam and Carolina.

"Where you from?" Bo said.

"Missouri."

"Missouri ain't back down that way."

"I've been working on a bone-picking wagon a while. Where are you from?"

"We ain't from Missouri," Bo said. "If you're a cowhand what you doing working on a bone-picking wagon?"

"Bad weather caught me out of a job. Where are you fellers headed for?" Carolina whooped and laughed at my asking questions. It wasn't clear to me what kind of a pickle I was in, but the laughing gave me a kind of straw to grasp at.

Sam Smith said, "I think he ought to go on about his business." It sounded like a friendly suggestion.

Bo said, "He wants to camp with us tonight." Then he pulled out the telescope with a *click, click, click* and began to look all around at the horizon.

It was clear as a bell that I had not fallen in with a gang of merchants, doctors, or lawyers. It was ticklish, but I figured I might as well test where I stood. I said, "Thanks, Mr. Smith, but I better go on about my business. I don't want to be any trouble. I enjoyed meeting you."

Bo was not having any of it. He said, "What you got against us? You claim you was going the same way before you seen us! Now you want to change your story, do you? What's your game? What you got against us?"

"Well, I might camp with you one night," I said.

We went on about a mile to a creek, which they said was a branch of the Picketwire River. There was not too much doubt in my mind that I was a prisoner, though the why of it was not at all plain. Any idea of making a run for it on Cricket seemed far-fetched; even if I got a half a day head start they would probably catch me. They did not act like enemies as we sat around cooking and eating, but Bo was sullen. I got the idea he was thinking and it put a strain on his brain. They had curried and brushed their horses' backs after taking the saddles off, and twice after supper Bo made Elmo go and stake them all on new grass. Once about dark I grabbed at the thought that maybe they were in the racehorse business, just traveling around making bets and staging races; but the idea was too fuzzy for me to swallow. All four of them slept that night with their saddles for pillows, their cartridge belts and holsters and Colt revolvers and right hands underneath the saddles. I could not make myself believe that they merely wanted to keep their right hands dry in case it rained.

Two of them snored, one high, one low, like someone practicing a fiddle. I did not sleep much.

The next morning Bo Smith got the idea that I was watching him in some indecent way, and he was quite sour about it. He said to me, "How come you keep looking at me? Want to remember what I look like, do you? Ever time I look up, there you are looking at me. I want you to stop it! It ain't none of your business how I look!"

I started to object. He was sure in a foul mood. In the first place he was nothing to look at; besides, if you glanced at him once in your life you would carry his ugly puss to the grave with you. Carolina began to he-he-haw-haw about it like a jackass. The laughter didn't give me permission to take the matter lightly, but it gave me the idea that the odds against me were not as bad as four to one.

"I aim for you to stop it," Bo went on to me. "Iffen you got to look some place, look some place else! I don't have to put up with it! You ain't seen me no place!"

He walked out to a nearby hill with his telescope to scan the surrounding country.

After some grub the four of them began talking together in low voices. They moved away from me and finally squatted down in a huddle, talking. I felt like the man in the dock must feel when the jury goes out. When the gab fest was done, Carolina came over to me and said, "We're pulling out, Charley boy. Get your stuff ready, so's you won't hold us up."

It didn't leave me much choice. It bothered me that the four of them seemed to be agreeing. We got ready, mounted, and headed north. Our way led along flattish sagebrush country. Bo raised his everlasting telescope to look ahead and behind every half hour.

Their horses all had a fast and easy pacing gait. I was not so lucky on Cricket. He could walk, dog trot, and lope. His trot was the joggiest, roughest movement a horse ever made. After about an hour of it I wondered if my old black saddle would come unwired from slapping my hind end. I started pulling him down to a walk, then, when they were a ways ahead, kicking him into a lope to catch up. Carolina laughed about it and said, "I'll give you four bits for that horse, Charley, and won't even ask fer a bill of sale."

I fell farther and farther behind before I would start to catch up. It was nice to imagine turning and making a dash south, but I knew I wouldn't get half a mile. I was maybe two hundred yards behind when Sam handed his lead rope to one of the others, turned, and came back to me.

He was almost casual when he said to me, "Bo says to keep up, Charley. He says to tell you to keep up or he's going to shoot you."

I was scared and sore, but trying to keep my wits and watch what I said. I asked him, "What do *you* say? Looks to me like he's got all of you under his thumb. What's he? A king or something?"

Sam laughed. "I'm telling you what he said. I'm not under his thumb and Carolina's not. Maybe Elmo. I didn't come after you because Bo said to. I came to talk to you in private. Listen to a little advice, Charley. Take it easy and don't cross Bo. Go along with him, and I'll help you if I can."

The whole business rubbed me the wrong way, but I had thought I saw some good in Sam from the first and it seemed time to call a spade a spade. I said, "You're a bunch of crooks, aren't you?"

"We ain't what you'd call lily white. That's for sure."

"You're on the dodge from the law."

"Well, you might say that. The less you know the better. To tell you the damned truth, I wish you hadn't come along. Bo's getting techy as hell. Don't cross him, Charley. Come on. I don't promise anything, but I'll help you if I can."

So I rode that day in a dog trot and kept up with them. I pounded blisters on my hind end and then broke the blisters. I'd begun to get softhearted about old Cricket, but in that one day of riding I lost all my kind feelings about him. Maybe friendship will stand a big jolt better than it will a steady pounding.

Toward evening we came off the flatland into the breaks on the south side of the Arkansas River. We made camp in the river bottom by a slough of water. Bo walked over to a small hill to scan the country. When he came back, Carolina asked him, "See anybody coming with a rope?"

Bo glared at him. "What's that supposed to mean?"

"You savvy what a rope is, don't you?"

"I savvy what I'm going to do to you if you don't quit being such a smart aleck! You think everything's so all-fired funny and humorous! Well, you'll see something one of these days!"

I thought I knew what Carolina's dig was about, maybe because I had already got the idea that Bo was born to hang. Carolina did not seem to worry about the threat but sang and made jokes while we fixed supper and ate. I was mulling over a scheme of action which I thought Sam would let me get away with if I could do it slick enough—pretend I thought they were brothers and in the racehorse business and had to go heavily armed on account of the chance of horse thieves and had to keep using that infernal telescope for the same reason. It would be a hard act to pull off, but when you are up against such a row of stumps you will try anything.

Carolina got a canvas bag out of the pile of packs, brought it up beside the fire, and began to rummage through it. Letters on the side of the bag said "Wells, Fargo."

Bo was furious. "Didn't I tell you to burn that damned thing?"

Carolina said, "Aw, come on, Bo. Ain't we ready to ask Charley does he want to come into the stagecoach business with us anyway?"

Bo acted dumbfounded. "You've give it away! You

sure have! Now you've give it away! He's got to come in
with us or we got to shoot him! You set right there and
give it away!"

I toyed with the idea of acting like I thought the
"stagecoach business" meant building stagecoaches, but it
seemed a little too much. Since the fat was in the fire, I
might as well go whole hog the other direction and get
them to adding up Bo better.

I said, "It's been plain to me from the start that you're
a bunch of outlaws, especially when you wouldn't let me
go on about my business like I wanted to. I don't know
what harm you think I'd do you."

Sam said, "They've got pictures of us in the post offices
and law offices down in Texas. All they need is somebody
going around talking about where they seen us."

"I wasn't going to Texas," I said.

He said, "We don't know what pictures they got around
Denver."

"Well, if the rest of you let Bo capture people and shoot
people, they'll get pictures of you all over the country."

Bo sat there scowling while the other three tried to per-
suade me to come in with them. They were going to scout
the stagecoach lines coming out of the mountains west of
Denver and try to find the ones that hauled gold or silver
or payrolls. If that didn't work too well they might go into
the train business. I would do things like hold the horses for
them. Also they could use me to go into towns to buy
supplies and check to see if any reward posters were stuck
around. There would be plenty of money in it for me.
While they were laying it on the line about my great opportunity, I was thinking about my folks and their fear
that I might turn out to be a disgrace like my Uncle Milt.
But Old Scratch was not tempting me at all. Going into a

gang that had Bo Smith in it was like trying to cozy up to a den of rattlesnakes.

They explained how they were really not bad fellows but had not been too friendly because they were only trying to protect themselves. Even Elmo tried to cotton up to me.

Finally Bo speaks up. "What if he says he'll do it, then he goes in after supplies, and the first thing he does he sics the law on us?"

They're quiet a while. Elmo says, like he's seen which way the wind is blowing, "If we shoot him and throw him in the river wouldn't nobody miss him. That's what I think, don't you, Bo?"

They all squat there, and I can't keep my eyes off the six-shooters they wear and their shell-studded belts.

Sam says, "That's a half-cocked idea. He'd bloat up and float down the river and probably come out on a sand bar right at Dodge City."

"Ain't nobody shooting nobody," Carolina says. "Bo, you're getting so techy they ain't no living with you!"

"And you keep on ragging me and I done told you about it once! You're going to see something one of these days!"

"I done seen plenty," Carolina says. "You been nervous as a whore in church fer a week. You don't calm down we ain't going to let you run this gang."

"I guess you aim to take charge and say what we got to do?"

Carolina says, "I may do it any time."

Bo's hand swoops down to his leg and comes up with his .44 revolver. It's not a fast motion, but powerful. He sticks it square in Carolina's face, six inches from his eyes, and thumbs the hammer back. "Do you see this?" he says. "I said you might see something!"

I think Carolina's a goner. Bo is mad as a wet hen, also nervous. His hefty arm with the black hair sticking out of his cuff shakes as he holds the gun. Carolina's only move is to cut his eyes over toward Sam.

Sam eases his own revolver out and raises it toward Bo's head, all the time speaking softly. "Now, Bo, don't none of us want to do some half-cocked thing they'd be sorry for soon as they done it. We can't afford to settle nothing this way. We got to use our heads and not do anything crazy." You can tell Bo doesn't catch on to what's happening until the barrel is six inches from his ear.

Elmo has turned pale, but he wants in the game, only he doesn't figure out the rules. Instead of pointing his weapon at Sam, he follows the lead of his hero and sticks it in Carolina's face.

Sam says calmly, "Let your gun down, Bo."

I get tensed up ready to run when the blood starts flying. Bo seems so worked up he might blast away in spite of the gun barrel sticking in his ear. He shouts at Carolina, "You ever see anybody get hung?"

"No," Carolina says.

"Well, I did! I seen it! It like to pulled his head off! His face turned black as a nigger! You ain't messing around and causing me to get hung! Ain't nobody! I won't stand for it!"

"Let your gun down easy, Bo," Sam says. "Nobody will get hung. We got to use our brains."

They discussed my fate there in front of me like I was a stick of firewood. Mostly Bo repeated his determination not to get hung and to shoot anybody who might get him hung. He began waving his gun around as if to give strength to his words and finally put it back in his holster. All the guns were lowered. Bo was still ready to shoot someone but not sure who it should be. It was clear that he and Elmo would get rid of me without batting an eye as soon as they were sure there was any advantage in it.

The next morning we forded the river, which was only stirrup deep and no trouble. On the north side we had to cross a wide sand flat. Cricket's hoofs were sinking six inches deep and he was working hard at it, so I piled off and led him. The four Smiths stayed in the saddle. Elmo was leading all four extra horses on ropes of different lengths. One of them veered out into a wet spot, began sinking to his knees, then began fighting it. Elmo dropped the one rope and got out of there to solid ground.

Bo dismounted and ran back cussing to high heaven. The loose horse lunged in the quicksand and came free, but he staggered on three feet. One front leg was broken.

Bo cussed the horse. He grabbed out his six-gun and shot him in the head. He blasted away—*Blam! Blam! Blam! Blam!*—the last three times after the critter was already dead as a doornail.

Carolina yelled, "That's my horse!"

"You saw his damned leg is broken!" Bo said. "Get the pack off of him!"

"How come you shot him four times?"

"What do you care? A dead horse is a dead horse! Get the pack off of him!"

They got the pack and halter off. Carolina was sore. He said, "You let me shoot my own horses!"

We rode north and around noon struck a small stream Sam said was named Horse Creek, where we camped. They were out of meat and wanted to get a deer or at least a turkey or some prairie chickens. Bo threatened me a while about not trying to escape; then he took Elmo and rode off hunting.

The two of them had not gone half a mile when they stopped out there. Sam said, "Look at that!" Bo was studying us with his telescope. Carolina and Sam watched the big man and looked at each other.

"What do you reckon," Carolina said, "he would do if we said we're cutting out, we don't want to run with him no more?"

Sam said, "He'll pull his gun and say he's going to kill us."

Carolina agreed. "He's got so edgy he thinks nobody can't trust nobody."

I put in my two cents' worth. "Well, Carolina, at least your horse won't turn him in and get him hung." They didn't laugh, but I think they got the point. A man who will boil up so high he shoots a dead horse three more times is something like a mad dog.

"He don't give us much choice," Carolina said. "We got to beat him to it. We got to shoot him."

Sam said, "It'll come to that. The best chance we got to come out with a whole skin is to go ahead and do it. When they get back here after while, quick as he gets down on the ground you get behind him and let him have it. I'll draw down on Elmo. We'll take Elmo's guns and hold them a day or two; by that time it'll sink into his thick head that Bo ain't around no more and we can show him we had to do it."

Carolina thought about it and said, "Well, quick as Bo gets down, say I get behind him. Whereabouts should I shoot him?"

"Right in the middle," Sam said. "You can't miss him."

"You wouldn't shoot him in the head?"

"It doesn't matter," Sam said. "Any place you want to. I'd say in the middle. Then soon as you see you've got him you can come over and lift Elmo's guns. I'll guarantee to hold Elmo off of you while you take care of the main business."

Carolina took off his hat and walked around scratching his bald head a while.

Sam said, "He don't leave us any choice."

"Only thing I was thinking," Carolina said, "you could get behind Bo and shoot him and I could hold Elmo off of you."

"I didn't figure you'd be scared to do it," Sam said.

"I reckon you know I ain't scared to do it. Only you just line it out here where I'm the one that does it, and you could do it just as well. You ain't scared to do it, are you?"

"No. But we got the plan already laid out where you do it. Why change the plan?"

"*You* got the plan laid out," Carolina said.

"Look," Sam said. "We ain't trying to do a thing but save our own lives the only way we know how. Bo is like a cow on loco weed. Suppose he comes in here and says he wants to split up the gang, we don't get along, so he's leaving. What do we say? We tell him good-by and good luck. But will he let us leave? No. He don't think of anybody but his own skin and he don't leave us any choice. It shouldn't bother you to shoot him any more than it would to shoot a rattlesnake."

"That's what I say," Carolina said. "So you shoot him and I'll hold Elmo off."

"You're the stubbornest feller I ever seen."

"I ain't no more stubborn than you," Carolina said.

The plan had seemed a good idea to me. I thought about offering to do the dirty work myself if they would loan me a gun, but when I got right down to thinking exactly how to do it, it was all off with me. So the two absent Smiths came back, Bo riding, Elmo leading his horse with a red mule deer across the saddle. Bo dismounted and nobody shot him. We dressed out the deer and things were about the same as before. That night I thought about slipping out to Cricket and heading south. If they didn't miss me till morning I could make it back to the Arkansas River and lose my tracks in the water before Bo caught me. Only at night I'd probably hit some of those patches of quicksand.

The next day we followed on up Horse Creek. The day after that we cut west across a divide. It was all sagebrush foothills country. The four of them argued with each other but did not settle anything. Bo located a man driving a one-horse buggy so far away that it was only a small spurt of dust to the naked eye. He tried to get Sam and Carolina to go and capture the man, but they wouldn't. He said they had to have a man to go in after supplies and scout around for reward posters and information about stagecoaches. They argued that it would just be one more man that couldn't be trusted. They didn't settle anything.

The morning after that we could see the Rocky Mountains like a dim cloud bank out to the west, pale snow on them. The light had to be right to see them at all. When you could no longer see them you would wonder if your eyes had been playing tricks on you.

Before noon we stopped at a water hole. Bo rode toward a knoll a half mile away to use his telescope. Elmo had got to repeating every word he could remember that Bo had said. Carolina told him not to leave the meat uncovered because the flies were getting bad. Elmo said, "Get off my back and quit ragging me! I don't have to do what you say!"

"Don't get on your high horse," Carolina says, grinning.

"You think it's so humorous and funny," Elmo says. "Bo is probably looking at you with his spy glass right now. I don't have to put up with nothing like this. You're going to see something one of these days!"

"Young feller," Carolina says, "it ain't funny any more to me, and that's a fact." He pulls the canvas over the deer hindquarter which lies in the opened pack.

Elmo grabs out his .44 and sticks it in Carolina's face. "I guess you'll change your tune now! You ain't far from dead!"

Sam is circling to come around behind him, but Carolina doesn't wait. He slaps the gun aside and plows into the younger man like a charging bull.

I don't think animals ever fought like those two. They're both mad, also scared and spouting out feelings that are capped up in them. They swing and cuss and grunt and grit out noises. They flail and strike and roll through grass and a thicket of plum bushes. Sam and I watch.

Carolina is stronger than you would think. He's built, as they say, like a brick outhouse. Down or up doesn't mean much to him and he's got staying power. Finally he fastens onto Elmo like a bulldog and gets him down. They pound each other in the face. Blood is smeared on their heads and fists. Then Carolina gets up and runs over and gets the revolver Elmo dropped. One of Carolina's boots has come off.

"Don't kill him!" Sam yells.

"I'm just going to make him eat this goddam gun!" Carolina pants.

Elmo's trying to get up. Carolina piles back on and tries to do what he had said. Elmo gets a busted lip and a couple of broken teeth out of it. Carolina's going full steam and can't find a stopping place. "You'll eat the shells then, damn you!" he says. He throws out the cylinder and drops the cartridges on the ground and grabs them up, dirt and all, to cram in Elmo's bloody mouth. He's slapping him to make him swallow when Sam drags him off of the younger man.

"I reckon he et one or two," Carolina gasps.

Elmo had worn two six-shooters. They find both and fling them out into the plum bushes. Carolina walks around feeling of his head, looking at his torn clothes, and getting his breath. Elmo manages to sit up. Then Bo comes riding full tilt, his horse in a lather. I stand back thinking if they tear each other up bad enough I'll get on Cricket and ride off.

Bo must have seen some of it in his telescope. He hits the ground and heads for Carolina with his brawny arms spread out like a man trying to pen a pig. Sam enters the contest quicker this time. He runs up and jams his gun hard into Bo's backbone. When the big man turns, frowning, Sam says, "Put up your hands, and I mean it!"

It's funny. Bo slowly raises his arms. He doesn't want to, but it's like he doesn't understand anything except a rule: If somebody points a gun at you and says you must do something, then you must do it. Carolina takes his gun and gun belt.

Sam says, "We got to split up the gang, Bo. You don't leave us no choice. Me and Carolina are going to take our three horses and our gear. We don't want nothing of yours except your shells. We don't want to get shot. All we want is to get loose from you. You don't trust nobody for nothing. You don't leave us no choice."

They collect cartridges, everything, even shotgun shells,

and start getting ready to go, meanwhile holding cocked revolvers in their hands.

Bo finds his voice. "You ain't doing this to me! I'll foller you!"

Carolina stops what he's doing and says slowly, like a judge, "Wait, Sam, maybe we better let Bo help us decide. Iffen we ain't doing nothing but getting loose, and he aims to foller us anyway, we'd be damned fools to go off like this without shooting a few holes in Bo first. How about it, Bo? Can we get loose from you peaceable? Or ort we to make sure we can trust you?"

"You ever see a man get hung?" Bo says. "Ain't nobody getting me hung!"

"No. And ain't nobody spending the rest of their life worrying about you getting hung, neither. We ain't going to turn you in. All we want is loose."

Bo asks, "How do I know you ain't going to turn me in?"

"You don't know," Carolina says, "but you can try your best to believe it, can't you? Help us decide real quick: have we got to shoot you or not?"

"I don't guess I'll foller you," Bo says.

They get mounted and I jump on Cricket without being told because I sure don't want to remain. As we ride off Carolina says, "Don't hit Elmo in the stomach; he might go off. He! He! He!"

We rode north up the valley, looking back. Bo had sat down in the grass not far from Elmo. We held an easy lope for half an hour, then settled down to a trot, and I did not even mind Cricket's rough gait as long as it covered the miles. We circled up over a hill to look back. Nothing. We went on making good time. It was warm. At nearly sunset we came down to where a spring came out of a rock outcrop and a meadow of good grass grew. They said we'd make camp.

I take my stuff off of Cricket, rub his back a little, put a stake rope on him, and lead him around to graze and cool off before he waters. Carolina yells, "Tie that bag of bones some place, Charley boy, and help drag up some wood." I pay no attention to him.

I water Cricket, lead him back, and start putting the bridle on. They both come toward me. Sam says, "What the hell are you doing? We're going to camp here!"

"I'm not."

They both seem to see they've got mutiny on their hands at the same time. Carolina says, "You ain't leaving, Charley. Put that saddle down. Right now!"

I swing my black saddle on my horse.

Sam says, "We ain't playing. The law is after us, boy! You're going to stick around and we'll talk it over. We're not like Bo. You can talk to us. But we got to figure out what to do."

I cinch the saddle down. Cricket swells up his stomach as usual to keep the cinch from getting too tight.

Carolina says, "We can't let you go right now, boy. You better pay attention. We've got you covered."

I pick up my pack, throw it across behind the cantle, and say, "I know you have. I hope you enjoy it."

It's hard to say exactly what had got into me. Sometimes you can get so sick and tired of a thing that you can get mad enough to bite nails in two. One time when I was maybe half grown I had got in a fight with a boy my size and another boy got on me too; I fought them both, crying like a baby, not because I was hurt or scared but because it wasn't right. And after that the kids would say, Don't get Charley to crying; he'll tear you to pieces. I remember that

90 THE TRUE MEMOIRS OF CHARLEY BLANKENSHIP

now because I feel the same inside. My mad feeling must be
plain. I look up at Carolina and as soon as he sees my face
he lowers his gun. They both stand there with guns in their
hands pointing at the ground.

"Now, look, Charley," Sam says. "You got us all wrong.
We ain't like Bo."

"It's a small choice in rotten apples," I say, sure they
won't shoot me. Anybody that can't shoot Bo Smith when
he deserves it can't shoot a man when he doesn't want to do
a thing but go about his own business. I tie my saddle strings
around my pack.

Carolina says, "Come on, Charley. You got us wrong. We
ain't like Bo."

I swing my leg over my horse and say, "Lay down with
dogs; get up with fleas."

"But, no, wait, Charley," Carolina says. "How do we
know you won't turn us in? That's all we thought. You
can see that."

I touch Cricket in the sides with my boot heels and start
north. The two of them trot afoot after me and seem to
have forgotten the guns in their hands.

Sam says, "Wait! You can leave when you get ready!
Come on! We swear you can leave when you get ready!"

Carolina yells, "It's pretty nigh dark, Charley! Come on
back! Don't go off sore! You can leave when you get ready!
At least say you ain't sore, Charley!"

I look back at them in the dusk a hundred yards behind
me and see them standing with hands on hips staring at
each other.

If you want to know the truth, I wanted to go back
and spend the night with them. Oh, I thought about how it
had been those two particular Smiths that captured me in
the first place. But the real reason I didn't go back is

harder to see. Although I thought eighteen is pretty old, I knew I couldn't do all night what I'd just done. I'd got my power from being right and mad at the same time, and that's why they trotted after me afoot, begging me. What I had over them, I couldn't keep it overnight. And when a man gets on his high horse, it's hard to get down on plain old dirt again.

Chapter 4
The Jonah

I DON'T RECKON ANY MAN can explain every month of his life, what he did, especially why. That spring I thought I was headed for buffalo-hunting country, where I thought big money could be made. But in Sheridan, Wyoming Territory, I ran into a man looking for cowhands and he offered me a job. He had a lot of grass east of there in the Powder River country. Why I took him up I don't know. Maybe it was because I wasn't sure I was a cowhand and wanted to prove it. His main brand was a Circle Four on the left side, but he also ran some Lazy T and Rail P cows for a partnership or a company. The old Powder was said to be a mile wide and an inch deep; the rolling country along it was good cattle land.

We called the outfit the Circle Four. It had no head-quarters but had three sod houses and three or four dugout camps miles apart. They had me keep Cricket in my saddle string of five horses, but I seldom rode him on account of his rough traveling gait. The second payday I bought me a good double-rigged stock saddle in Sheridan. The man would not buy my old saddle for any money; I threw it in a wash south of town.

I'll always remember the roundup that fall. We would gather a herd out of the hills and creek bottoms toward a good flat area. It would take a half dozen mounted hands to hold them and another half dozen to work them, two ropers on horseback, two flankers on the ground, a branding iron man and a knife man. It was sort of grand work because you see the way men can control animals, but hard and dirty too. Your sweaty clothes would catch the dust and they would get stiff from the salt and dirt in them.

We worked all young stuff, about three months to yearlings. I got stuck with a flanking job. The ropers would drag them out of the herd toward the branding fire. They would be maybe bawling, jumping stiff-legged and scared and stubborn. The flanker would grab the rope and run down it to the critter and grab over his back to the opposite flank and wrestle him down. The roper would sit up there easy in his saddle till the peons gave him his loop back. One flanker would hold down the calf's head, but I usually got the back legs. I would jam my right boot into the hock of the bottom leg, push for all I was worth, nab the top leg with both hands, and hang on. The foreman did all the castrating, and he would say, "Hold him still, Blankenship! Hold him still! I can't do a thing if you don't hold him still!" If you would get ahead of a ten-month-old bull and really get him stretched out, you could hold him. But when three or four hundred pounds of steak gets to kicking, you have got a handful. If you let that top leg get free you are going to get the soup kicked out of you before you get it again. We held them all down without any ropes to save time. If you are straining your guts to hold those back legs, you will learn to lean over and not let the brand smoke get in your face, or you may not feel like eating any supper.

We'd been branding maybe two weeks, and one day we had about two hundred head of cows gathered with some hundred and fifty calves by noontime. Out of the clear blue sky the foreman asked, "You want to rope this evening, Blankenship?"

If he'd given me time to think it over, I probably would have given a different answer, but I said, "Sure!" I figured I would rope some calves or get fired.

"Catch your best roping horse and you can rest off from this wrestling," he said.

You wouldn't believe it, but I did rope some calves. Two of us roped. The other one was an old gray-headed man who never missed, but took his own good time in all he did. I worked twice as hard as he did and kept up with him.

But something I didn't see till I started doing it: Calling out the brand was more important than the roping. I'd been watching and knew what to do. Only when I dragged that first six-months-old bull out toward them, it struck me sharply. Not a soul in the world knows what mama this calf follows but me. I'd better know and also sound like I know. It's embarrassing to have a Rail P calf sucking a Circle Four cow, or a Flying U mama licking a Bar X offspring; somebody has got some explanations to make. So when I came out with that first bucking little bull and the flankers got hold of him, I turned toward the man waiting at the irons and yelled, "Circle Four!" The sound of my voice said, If anybody disputes it I may climb off this horse and punch you in the nose! I didn't keep that tone all afternoon; it became a singsong. But it's a part of the glory of being a roper in that kind of operation to sit up there above those fellows fighting down in the dust, waiting patiently for them to give you your loop back, and turn toward the fire and sing out clear and sure, "Circle Four!" or "Lazy T!"

or whatever it is. Luckily for me only a couple of outside brands were mixed in with the three we ran, and I knew them all.

Why that foreman trusted me with that rope I'll never know. Maybe he thought I'd done my share as a flanker and deserved a shot at something else. It is true that a boss will usually give you a chance if you work hard and grin a lot. The rest of that roundup I spent in the saddle, and if I didn't rope I helped hold the herd.

Besides getting to try my lariat rope, I remember that fall because the cook knew how to fry up mountain oysters, and I learned to like them. Some of the hands said, the first time we had them, "Man, oh, man! Mountain oysters! Ain't had any in a year!" When I tried them I agreed they were real good. I guess we'd had them twice before I asked myself, What are mountain oysters? There were no mountains around there close. Well, the cook would come piddling around where we were branding, carrying a bucket. There was so much to watch and learn that I paid no attention to him, because I sure never wanted to be a cook. I'd seen calves and pigs cut when I was a kid; you throw the nuts out in the litter and maybe an old barn cat comes and drags them off to eat. Now the cook was coming around with his bucket and the foreman would throw the nuts in it. I thought, Maybe the old fool wants to give them a decent burial. It took two or three weeks for me to put two and two together and get the connection between mountain oysters and the process of making bulls into steers. Then it was too late to get finicky; I already knew how good they were. Well, they say Frenchmen eat snails, and it says in the Good Book that John the Baptist went out in the wilderness and ate locusts, which probably means grasshoppers. Everybody to their own taste.

It was hard to save money on the Circle Four. We would

ride to Sheridan every payday. It was a crude wild town. I stuck with the other hands and we had some big times.

As I mentioned, the ranch had no headquarters. In fact the ranch was just in the owner's mind to a good extent. He owned the livestock and a few wagons and had a first-come-first-served claim on a broad sweep of free range, on which he had pitched some tents, thrown up some sod houses, and dug some dugouts for cow camps. I spent that Wyoming winter in a dugout in the south side of a hill and learned how wrong I'd been in thinking western Kansas could get cold. Weeks went by when you couldn't even get a drink of water without thawing some ice or snow. We dug big holes in the floor, put our canned goods and potatoes and onions in them, then spread our bedrolls on them and slept on them to keep our grub from freezing and spoiling.

During that year on the Circle Four, besides my new saddle, I bought a good-looking bay gelding named Chili Beans and a Winchester rifle, .44 caliber, from another hand, both for ninety-five dollars. Those boys enjoyed a night on the town so much they would sell anything if they got short of money. I cut down the horse's name to Chili.

In March I quit my job. On my birthday when I turned nineteen I wrote my folks a letter from Sheridan and rode north. The weather was still cold, but my equipment and outfit was better than I'd ever owned before. I rode Chili and led Cricket with a pack on him. It was lonesome sagebrush country. The idea came to me that I wouldn't mind riding this saddle and horse home if I had some better clothes and maybe a pair of silver-mounted spurs. Then the idea came along that there could be big profits in buffalo hides and I could get my thousand dollars this very summer and I could go home by Christmas. Or maybe I would run into Buck.

I followed the Tongue River up to Miles City on the Yellowstone. The town was booming. It had started as a collection of log shacks outside the cavalry post of Fort Keogh and now the Northern Pacific Railroad had come in. The place reminded me some of Dodge City, the excitement, the feel that things were happening. Right in the middle of town they were in the process of building a three-story brick courthouse, but at the same time you could see business places built out of tar paper—not lumber covered with the stuff, but just shaky frames tacked over with tar paper.

The main boom that spring was made out of hundreds of people, men and women, cowhands, dudes, miners, bums, farmers, you name it, who had heard about the fortune everyone could make out of buffalo hides. I figured I had got here none too soon. I talked to a man from Indiana who came in on the train. He showed me his Sharps, .50 caliber, with a telescopic sight on it, a beauty of a gun. He didn't know a damned thing about the hide business but thought he ought to have the best gun money could buy, because he planned to make buffalo hunting his profession and stick with it the rest of his life.

Big operators stood up on the spring seats of wagons in the streets trying to hire help. By the time I'd hung around town a day and a half I'd seen enough crews outfitting to know that I would not be able to hunt any buffalo on my own. It took too much gear and supplies and know-how. They were hiring skinners for fifty a month and experienced shooters for twice that, and in some cases paying on percentage.

I got to talking to one big operator named Mr. Arnold. He was sending out seven wagons in all, each in the charge of a shooter. The two skinners and the hide pegger would get thirty cents a hide to split between them. He would pay all expenses, but the employees would have to spend a day or two a week salting and smoking meat for no pay. He had seen two skinners take off a hundred hides in one day down south. A little figuring told me that one man at that rate could make ten dollars in one day. Ten dollars a day! I signed on.

The next morning we loaded our light wagon and forded the Yellowstone. It was dangerous water with patches of snow-covered ice drifting down. The shooter, Luke, rode a big gray stud horse, and he tied on with a lariat to one front corner of the wagon box. I rode Chili and tied onto the other front corner. The pegger, Dominique, rode Cricket bareback. The single span of mules to the wagon was driven by the other skinner, Mr. Crankshaw. Mr. Arnold rode horseback across the stream shouting advice to us. We had to hurry not only to dodge the ice but to get out of that cold water. We came across safely and my feet and legs were numb.

When we got our ropes loose from the wagon, Luke said to Mr. Crankshaw, "Drive on." To me he said, "Get off and walk till your britches dry out."

Luke wore buckskins that were shiny with grease and wear, also moccasins. I never knew whether he had another name. He didn't talk much and when he did it was usually to give an order, short and sweet. He waited and talked to Mr. Arnold a few minutes, before Mr. Arnold recrossed the river and went back to Miles City.

Me and Dominique poured the ice water out of our boots and followed the wagon, leading my two horses.

Not a half mile north of the Yellowstone, Mr. Crankshaw turned the wagon over. It was only a shallow gully, and I did not understand how you could turn a wagon over in it, but this was before I knew my skinning partner Mr.

Crankshaw very well. He stalled in it, got to sawing the team left and right, and turned over the whole kit and kaboodle. It was only God's mercy that the powder didn't go.

We unhooked the team and the three of us managed to lift the wagon upright. Luke rode up. He clawed through the tangled mess of gear and supplies, found his needle gun, and inspected it to see that it was undamaged. He said, "Get this stuff in the wagon." To Dominique he said, "You drive." He looked at Mr. Crankshaw a minute and spat, saying nothing. Luke chewed large wads of tobacco and had a forceful way of spitting. He rode on ahead, leaving the reloading to us.

We had canvas, groceries, cooking pots, axes, shovels, powder, lead, bedding, knives, whetstones and sharpening steels, arsenic, and other things. I satisfied myself that the tins of arsenic had not mixed with the groceries. We got it loaded and followed Luke.

We traveled three days, during which time Dominique drove the wagon, Luke scouted around, and I became better acquainted with Mr. Crankshaw. He was a tall, skinny man, maybe forty, with a large nose and a mouth that drew down at the corners. He always looked sad. He told me that he had not meant to be a skinner and had got another job only the week before as boss, head scout, and shooter of a buffalo-hide crew. His employer had handed him a buffalo rifle to inspect and naturally he had tried the trigger pull the first thing. To his surprise the gun had been loaded and he had shot one of his employer's mules, which had fallen down dead on the spot. Unfortunately the employer had not been a reasonable man and had fired him before he hardly got started, giving his good-paying job to a half-breed from Canada. Now Mr. Crankshaw had agreed to be a skinner, though he came from a good family. He had a gallon of whiskey in his duffle and pulled on it once in a while, never offering anyone else a drink.

We went up into that broad wilderness bounded by the Yellowstone, Musselshell, and Missouri rivers. It is sagebrush country. Here and there pools of water lay from melted snow, and some of the creeks were running. On the same day we camped Luke shot a young cow buffalo for meat. He must have figured out how green his crew was by that time, because instead of handling her like you would for meat he showed us how he wanted them skinned.

You cut around the head, tail, and feet, slice the hide down the belly and up the legs, then peel the hide enough so that it's started. You gather up the neck skin and tie it good with a rope. You drive two stobs into the ground on each side of the neck to catch the horns. Then you bring in your team, hook the rope to the doubletree, and tug the hide right out from under the critter. If you are saving tenderloin and hams, as we did later on, you need to roll the animal onto a canvas sheet first to keep the sand off the meat. You chop out the tongue with a hatchet and shear off the mop of wool on the forehead. If during this work you get your hands dirty, wipe them on your trousers.

According to the plan of Mr. Arnold and Luke, we were supposed to haul the hides in to Dominique and he would take care of the rest. They had to be sprinkled with arsenic water on the hair side to keep the hide bugs and moths from eating them and then pegged out flesh side up to dry. Any meat left on the hide had to be peeled off.

We made our first camp in the fringes of the great herd. We had seen straggling buffalo and small bands of a half dozen. Sometimes we heard faintly the booming of big rifles miles away on all sides. Luke's work scouting was as important as his work shooting, for the picking of camp spots and knowing when to move made a big difference.

The first day of operations Mr. Crankshaw and I drove up to where Luke had downed seven buffalo inside of about an acre of space. We didn't waste any time. Mr. Crankshaw picked up a skinning knife in his right hand, with his left hand grabbed hold of a buffalo hoof, then proceeded to slice the palm of his left hand clean to the bone.

"For the love of God!" he said. "Blankenship, help me!" He dropped the knife and grabbed the left hand with the other. Blood squeezed out between his fingers.

How anybody could do what he had just done was beyond me. I mean, he was either going to cut around the shin bone or else start splitting down the inside of the leg. In either case how could you slice straight across your palm that way? You had to have your eyes closed or do it on purpose. But that look on his face! Mr. Crankshaw was not blessed with good looks anyway. As I mentioned, he was skinny, but he had a heavy appearance about his nose and eyebrows. His mouth turned down at the corners. As he backed off holding his hand with blood dripping down his sleeves, his face showed surprise and dismay like I'd never seen before.

As I helped tie it up the idea struck me that I had a Jonah for a skinning partner. All we had to wrap it with was his handkerchief, a blue bandanna that looked like it had been washed last year. He sat down on the ground, panting as if he'd been running.

I started skinning. In a minute he chuckled and said, "Well, it's all in a day's work, I guess."

It took me most of the day to skin the seven shaggies. During that time Mr. Crankshaw strolled around making comments. "It's a good thing I heal fast. Ha! Ha!" "You know anyone may cut himself until he gets used to the work. Ha! Ha!" "I believe there is money in this business. Ha! Ha! When we get started." "Thirty cents times seven is two-ten. Then we have to divide with the pegger, of course." I could not tell whether he was talking to me or the dead buffalo.

That day I ran into a thing which I got to thinking of later as the buffalo's revenge. If you come up to a fresh-shot buffalo and look around through the hair at the skin, especially on the belly or where the legs join the body, you see ticks hanging on and fleas scurrying around. The body is still warm. The ticks are slow to catch onto what has happened, but not the fleas; they are ready to abandon ship. You watch one and suddenly he disappears. Must have jumped. Where did he go? We would sure find out soon enough.

It's hard to tell what Luke thought about my skinning partner. Maybe he was too busy scouting and shooting to think anything. Mr. Crankshaw's hand became infected and he never did a lick of work. Dominique helped me skin and I helped him stretch hides and do everything else that had to be done. Mr. Crankshaw would stroll around holding his bandaged left hand against his chest. He had a strange way of getting right in the middle of the work like he was doing something. He would hold to a buffalo horn while we were skinning the critter. He would stand by the mules while they were pulling, trying to jerk a hide off, and would mutter words of encouragement to them. If we were pegging hides and I walked down to camp to get a bag of pegs we had cut the night before, Mr. Crankshaw would go with me. Now, if Dominique or I asked him to go after the bag of pegs, he might take a half an hour or come back and say he couldn't find them at all. Dominique and I worked our tail to the bone from daylight to dark. There was a big question in my mind as to whether Mr. Crankshaw would get his pay of ten cents a hide. One time I would think, Do you pay a man for doing nothing? But then I would think, Do you cut a man out because of a small accident? Of course, the rub was this: Maybe Luke or Mr. Arnold couldn't see it, but if the man hadn't cut his hand they would have probably fired him.

He couldn't even cook and I for one was satisfied that he didn't try. I was afraid he would get the flour confused with the arsenic. When he had thrown away his empty whiskey jug he came out with another one from his duffle bag. He took two or three nips each day and seemed to be able to handle the jug well enough with his right hand alone.

Mr. Arnold had a big meat-smoking shed on Redwater Creek. His freight wagons worked out of there, and he also bought some hides from independent hunters. They called the place Arnold City. It had two saloons with planks across barrels for bars, a gambling hall with room for four poker tables, and another freight headquarters, all of these establishments made out of buffalo hides stretched over pole frameworks. The only wooden building was the meat-smoking shed. Whenever we killed a number of cows within ten miles or so of Arnold City, we would butcher out the hump steaks, tenderloin, and hams, let them chill during one of those cool nights, and haul them to the smoking shed the next day. As for the tongues, we cured them in our own camps with a salt-sugar mixture and by stringing them up on a wire to smoke.

Mr. Arnold had set up an icehouse and an ice-cutting crew down on the Yellowstone River the winter before. He had planned to use the ice to keep meat with and hauled several big freight wagons full up to Arnold City, but it turned out to be more trouble than it was worth. You could get by without it in May, and you couldn't hardly save any meat by using it in July. The meat would be too far gone before you got it on ice.

Every trip to the smoking shed we carried our skinning and butcher knives, of which we had about two dozen, to sharpen on a pedal grindstone there. We sharpened them every night in our own camp, but you could thin them down better on the grindstone. Nothing takes the edge off of a blade like cutting buffalo hide. I have read somewhere that it is because there is mud and dirt in the hair; that is bull. Any leather or rawhide dulls a knife, as any cowhand who has cut a lot of thongs can tell you. Come to think of it, if leather wouldn't wear steel how could a barber strop a razor? But thick buffalo hide beats it all. A knife will wear down to a toothpick in one season.

Mr. Arnold kept account of every penny we were due on all the hides that had been freighted out, and he was willing any time a man saw him to pay off part or all that was owed. I left mine lay. He was a big operator and good for any amount you had against him. One thing was clear; I sure wasn't getting rich. Evidently Mr. Crankshaw was drawing down some money, enough to keep him stocked up on whiskey from one of the saloons at Arnold City. The question stayed in my mind about splitting the thirty cents a hide between two skinners and a pegger. I guess I had a vague thought that some day Mr. Arnold, Luke, and us three would sit down and decide what was right. We would say that Mr. Crankshaw had not done a lick of work and was getting his meals free, which was mostly buffalo meat and free to anybody. We would say he signed on for ten cents a hide and the accident cutting his hand was not his fault. Such as that. We would agree on what was right to do.

One day it rained, and that was the first rest I and Dominique had got in weeks. All we had to do was work in camp, scratch fleas, and mold bullets. The four of us sat around on boxes and kegs in our hide house, Crankshaw holding his bandaged left hand against his chest as usual. Luke was particular about his shells and wouldn't let anybody touch them except to mold bullets. You can remold a bullet if a greenhorn ruins it, but not the rest of the shell. He washed all the brass hulls in hot vinegar water, rinsed them, and dried them. He looked every one over like it was a piece of jewelry before changing the primer section and crimping the mouth to size it. He would measure the powder like he didn't want to get one grain too little or too much. He would pick up a ball out of the pan full we had molded, look it over carefully, and about half of them he would toss back in the melting skillet.

I learned a rule that day the hard way. Reader, do not put anything wet into melted lead. The ladle was hot, so I dipped it in a bucket of water. Then I dipped into the skillet. Pow!

Hot lead flew every which way. It must be the steam that causes it. Pieces stuck into my shirt and one burned me on the wrist. I looked around and it didn't look like anybody else got hit. Luke stared at me a minute, then said, "You do that damned fool trick again and hit this powder and we might all go to Kingdom Come!"

I got sore at that, but also it set me thinking. Here I was doing half or more of the skinning and pegging and meat handling, not getting anything on the meat. If this high and mighty shooter, who had probably not taken off his greasy buckskins in two years, would make Mr. Crankshaw work or else fire him, maybe I would be getting better pay for working my tail off seven days a week. Anybody is going to do a stupid trick sometimes. I did not hire on to be a genius. It struck me about then what Mr. Crankshaw had said that "anyone may cut himself until he gets used to the work. Ha! Ha!" Well, I was not going to apologize to Luke and say "Ha! Ha!" If he didn't like it he could lump it. For a minute I felt sympathetic with Mr. Crankshaw, even if he was a Jonah; but about that time he went to his jug and took a nip without offering one to anybody else. How can you feel sorry for a man so worthless?

One afternoon I saw what they called the "great northern herd." We'd been hearing the boom of big rifles around us all day and knew that there was plenty of action. I'd walked three miles back to camp to get a repair link for a busted trace chain, and caught Chili to ride back to the spot where we had the kill. Bunches of buffalo were scattered everywhere, from a half dozen to a hundred together, grazing. They seemed to be thicker out to the west. I rode a mile or two out of my way to a ridge. Below me clear to the horizon buffalo were so thick that in most places you could not see the ground. They had shed their shaggy winter hair by this time and their backs were smooth brown, shining in the sunlight. Some were standing, like they were waiting for something. You could see currents in them, moving slowly south. You kind of get your breath when you see such a thing; even then it takes a few minutes for it to soak in. In my first surprise I thought I would count them. Estimate, anyway. I know that I was looking at a hundred thousand but had to give up; there may have been five times that many. Out there a certain distance it was just solid brown, like the land was alive.

The great herd made you feel different from what a few

buffalo did. I cannot describe it. It was a little like a flock of blackbirds you see sometimes flying over, stretching from horizon to horizon, and you are struck by the numbers of live things. But it was more than that, because of the size of these animals. Somehow you had to think about all the hundreds of years they had grazed over the thousands of miles of plains.

I was lost a while, sitting there watching. Then I had a practical idea, which I have thought about and added to since. I don't know what the experts say, but I think the buffalo helped shape the land with their hooves and their crowding together. You can see broken country, badlands—malpais, the Mexicans call it—where there must have been good soil once. You can see mesas, and the top of them is where all the land was once. What happened to all that dirt? The wind, they say. The gully-washer rains. But it was the sharp split hooves of buffalo too. They will graze close and when they are gathered in a herd they will kill every stem of grass in their path. They will leave the ground pulverized. Some cattle ranchers say sheep will do it. I don't know. I know a buffalo is a lot heavier and they run in bigger bunches. The sight I saw that day in June of '82 left me with no doubt that they have the power to shape the land.

I'm glad I wasted a half hour and rode onto that ridge. Already I was guessing the truth. I could hear the *Boom!* ... *Boom!* ... *Boom! Boom!* ... *Boom!* around, and from where I sat on my horse I could see a dozen hunters' wagons or camps. The great middle herd was gone and the great southern herd. I'd helped pick up the bones without thinking much about it. Reader, this was the very last summer in all the time of the world when a man could see what I saw sitting there. I about halfway knew it and felt damned sad as I rode back to where Dominique and Mr. Crankshaw waited for me.

One day I loaned Mr. Crankshaw ten dollars. I knew better, but the trouble was that you couldn't guess that he had the gall he had. We went into Arnold City, and Mr. Arnold was not there. Mr. Crankshaw said to me, "Duke, let me have ten dollars for a few days." I had told Dominique that sometimes I went by the nickname of Duke, and Mr. Crankshaw had jumped on the name like a dog on a bone. "I need to buy a few things," he said, "and I'll pay you back when we see Mr. Arnold."

Well, he caught me by surprise and I didn't have any excuse made up. I loaned him the ten. About a week later he got Dominique the same way.

As the weather became warmer that summer we did better stacking up hides because we stopped messing with meat so much. If you can't chill it the night after you butcher it, you'll probably lose it. But with the warm weather the work got harder and more disgusting. Flies swarmed everywhere, big ones, little ones, black ones, green ones. Millions. And the putrid smell that spread over that country! Two or three times we moved our camp just to try to escape it.

Mr. Crankshaw complained quite a lot in a good-natured sort of way. Dominique and I would be slaving away skinning one of the shaggy critters, sweat dripping off our noses, and Mr. Crankshaw would be standing nearby, his bandaged hand tucked against his chest, using his other hand to scratch fleas and fight flies. He would say, "These flies are terrible! Well, I guess we just have to grin and bear it." After a while he would say, "I believe the smell is worse today, if it can get any worse. Ha! Ha! Well, I guess we just have to put up with things like that." Sometimes he would walk over and wave the flies off a carcass we had skinned or off a hide lying on the ground, as if he were helping in the work. Once in a while he gave us the news that his hand was healing and would probably be as good as new any day now.

I did not see him step in our pot of beans, but I know he did. We had our cooking fire out under a tree a ways from the shelter. The pot had been sitting beside the fire and it was turned over. Mr. Crankshaw had beans all over his boot. He did not say a thing about it but just seemed to take it for granted. Every time you get to despising a man like that you find yourself suddenly feeling sorry for him again.

One night Dominique said something about buying a horse after the skinning was over that fall, and I offered to sell him Cricket for eighteen dollars. We talked about it, what was wrong with Cricket and all. I told him he would be getting a good bit of horse for eighteen dollars. Dominique said he wanted to think it over.

In August Mr. Arnold broke up our crew. The skinners and others hanging around Arnold City had a rumor going that Mr. Arnold needed Luke and some of his teams free to start a new operation that winter: smuggling Chinamen across the Canadian border to work on railroads. If it was true I wanted no part of it. In fact, I was well satisfied to get out of the buffalo-hide business, but I got sore that day talking to Mr. Arnold. He paid me a hundred and thirty dollars, which was supposed to cover everything except about ninety hides we had drying out at camp. He told me I was to drive a freight wagon with a load of hides and pickled tongue down to Miles City, where he would pay me the last few dollars in final settlement.

I said, "I can't do it. I have two horses and my rifle and all my personal stuff out at the camp."

Mr. Arnold said, "The other crew members will clean

up the camp and deliver your things to Miles City. I need you to drive the big wagon."

I was not happy about that plan or the money either. I said, "Mr. Arnold, I don't like this. I'm not satisfied with the settlement."

We were standing at the end of his meat-smoking shed and he threw his big book down on the top of a barrel. "There's the account," he said. "Examine it. It's no secret. I'm not satisfied either. I had to break up one crew and I chose yours because you men are not delivering. You get exactly ten cents a hide."

"Well," I said, "you know why we didn't deliver."

"No, I don't."

"Why, Mr. Arnold, me and Dominique did all the work. Mr. Crankshaw didn't turn a hand."

"You're exaggerating, Blankenship. You made an agreement with me and I have to hold you to it. I have a great deal of money invested in my operations. I count on my men to live up to their agreements and I live up to mine."

I told him, "I'm not exaggerating. Mr. Crankshaw didn't do anything but stand around."

He said, "If you'll think it over you'll see that you're exaggerating. If you didn't think he was working hard enough you should have complained. You'll find that when you're in business on percentage or speculation, you must guard your own interests."

"Are you going to pay Mr. Crankshaw ten cents a hide?"

"I certainly am. I can't change the agreement at this stage of the game."

When I tried to think of exactly what Mr. Crankshaw had done, all I could remember was his driving the wagon a half mile that time before he wrecked it. It was hopeless to try to convince anyone that a man could be that worthless. The man who had really done me dirty was Luke, and evidently Mr. Arnold had already sent him up north somewhere.

I said I had agreed to help with the meat one or two days a week for nothing, but I hadn't agreed to do any freighting. Mr. Arnold said he wanted all his employees to be satisfied, so he would pay me four dollars extra for driving the six-mule team down to Miles City. I didn't like leaving my personal horses and gear to be looked after by Dominique and Mr. Crankshaw, but I agreed. The only bright spot I could see in the affair was that Mr. Crankshaw would have the money to pay back the ten he had borrowed from me.

The Yellowstone River was down. I forded it on a Sunday afternoon without any trouble, came into Miles City, and turned the load over to an Arnold representative.

Somebody had told me that it gets down to forty below in Montana and I did not want to spend the winter here. The idea that Buck might be down in Arizona country had crossed my mind several times; it was a vague hope, but I had a hankering to see that country anyway. I figured to ride up the valley of the Yellowstone to Billings, then cut south, taking my time. Actually, I believed that I could pass for a cowhand on anybody's ranch and would have no trouble finding work.

I bought me some clothes in Miles City, got a hot bath and a haircut, and waited. On Tuesday Mr. Crankshaw rode into town alone on a gray roan horse. He yelled at me like he hadn't seen me in a year. "Hey, Duke, how are you?" His hand was no longer bandaged.

He said Mr. Arnold and Dominique would be here in a couple of days and bring all my stuff. He was very proud of the new horse he had bought and said he'd paid forty dollars. It didn't look like forty dollars' worth of horse to me. Suddenly he said, "Oh! did I tell you, Duke? We sold your old horse Cricket for you. Dominique will bring the money."

"What did you get?"

"Well, eighteen dollars. Isn't that what you said? I'm sure that must have been what it was, eighteen dollars. Dominique will get the money when the man that bought him settles up out there at Arnold City."

He showed me his hand. He had a bad scar from the cut. It struck me that even though he was a useless and disgusting man, at least he had been honest about not being able to work. About that time he said, "Don't let me forget I owe you ten dollars, Duke. I want to be sure and pay you when I get things straightened out."

I took it for granted that he had some more money coming from Mr. Arnold. Actually, he had already drawn all he had coming. Mr. Crankshaw was not the kind of man you would choose to hang around town with, but he was the only soul I knew. We looked around and ate and had some drinks.

I remember sitting in one place drinking and the thought came to me: Mr. Crankshaw is not really so bad as you've got him painted in your mind. I had just got down on him on account of the cut hand. He told me that he came from a good family and had once owned a store in a small town in Illinois. His father and grandfather had been in the brick-making business. I told him about my plans to travel up the Yellowstone River to Billings, then cut south and make my way down to Arizona Territory.

The only thing that bothered me that night was when Mr. Crankshaw said, "I sure hope Dominique brings the eighteen dollars." I thought, What the devil does he mean? He had talked before like it was settled. Later he said,

"Surely Dominique will collect the money for your horse, Duke."

I went to the hotel before midnight. No telling where Mr. Crankshaw was staying. I didn't see him until late the next afternoon. He came down the main street on his dirty roan horse and a strange pack that bulged out on each side tied behind the saddle. He again greeted me like I was his best friend. "Hey, Duke, guess what! I'm going up to Billings with you. Yeah, that's right. I'll be going up there on business, so we can go together."

I was not exactly tickled at the idea. It seemed like he would mention what his business was or what he had in the pack, but he went along just taking everything for granted. In fact, we headed for an eating place together and he reached in his back pocket and pulled out a pint bottle and had a big drink. We'd been drinking together the night before, but he never offered me a drink or said Excuse me or By your leave or Go to hell.

On Friday Mr. Arnold and Dominique came into town in the light camping wagon, leading my horse Chili. No sooner did the wagon stop than I began pawing around and made sure they'd brought my rifle and saddle and clothes and everything. Then I asked Dominique, "Did you get the money for Cricket?"

"I don't know what you mean," he said.

Mr. Crankshaw was standing there and he said, "The eighteen dollars. Wasn't that the amount? I thought that's what Duke was asking."

"I didn't have anything to do with it," Dominique said, "and you know I didn't."

"Surely he paid you!" Mr. Crankshaw said. "The man. . . . What was his name?"

"How do I know?" Dominique said. "I didn't even speak

to him. I didn't sell the horse. Charley didn't tell me to sell the horse. Nobody paid me anything."

Mr. Crankshaw said, "Well, I'll swan! I'm afraid some bad mistake has been made. It's a good thing we didn't sell your best horse."

"Stop saying 'we,'" Dominique said. "You did it."

I told Mr. Crankshaw, "You're going to pay me for Cricket. I want my money."

"You'll sure get it, Duke. I'll guarantee that. I swear on my grandmother's grave."

Dominique and I went into the office with Mr. Arnold and he paid us each nine dollars in final settlement of our agreement, plus the four extra dollars he had promised me. I asked him if Mr. Crankshaw had anything coming and he said, "No, I paid him in full out on the range in order to get rid of him. I don't like the fellow."

I asked Dominique, "Did he pay you the ten dollars he borrowed?"

"No, and I'm not waiting around for it. I want to get away from him."

I was getting mad. Why should I have to let Mr. Crankshaw beat me out of my money in order to get away from him? I went outside and he was standing by the hitch rail holding that roan with the bulging packs behind the saddle. He said, "Well, Duke, did you get all settled up?"

I said, "Listen, Mr. Crankshaw, I want my money."

He said, "You'll sure get it, Duke. There's no question about that. I'm going to take all the blame about your horse and pay you the money out of my own pocket. It's only right. My money is tied up at this time, but I'll have the cash when we get to Billings. I swear it on my grandmother's grave. And remember the ten I owe you also. We don't want to forget that."

I didn't want him to go to Billings with me, but I was mad and thinking some stupid thoughts. Why should I let him beat me out of twenty-eight dollars even if I had to put up with his company? I had another feeling too that made even less sense. He had sold my horse Cricket. I had spent a lot of cold days and hot days on that horse, with him feeling the weather the same as I did. We had looked for water holes and he had appreciated a good drink of water as much as me. I had ridden him until I was dead tired and knew when it came time to rest that he was worn out as me. I had talked to him when I was lonesome. Now, he had been a naturally bony horse and had a rough trotting gait, but that didn't keep it from being sad to get rid of him. That son-of-a-bitch Mr. Crankshaw had sold him without even asking me.

Those feelings and ideas rolled around in my head a while; then I asked myself, What has that got to do with it? Good old Cricket, my eye! I'd been ready to sell him myself for eighteen dollars. There was no use in painting Mr. Crankshaw any worse than he was; he was bad enough at best.

I bought a side of bacon, ten pounds of flour, two pounds of coffee, and four pounds of dried apricots, and rode southwest up the south bank of the Yellowstone with Mr. Crankshaw. We found a beautiful camping spot beside that clear stream about sundown with good grass for the horses. I was rustling around building a fire and breaking out my cooking gear when suddenly I guessed what I should have suspected: the man did not have any camping gear nor a speck of food.

I said, "What did you mean to eat on the way to Billings, Mr. Crankshaw? You don't even have a gun to kill game."

He was strolling around doing nothing, like he'd been

doing the last four months. He said, "Why, I thought we'd just go in together, Duke. I guess we're used to each other by now. Ha! Ha!"

I said, "Mr. Crankshaw, I don't understand you. I think we better have a talk and lay some cards on the table. I'm just a youngster myself. I don't aim to be mean, but I can just barely take care of myself and get by."

He said, "Aw, Duke, don't run yourself down. You're one of the best hands I ever saw. I believe you can do anything you decide to do. Don't run yourself down. I respect you."

"I'm trying to tell you something, dammit! You may eat free off of Mr. Arnold and screw me and Dominique out of ten cents a hide, but you're not going to follow me around and have me take care of you. I'm nineteen years old. I'm trying to tell you that I have got all I can do to support myself."

He said, "I hate to hear you belittle yourself that way. Duke, you can do as much as most men twice your age. I'm sincere. I want you to know that one of the best things I've found in the West is the chance to live with you and be your friend. I value your friendship, Duke. I really do."

"Dammit!" I said. "Will you listen? I'm not your friend! I don't like you. I don't like your looks. I don't like anything about you. We haven't ever been friends. I don't like it when you borrow ten dollars and say you'll pay me in Billings. I don't like it when you sell my damned horse when I didn't tell you to and then try to act like Dominique had something to do with it. We're not friends! Can't you get it through your head?"

"I'm sorry you feel that way, Duke," he said. "I've always thought quite a lot of you."

I clammed up. He sat there nipping at a bottle of whiskey

while I made supper. After I had got it done he helped himself, ate, then stood and watched me while I rinsed out the dishes. For two days it went along that way. He would try to make conversation, but I wouldn't answer him. Finally I shot an elk and butchered out the hindquarter. I fried myself a steak and thought I'd just wait and see whether he'd do the same or starve. When he saw I was eating all I'd cooked, he began to hack at the meat, got some off, and cooked it himself. It struck me that one reason why he didn't do much was that he didn't know how and another was he was scared he would botch the deal.

Chili was already loaded fairly heavy carrying my things, without adding any meat. I asked Mr. Crankshaw, "What do you have in your packs?"

Then he told me his stupid scheme. He had two five-gallon kegs of whiskey, which he expected some way to sell to the Indians. When I asked him what Indians, he didn't know; there would surely be Indians of some kind up around Billings. There was big money in it. What you did was pour five gallons of whiskey into a fifty-gallon barrel, add water and vinegar and pepper and tobacco, anything to give it body, and you were in business.

I asked him if he had any money at all. He said he didn't; he'd tied up all his money in his horse and ten gallons of whiskey.

I asked him, "Where are you going to get the barrel and pepper and vinegar and tobacco?"

He hadn't thought of that. In a minute he said, "Would you be able to let me have another ten, Duke? You'll get all your money back. You can be sure of that."

I told him that his business plan was the craziest thing I'd ever heard of and he would probably lose his scalp or get arrested. He gave me a lot of argument, saying many people were in the Indian-whiskey business and after he got used to the way it worked and located the right Indians he could sell for cash or ponies; he figured he had at least two hundred dollars' worth of whiskey, that is, after it was mixed.

We came up to where the Big Horn River runs into the Yellowstone, and I bought some more grub there at a trading post. Then I told Mr. Crankshaw the bad news. "I've decided not to go up to Billings with you, Mr. Crankshaw. I'll cut south up this river. I wish you good luck."

He followed me, arguing. "Why, Duke, I can't let you do that. I owe you money and I want to pay it."

"I've decided to give you the money you owe me so I can get away from you," I said. "Good-by and good luck."

He kept on following. "But I want to pay you, Duke. Besides, we've been friends a long time. We'll total up what you spend for grub and I'll owe half of that to you too. You'll get all your money back, Duke. I swear on my grandmother's grave."

He followed right behind me for an hour; then I stopped and asked him, "Mr. Crankshaw, do you know why I don't want to go with you and don't want you to go with me?"

"Why, Duke?"

"Don't you know?"

"No, I don't. What is it, Duke?"

"You're a damned Jonah. You can't do anything, and when you do, you do it wrong. You're lazy. All you do is stand around and drink."

"I'll never drink another drop as long as I live," he said.

"Besides that I don't like your looks or anything about you. You're always making mistakes. Always bungling."

He looked sadder than usual even. He said, "That's the truth, Duke, and I can't help it. I have bad luck. I'm glad you brought it up, and I'm going to start being more careful from now on. I don't blame you for saying I'm a Jonah, but you know I can't help it. You couldn't help it when you blew up the lead skillet that time. But I don't want to mention that. Forget I said it."

He had almost got me feeling sorry for him again when he brought up the explosion in the lead skillet. I said, "No, Mr. Crankshaw, I've been telling you wrong. The reason I don't want you to go with me is this: You tell lies and you're crooked. You're low-down. You're sorry. If you want people to be your friend don't lie to them. Don't cheat them. How do you expect anybody to be your friend if you don't act like a friend is supposed to act yourself?"

"That's my trouble," he said. "I needed somebody to tell me that, Duke. I'm going to turn over a new leaf. Sure enough. I'm ashamed of myself and I'll be a new man from now on. You'll see."

And so Mr. Crankshaw followed me south. Nothing changed except that his bottle became empty and he started nipping on the kegs. Every day or so he would say something about trading with the Indians, but how he expected to get a new stock after he drank up the old one he never said. For over a week we followed the Big Horn River; then we cut west over into the Wind River Range.

I got sore at him one morning. Up in a high valley we saw a half dozen antelope and we needed some meat. I was about to get a good shot at one when he trotted up on that dirty roan yelling and pointing at one a half mile away. The whole bunch spooked and took off for low country.

That evening we camped in a pass with peaks all around. Up to the north the mountains had snow on them. You could see a long ways west. Later I learned that this was named South Pass on the Oregon Trail. The air smelled sweet and the ground was soft with rotten pine needles, but I was out of sorts on account of losing the antelope. I fussed about this and that, then began griping about the whole summer's work skinning buffalo. Mr. Crankshaw fell in with my mood and said that after all that time with Mr. Arnold when he settled up he only got forty dollars.

I said, "He paid you ten cents a hide, but you drew some before that and spent it, and when you settled up you got forty dollars?"

"That's right. And forty dollars isn't much."

"I believe you said you paid forty dollars for your horse."

"That's right, Duke. I had to pay every cent of it for my horse."

"What did you give for two kegs of whiskey?"

"I got it at a bargain for eighteen dollars."

He began to ramble on about the prospects of making big money selling whiskey to the Indians, but I cut him short.

"Mr. Crankshaw! You've made a bad mistake following me out here to this lonesome country, because I'm fixing to beat the living hell out of you!"

"What's the matter, Duke?"

I'm so mad I can't talk. When angry, they say, count ten; but who remembers old sayings at a time like this? When I rush him he's trying to get to his feet, also backing up like a crawfish and at the same time saying, "I meant to tell you the truth, Duke! I meant to tell you I got the money for Cricket! You'll get your money, Duke! You can be sure of that!"

The first swing I hit him on the arm and the second I get him a good one on the nose. He begins flinging his fists but can't fight worth a hoot. We grab each other and roll; the worst damage I get is some bruises on my back from rolling over the rocks. We turn loose and scramble around trying to sock each other. At the time I'm so mad I can't hardly see but I remember the silly look on his ugly face with the blood running out of his nose while he tries to put up a fight; he's trying harder than he's tried anything since I met him. He throws a looping right that misses me a foot and hits the trunk of a tree; his weight is so solid behind it that he goes on and stumbles into the tree. About that time I get him another glancing blow on the mouth.

I feel like pounding on him for hours. Here is what stops it: he backs through the campfire and kicks a burning chunk out on my saddle blanket and catches it on fire. Of course I begin to try to save my stuff.

We're both panting like a steam engine. He sits down over there swabbing at his nose and busted lip. Finally he says, "I say one thing, Duke. You whipped me fair and square." What can you do with a man like that?

The next morning his right hand was swollen up as big as a ham, giving him an excuse again, if he needed any, to do nothing. We rode southwest.

That was the longest trip I ever made of steady traveling, from late August into November. I saw every kind of scenery, all of it grand and wild and lonely. We passed mountain peaks that rose way up past the line of firs and pines and aspens, just bare cold rocks with snow in the cracks and hollows. The places, though, which seemed to give the biggest sense of distance were the sagebrush flats in Utah that stretched on and on. We went hundreds of miles without seeing any houses except two or three stage-coach stations.

Most of the time we had no road but wound this way and

that, trying to find the best way to go south. One canyon we followed east three days before we found a way to cross it, and I think the trail might have been made by mountain goats. Also, we had to locate decent fords across the streams and passes through the hills and mountains. I was worried about Chili's shoes. They had been nearly new in Miles City but were getting thin. In rocky ground I let him pick his own easy way.

The weeks of riding led into months. We came through country that had high brown cliffs and orange cliffs and bare clay hills. Then we threaded our way through land that had mesas and natural monuments sticking up. It seemed drier. We were coming into Arizona Territory.

I'm glad I made that ride before I got sense enough not to try it.

Some of that country—a man wants to look at it alone or else with a person he likes. The big fly in my ointment was Mr. Crankshaw. I went along hating him one day and feeling sorry for him the next. The one five-gallon keg which he had emptied did come in handy for carrying water. One time I got the idea not to give him any more food, but he was so friendly and understanding watching me eat that I could only do it two meals, then gave in.

Somewhere north of Winslow the second keg of whiskey petered out. I guess Mr. Crankshaw gave up his business plans, because he started saying, "I don't think we'll have any trouble finding work down here, Duke. We'll surely find work." I was feeling desperate about him.

That was Navajo reservation country. We stopped at an Indian trading store one morning early. They had a post office and groceries and nearly anything you wanted to buy. My bankroll was down to fifty-six dollars, so I bought only two pounds of coffee and a box of shells for my rifle. Mr. Crankshaw looked around in the store a minute, then said, "Let me have ten, Duke. When we find work I'll pay you back the first thing." I did not answer him.

We rode south along a faint road, and around noon it began to shower. Rain would be pelting down one minute; then the cloud would pass over and the sun come out bright. When those cactus and Joshua trees and everything get the dust rinsed off so that they shine in the sunlight they make a sight to look at. The road came to a wash which had probably been dry as a bone a few hours ago but now had about a foot of muddy water rolling down it. The bed was full of rounding rocks, some of them sticking out of the water. You couldn't see where the crossing was supposed to be. I gave Chili his head and he picked his way across.

Behind me my leech of a partner begins yelling, "Duke! Duke!"

He's floundering in the water. His roan comes on out and I catch him. I never knew whether the horse stumbled and went down or Mr. Crankshaw just flat fell off. I wade out and drag him to the gravel bank.

His left leg is broken between the knee and the ankle. His hand he busted swinging at me had just got healed and now his leg is broken. I put him on his horse with him grunting in pain and we ride on to try to find some help or at least a place to camp. I know we can't go far, because Mr. Crankshaw is pale as a ghost and yelping every rough step his roan makes.

About a mile past the wash we see a log and dirt house, which the Indians call a hogan, not far off the dim road. A man is working on some sheep pens, wiring crooked sticks of driftwood up to repair the fence. It's a poor-looking place. A half dozen skinny wet chickens run around.

A woman looks at us from the door of the hogan as we ride up.

The man, barefooted, wears a shirt and pants and shoulder-length hair with a band of cloth around his forehead. He grins broadly, answers my "hello," and right away tells me that he's a corporal. I take it to mean that he's been a scout for the army. Grinning all the while, he helps me get Mr. Crankshaw down and lay him beside the sheep fence.

He seems like the friendliest Indian I've ever seen. I take all the silver money I've got in my pocket, nearly two dollars, hand it to him, and say, "I'll go get the doctor!"

With him grinning that way you can't tell how much he understands. I'm having a quick argument with Old Satan as I start to mount my horse. I stop, get a ten-dollar bill out of my pocketbook, and hand it to the Indian. As I get into the saddle Mr. Crankshaw says something, but I'm in too big a hurry to listen. Chili probably wonders why I'm kicking him and yelling at him to get out of there.

If there was a doctor in that country I never knew it. For two days I made good time and could not help looking back every once in a while to see if anybody was following.

It has been said that the white man did wrong by the Indians. I've only done one of them wrong that I know of. Sometimes my still small voice says to me, Why did you do it to that friendly Navajo, who had never harmed you? My only hope is this: He didn't look too savage, but maybe he had enough in him to take his knife and do right by Mr. Crankshaw. Or if he didn't have the guts to cut his throat, maybe he had the sense to foist him off on somebody else, sort of pass him around.

Chapter 5
You Can't Miss It

NORTH ARIZONA IS HIGH PLATEAU COUNTRY, not like that on the east side of the Rockies. It's rugged. Rough peaks stick up and canyons cut through it. A poorly kept road led me into the new little town of Flagstaff, which is surrounded by mountains.

I walked down the street looking it over and laughing a little at myself. When I'd see a man some distance off or with his back to me I'd say, Could that be Buck? No, not this time. Then I'd realize I hadn't really expected it to be. After I had arrived some place it always seemed that my expectations to find him would fade. He could really be in Arizona Territory somewhere, but farther on, maybe in Prescott, beyond the horizon. At the same time I couldn't help looking.

One store had a long boardwalk in front with a canvas shade over it. On one end of the walk squatted an Indian in baggy blue and red calico shirt and trousers, his hair tied out of his face with a sweatband. Before him on a folded blanket he had arranged silver jewelry, buckles, bracelets, necklaces, brooches, conchos, and other things. I saw two women stop and look at the display a minute. When they left I went over to look.

I asked the man, "Are these things for sale?"

He grinned and answered in an Indian language. It didn't seem to bother him in the least that we could not talk.

Some of his jewelry was rough, sort of chopped out. The batch looked like it had been made by different people. But my eyes lit on a solid bracelet of silver that looked like whiter metal than the others. It had four small pieces of blue-green turquoise spaced evenly around it. I could not help remembering the brooch Buck had brought home to Ma. I touched it and the Indian did not mind, so I picked it up. You couldn't hardly tell how the sets had been put in. The silver seemed all one piece. Fine tracks led up to each bit of turquoise in a beautiful design. It looked like it was made for a queen, and I wanted it so bad for my ma that I would almost have given my left arm.

I took out two five-dollar bills and offered them to him. He shook his head no. I made it twenty and it was still no.

His grin hadn't changed. The bracelet had really caught my fancy. It was not just the silver and turquoise; the way it was laid out and put together made you want to look at it. The Indian evidently knew it was something special. I had almost exactly forty dollars to my name and no job, but I raised the ante to thirty. The answer was still no.

I walked around town asking about work. The only possibility was a job stacking green lumber for a man who had a steam sawmill. I spent the night in town and got ready to move on the next morning. The Indian was still on the boardwalk of the store when I tied Chili in front and went inside to buy some grub and a box of shells for my rifle.

When I was paying up I said, "That old Indian outside sure wants high prices for his stuff."

The storekeeper said, "Some of it. He's got one bracelet

that's a beaut. I offered him twenty, but he wouldn't take it."

"I offered him thirty," I said.

"Silver money?"

I told him no.

"Try silver," he said.

I got thirty silver dollars and went outside and put my stuff on my horse. I went over to the Indian, put the dollars on his blanket, and pointed at the bracelet. He examined the dollars one by one and tested them with a knife point, then nodded at me. He seemed sorry to sell it.

I wrapped the bracelet in a clean handkerchief and a clean shirt and put it in my saddlebags, then rode southwest out of Flagstaff.

It was a three-day ride through rugged country to Prescott. I don't know why I went there unless it was because it was the capital of the territory. It was a larger town and had considerable mining around it. A lot of the houses and buildings were adobe.

A Mexican was selling hot tamales out of a basket which he carried on his arm. I ate six. They were good, but I got sick and didn't feel worth a hoot for two days.

Nobody seemed to be hiring cowhands that time of the year. I was nearly broke and wondering if I'd have to get a job in a store or some place. The only lead I got was about a rancher named Colonel Searcy, who had a spread over a hundred miles east of Prescott and had been in town the week before trying to hire hands. I got the information from two places, the postmaster and also a bartender, so it seemed worth checking into.

I rode east across the valley of the Verde River, through stretches of cactus and agave, yucca, ocotillo, mesquite. The nights were cold, and I slept as close as I could to the coals of my campfire. On Tonto Creek I got directions to the outfit of Colonel Searcy and headed north into the foothills. This country gets rougher to the north, with canyons and rocky peaks, but has forests of ponderosa pine. From high ground near the Searcy ranch house you could see in the distance a sheer bluff, the Tonto Rim.

My memory of this country is partly good, partly bad. The first thing the colonel put me on was tanking. It got me off on the wrong foot. He was a nut about building tanks. He used to come out in his buggy to where we were working, a heavy old man with a backbone like a wagon rod and white muttonchop whiskers like a retired sea captain. He would look at us slaving away, loosening dirt with a plow and moving it with a fresno, doing what he had told us, and say, "Yes. Yes. Yes." One time he said to me, "You see, Mr. Blankenship, we have all the water we need. It must be held where it falls." He worked you like a slave and called you Mister.

Colonel Searcy had come into that country a few years before and had started building tanks, or "ponds" as they are called back east, right away. Being a hog for water, as you are bound to be in Arizona, he had chosen the big washes for sites and put dams across them. Everything he built the first two years had washed out with the first gully-washer that came along. Now he had wised up. He was building tanks on the side of a rise, anywhere it looked like a trickle of water might run down. Of course he was right. The range he claimed had only a little frontage on the creek and he was watering cattle as much as ten miles back in the hills. I saw it rain a few times there, and that's when the colonel really got excited. He would get out in that buggy miles from the ranch house and watch the water trickling around on the land. He said to me once, "Mr.

Blankenship, nature is the best surveyor. If you want to know which way the water runs and how much water, go look when it's raining." Come to think of it, I guess he was pretty smart at that.

The tanking crew was an old man called Sergeant, a Mexican named Eduardo, and me, and six mules. Sergeant did the plowing by himself with the lines tied behind his back. I and Eduardo ran the fresno, one driving the four mules, one loading and dumping. You would not think that a big iron box contraption that you drag around to move dirt could be as much work for two men. The first trouble is that you are always walking in a footing of loose dirt, clods, uphill, downhill, stumbling over mule tracks, your feet sinking in and cocking sideways. Around and around you go, taking a load out of the tank, up on the dam to dump, and circle to the bottom again for another load. The fresno will ride pretty free by itself. The man on the handle rope pulls to right the scraper when you come into the tank bottom, then lifts up on the handle just enough to take a thin bite with the blade and get a load. Of course, it wants to take a thick bite or no bite at all. He fights it. By the time he gets a load he's off balance and has lost his hold. He runs in the cloddy footing to catch up. At the right place on the dam he gives a mighty heave on the handle to dump it. This makes him lose his balance, and he has to run to catch up.

Me and Eduardo switched off. Driving the team should have been easier except for one old mare mule we had, named Victoria. She could loll out her tongue a foot. She would roll it around on her bit, flap it around and feel of her bridle, put it in her mouth and chew on it. Victoria woke up to a new world every day. She had not learned a blessed thing since she was a colt. She would dream off into some mule's happy hunting ground. If you struck a shelf of rock and had to stop the team, when you started them again she might take off sideways for home or goodness knows where. She would step on her singletree, put her feet out of the traces, hang her neck over the mule beside her, and gaze into the sky. When you got her jerked into line, she would start flapping that tongue.

To tell the truth, I didn't think it was any work for a cowhand. I could have driven idiot mules like that and stayed in Missouri.

In the middle of the winter the colonel announced that sooner or later we were going to have an Apache uprising. He wanted to get all his *cimarrón* cattle out of the back country and sell them. I was happy to find myself horseback again.

I had plenty to learn. They don't work like they do on the plains east of the Rockies. It's because of the rougher country and thinner grazing. You can ride for miles in Arizona and never see a cow unless you know where to look; they go where the water is, where the grass is, where it's cool in summer, and where they can get out of the wind in winter. Colonel Searcy branded a Star. He had it on his red and roan Durhams. Then he had bought out a mixed-up mess of Mexican cattle and longhorns range delivery, most of them branded with a Twelve Bar; he didn't know how many Twelve Bars he had, much less where they were. He didn't want us to bring in the stock from the easy valleys, but only those which had taken to the rough country away back; they were about like deer or elk as far as handling.

We would eat a big breakfast of steak and potatoes and biscuits because it would be the last food till night. At daylight we'd hit the saddle, ride about three hours, then separate to hunt cattle. The going was slow on account of the steep slopes and rocks, and because the critters would hide in the pines and cedar brush. Whatever you found that would drive, you got them headed for some point where the hands meant to come together. Of course, some animals had no intention of being driven and that's where the fun came in.

We each carried a couple of tie-down ropes, besides a longer lariat rope. We would find these flighty stubborn old cows and steers that had so much independence you couldn't do a thing with them. They wanted to go, the faster the better, but not where you wanted them to. We would simply run them till they were winded, then rope them and tie them down or neck them to a tree. When you came back and turned them loose the next day they would be ready to holler uncle and let you lead them or drive them. In one canyon so far back in the hills it didn't even have a name we found a herd of scrub Twelve Bars, eight old grandma cows, two longhorn steers, and twenty-nine long-ear offspring up to three or four years old which had never seen a man. We had to rope about half of them, but finally got them all out except a two-year-old bull which went over a cliff.

It was hard work and dangerous, because of the rough country and the wildness of the stock. I probably tied onto fifty or a hundred brutes during two months of time which would have preferred to kill me rather than be captured. But I liked the work because it was a real plain struggle and no baloney and I learned a lot about roping. There is something satisfying about proving that skill and savvy can come out ahead of muscle. Chili learned to be a mountain horse and a roping horse; if you were going to keep a personal mount on Colonel Searcy's place you had to work him, so I rode Chili twice a week.

We gathered those critters toward a loose herd on Tonto

Creek. We brought in fewer and fewer all the time because you had to go farther to get them and three hands
had to stay home and keep the herd together. I remember
one day four of us only brought in one cow as old as
Methuselah; she had broke four ropes and practically run
our horses into the ground.

The colonel said that was all. We drove the herd, some
three hundred and fifty head, to the town of Phoenix down
south and delivered to a buyer for the military.

Altogether I worked a year and a half for Colonel
Searcy. I want to tell about one last task I did for him in
the spring of '84 because it shows what kind of roads we
had out there in those days. Anybody could tell the same
story before the railroad came in or even after the railroad, in the back country. The colonel had bought out

an abandoned ranch away over east, evidently in partnership with his brother, Mr. Adam Searcy. I was given the
job of hauling a load of lumber over there with the help of
an overgrown kid named Bert. The old man called Sergeant
was supposed to know all that country, and he gave me
directions.

"Go down to the crossing about three miles, then head

east," he said. "Hold to the right till you get through
the sand, then hold to the left. You can't miss it. Take it
easy when you drop off into Rattlesnake Canyon; the road
ain't none too good."

I asked him how far it was.

"You can make it in daylight if you'll harness up and
go on," he said.

"Hold to the right till I get through the sand? Then hold
to the left? Then down into a canyon?"

"You can't miss it," he said.

To my sorrow I found I couldn't make up a four-mule
team without using that old tongue-wagger Victoria. And

to my surprise I found that Bert and I were to have a passenger, Mr. Adam Searcy himself. He brought a blue cloth cushion, which he carried up to the middle of the load of lumber and sat down on. I thought, Well, if he can stand our company, we can stand his.

He looked like the colonel only his beard was whiter and his shoulders stooped. He was dressed like a dude with a string tie and celluloid collar and black derby hat. He put me in mind of a rich Scotchman or Englishman—not that I know much about such people, but only what a cowhand thought about the kind that would go out west and couldn't do anything but stand around and look and frown. It seemed like they took it for granted that things would be done for them. Mr. Adam Searcy was making a mistake crawling on my loaded wagon, because it wasn't my job to haul him, only the lumber, but it wasn't my place to explain to him either.

It was a clear day in early spring. We made it across the creek all right and headed east along a dim wagon road. Before long I saw what Sergeant had meant by the "sand." The land got sandier and sandier. It was yellow-brown. It stood up in little hummocks around the roots of scattered mesquite brush. In places the tracks of the road were covered so that I had to stand up and look ahead to see it. Bert chattered off and on. He asked, "Did Sergeant say hold to the right in the sand, or to the left?"

"The right," I said. "Don't get to talking about it; you'll get me mixed up." In fact I could barely see any kind of road, much less take the right forks.

About the middle of the morning Mr. Searcy asked, "Will we arrive in time for lunch?"

I told him, "No, sir. I don't know how far it is, but I think it will take all day."

The hummocks got as high as the wagon. Some of them

had bunch grass on them; others were just pure piles of sand with mesquite or stunted oak growing out of the top. The road disappeared. I rested my hope on the idea that there were precious few places a wagon could go through here, so we must be on the road. Victoria was the off wheeler. Her dreaming had not mattered much before, but as the wagon tires went to sinking about six inches into sand the pull got to be all the team could handle. I got down and cut me a mesquite branch six feet long that I could reach her rump with.

About noon Mr. Searcy asked, "Are you certain we are on the right road?"

I started to try to ease his mind but then thought, Why should I? I said, "No, sir."

"You should have asked directions before you started," he said.

I tried to explain but my explanation didn't make much sense, so I quit. It was becoming clear that there were at least three simpletons involved in this business: Sergeant with his you-can't-miss-it directions, me who had been simple enough to take them, and that old man sitting behind me on his little blue cushion. I should have told him that since he was one of the big augurs around here I would drive right where he told me to.

For lunch me and Bert had a drink of water out of my canteen. Mr. Searcy said he didn't care for any. He doubtless thought we had hoof-and-mouth disease and didn't want to drink after us.

Soon after midday I turned into a blind alley in the sand hills and couldn't back out. First I put Bert to jumping on the spokes of a back wheel, but it did no good. Then I gave him the lines and got down and took the near wheeler's bridle and tried to back them. We yelled, "Whoa-o-o-o!

Back!" till we were red in the face. No soap. You can't
hardly back a four-mule rig that way. The wagon tongue
rared up and like to have pulled the harness off the team.
The wagon tires were bogged a foot in sand. Victoria was
enjoying her tongue and staring at a pipe-organ cactus.

I and Bert began unloading the lumber and carrying it
out of the way. Mr. Searcy got down with his blue cushion
and watched us, standing with his hands together behind
his back. Most of the stuff was two-by-twelves, twenty
feet long, rough and covered with splinters, what they
call "rawhide" lumber. It was work slogging through the
sand wrestling that stuff. When we got the bed empty, we
scooped out from in front of the wheels with our hands. I
had me a route picked out and I whipped up the team and
blasted out forward and got her in the clear again. Then
we packed the lumber up to where the wagon was and reloaded it. The day wasn't hot, but I and Bert were soaked
with sweat.

I told Bert to drive and I would walk ahead. Mr. Adam
Searcy, perched on the load like a bird on his nest, said,
"Perhaps we are going around in circles."

I didn't answer that. The sun said we were going east.

My boots got full of sand climbing hills trying to see
how to go. I would scramble to the top of one, then wave
madly to Bert. In the middle of the afternoon he went to
the right around a hummock when I meant him to go to
the left. He stuck her again. I could nearly read Bert's
mind. He was thinking, No, it's too big a job to unload
this lumber again! He was wondering how he could escape it. Bert must not have been over fifteen or sixteen
and he had got his growth real fast. Work is hard for a kid
like that; they are all thumbs and big feet and their muscles
don't work together. Also, I was used to going on two

meals a day on account of hunting wild cattle, but he was not. I told him to come on, let's get on it, and started laughing. He saw there was nothing to do but laugh or cry, so he grinned a little, then got to laughing. We unloaded that mess of lumber, got the wagon free, reloaded. That stuff seemed heavier the second time around.

After we got her rolling again, Mr. Searcy remarked, "The roads seem very poor in this country."

Near sundown the sand hummocks got smaller and farther apart. The going got easier. I stood on top of the load and scanned the country. With the sun rays low, small features on the ground stand out. I spotted a road a half mile south of us. We got on it.

At dark Mr. Searcy said, "It appears to be getting dark." I was thinking, Yes, you old bastard, if I was like Joshua and could make the sun stand still, I guess you would take it for granted, sitting there on your blue cushion.

I got down and walked, pulling the nigh leader by the bridle. A thin moon behind us gave a little light. I even found a "Y" in the road and took the left fork. It must have been getting along toward midnight when I stopped seeing ground out in front of me and stopped the team. I edged forward. It got rocky and steep real fast.

I want back and climbed on the load and said, "Mr. Searcy, we'll stop here and take the wagon on in daylight. I think we're on the right road. If you want to walk on, one of us will go with you."

"Good heavens!" he said. "How far is it?"

I said, "I'm sorry. I don't know." Then I couldn't help laughing right at him—the whole thing was so far-fetched and unlikely. It was probably just as well that I couldn't see the expression on his face.

Bert said, "Man, I'm hungry. I could eat a mule." I had

the sweet thought that he could eat Victoria, but it didn't seem practical.

I told Bert he could walk on if he wanted to. He thought about the name of what this place must be, Rattlesnake Canyon, and gave up the idea. He figured there were snakes all over. Actually it was too early in the year for them to be out. We left the mules in the harness but let the wagon tongue down. Bert and Mr. Searcy slept on the load. I slept on the ground. It got so chilly I had to get up twice and run around to warm up.

Soon as it got light we could see some buildings and corrals about three miles down in the canyon. A wisp of smoke rose from the adobe house, probably from a breakfast cook fire. We had undoubtedly found where we were headed for. But the road! I walked down it a couple of hundred yards. It had been traveled a good bit in the past few weeks. Plenty of horse tracks showed, and the marks of iron wagon tires on rocks, but whether a freight wagon with a load of lumber could make it was anybody's guess. The road hugged rocky walls on the left. Some places the road was caving.

When I came back to the wagon with Mr. Adam Searcy perched up there, I should have forced him to make a decision—say whether we should put off half the load or walk in and get help or what. At least he might have decided whether he would walk or ride; come to think of it I guess he did decide; he rode.

The brake blocks and linkage seemed stout. I got on the load, woke up the tired mules, and pointed them down. Bert was on the brake lever with me. Most of the way it was a matter of holding the wagon off the team.

When she would get to bouncing, the team trotting, the wagon tongue trying to pull the collars off the wheelers, we would come down hard on the lever. The back wheels struck a stream of sparks from the rocks. Mr. Searcy sat on his blue cushion, clutching at the lumber, and said not a word.

About a quarter of a mile below the rim we slid along with the back wheels locked. The right-hand bank started to sink. I pulled left as far as I could but she went anyway. We came to high center on the back axle on a boulder buried in the roadway dirt.

After I look it over, I tell Bert we'll have to unload the lumber. He looks at me and Mr. Searcy and looks up the road and down the road, then says, "I don't see how we can do it; we're too weak." I tell him I know he's not a sissy and let's see if we can do it. He paws at a plank a minute, finally gets hold of it. He grunts at the work, and the sounds slowly change while we stack the lumber till he's not grunting but laughing. He's not smiling, only laughing. We get the stuff off. One good thing, we have plenty of prize bars. We prize with the two-by-twelves, dig with our hands, and carry rocks. In an hour I whip up the team and they jerk the wagon out of there. We carry the lumber and reload. Mr. Searcy mounts his perch. We ease on down. Three of the mules got waked up and warmed up; Victoria is in her usual mood, dreaming and wagging her tongue.

I figure up a plan about the heavy wagon and the caving road. Like they say, on thin ice our safety is in our speed. I think, Hold hard left and move along! It works in two bad places. Then it doesn't.

A moss-grown boulder as big as a house stands on the left. I mean to miss it an inch. The team has been pushed into a lope. The rough road bounces the wagon and steals my inch clearance. The hub of the left front wheel strikes the rock like a cannon going off. We hit the brakes and jerk right, and that wheel goes on alone down the road. Fortunately, at the same time Mr. Searcy slides off the back of the load on his cushion.

But the wagon and team both are still traveling. Victoria goes halfway down with two feet off the edge but is jerked back by the plunging of the other three mules. I don't even have time to know what all is happening. We break the fifth wheel, smash in the side of the wagon box, throw the lumber down the bluff beside the road and lose one back wheel too. Bert jumps in time. I hang onto the brake lever and don't go out till the wagon turns on its side. The team stops sideways in the road, the wagon, what's left of it, teetering on the edge. That back wheel runs and jumps a mile down through the malpais and juniper.

Mr. Adam Searcy walks down the road to where I am getting up. He's dusting off his derby hat and trying to get it straightened out. I expect him to look at me as if I'm a monster, but he only says, "You have wrecked the wagon." One thing I notice that I like about him right then: he's walked off and left his cushion. But I get the idea he doesn't like anything about me at that time. The three of us limp along, me driving the team, to the new division of the Searcy Ranch.

I rode horseback out of there four days later and made it back to main headquarters in less than half a day.

Colonel Searcy huffed and puffed at me a while and finally said, "Mr. Blankenship, the plain truth is . . . well, my brother is investing in these enterprises. You wrecked a good wagon. I've got to fire somebody. So . . ."

I laughed. He wanted to talk plain, yet he didn't want to say what he meant. What he didn't know about me was that I was sort of looking for a reason to quit anyway. Rumor said the colonel was planning on building a private fort out in that canyon; then he was planning to go in with other ranchers and build pens and watering places all the way from the Tonto Basin to Phoenix. I wanted me a job as a cowhand, not a general laborer.

The colonel paid me off and I gathered my gear and rode Chili east the next day. I had a hankering to see New Mexico Territory. Also, I was thinking that if I could sign on with an outfit good to work for, without so much construction and tanking and posthole digging, I would like to stick with them and keep my nose clean and save my money and cease some of my wandering ways. Like they say, the road to hell is paved with good intentions.

Chapter 6
Shivaree

THE NEXT PLACE I STUCK for any length of time was on the Lazy Eight in eastern New Mexico Territory. It was a good outfit to work for, and I stayed with them two years. Some Scotchmen had bought into it, but Mr. Robertson, who had started the spread about ten or twelve years before, still ran it and maybe still held an interest for all I know; anyway, he knew cows and didn't get much nonsense from outside owners.

By being good to work for, a hand doesn't mean that it's easy. That part of the country is too hot in the summer, too cold in the winter, always too dry. The distances are too long to ride and it takes too many acres of that cedar brakes and creosote bush and bear grass to feed a cow. But if you put in rough twelve- or fourteen-hour days and know that Mr. Robertson and the ramrod Bull Vaughan have done the same thing, you feel like you get credit for it whether you ever collect or not.

Lazy Eight cattle watered along the Pecos River and back toward the Valencia Mountains at a couple of springs and three or four dirt tanks. The Robertson house was a

two-story wooden structure painted white with a gallery around three sides. It overlooked the river. Not far behind it was the bunkhouse, a long adobe building with a flat roof. It had a dirt floor but was a comfortable place. The big old cottonwood trees scattered around there seemed a hundred years old. They had a peach orchard, which never seemed to grow any fruit. The garden down on the edge of the river would grow anything you planted: squash, beans, pumpkins, cantaloupes, peppers.

Out of the eight of us who lived in the bunkhouse, four men, Bull Vaughan, Henry Shaw, Mexico Ortega, and Skinny Lambert, had helped Mr. Robertson drive the first herd here, had seen the ranch grow up from nothing, and had been through a lot of Apache scares together. They were sort of permanent fixtures. In fact the outfit did not use temporary help much; if you hired on you could stay about as long as you wanted to. The rest of us, Joe Lefors, Orval Tanner, Ab Brown, and me, were accepted as part of the family. They were a hell-raising crew in town but knew how to get the work done on the ranch.

The astonishing news that spring after the roundup and after we turned the big steers over to a trail crew was that Henry Shaw was going to quit and get married. He had kept a picture of the girl, Gloria May Adams, tacked up on the front of his clothes closet until it was turning brown. He had been in the habit of going a couple of times a year, when the work was slack, to see her in Texas somewhere. He had taken a lot of ribbing from the other hands when he wrote her. They would say, "Tell Gloria May I still love her," or "Tell Gloria May I said she better quit running around."

I guess all the hands had fooled around with the fast women in Almas Muertas, but this was different. Now the word was that Henry was quitting, leaving the next day, hooking up with this Adams person, and that was that.

We had chow a couple of hours before dark that afternoon and everybody was beginning to shine up to go to town the next day. Joe Lefors was doing a few jobs of amateur barbering; they were shining boots, shaking the wrinkles out of their good clothes.

Skinny Lambert said, "Well, Henry, they tell me soon as you marry this gal you are going to Albuquerque to work in a store."

Henry said, "Yep."

"You won't be doing any more of this dirty old cowhand work, will you?"

"Nope."

"Just be a store clerk instead?"

"Yep. When a man takes on a family he's got to try to better himself if he can."

After Henry said that, everybody was quiet a minute like they were letting it soak in. Skinny Lambert had a lot of energy, not especially the working kind but the kind that always wants something going on. He was outside man for the Lazy Eight and repped all up and down the Pecos River. If Bull Vaughan had not been around he would have been ramrod.

Skinny said to Mexico Ortega, "You been married once, Mexico. Looks to me like you would be an expert. Right?"

"Yes, sir-ee," Mexico said.

"Well, now tell the truth. You think Henry ought to get married and be a store clerk?"

"No, sir-ee. I think he ought to stay here like he always did."

"Now, Mexico, you've got a girl friend, haven't you?"

"I have two in Almas Muertas, one old and one young. I have one in Roswell and one in Santa Fe. I haven't seen my love in Santa Fe for a long time, and maybe she is not true to me any more."

"All right," Skinny said. "Some women are fickle. The point is, would you marry any one of those gals and go off and leave us here by ourselves?"

"No, sir-ee."

Mexico was a chubby fellow with a little black mustache. He liked to have fun and would usually keep as solemn as a judge, but his eyes would be shining and crinkled up.

We were all in a mood to rag Henry some, but it was clear we were flirting with trouble. Some subjects you can talk about any way you get ready, but when you begin to talk about what might be called a "good" woman, or put her up beside some that are not too good, then you may get a fight on your hands. And the idea that we couldn't hardly even talk about Gloria May Adams was bothersome. Actually, no doubt we all figured her a nice, innocent, decent girl and did not blame her for anything. But it seemed like we had it coming to blame Henry if we could find what to blame him for.

Skinny said, "It ain't the getting married so much, Henry. But you can't seem to wait to get away from here. It looks like you would be walking around looking the place over before you leave and talking over old times. Don't your old friends mean a thing to you?"

Henry grinned and said nothing.

Ab Brown said, "I've saved Henry's life many a time."

We nodded at this far-fetched lie and said, "Sure he has." "That's right." "Yes, sir-ee."

Henry said, "How many times, Ab?"

"Plenty."

"Would you say six? Did you save my life six times?"

Joe Lefors said, "A man don't keep exact count of things like that, Henry."

Henry couldn't let it rest. They were joshing and at the same time arguing about something, though it wasn't exactly the thing they were talking about.

Henry said, "Ab, just tell me one time. Never mind all the rest. Tell me one time."

Skinny said, "You ought to know a man don't like to talk about things like that, Henry."

"All I want Ab to do," Henry said, "is name me one time he saved my life or else back down."

Ab said, "All right. Remember way up on the Canadian that time. The river was up, really rolling. It was dangerous. My horse went clean under and I nearly got strangled and swallowed about a gallon of muddy water."

"Yeah," Henry said. "And I came running along the bank and threw you a rope and helped get you and your horse out."

"That's right," Ab said. Everybody laughed.

"It's a good story," Henry said. "And true. But did you notice who got saved?"

We said, "It's all the same." "Yeah, Henry." "What difference does it make?" "Yes, sir-ee."

Henry said, "You all are a bunch of idiots. I got nothing against Ab, but I and him are not the same. I think he ought to name me one time or else back down."

Ab said, "I'll name you one about two or three winters ago. You and Orval were in that camp way up through Kelly's Gap. It was snowing and cold enough to freeze the horns off of a brass billygoat. I went up there in that blizzard with a pack horse of grub for you and Orval. We had some stock to freeze in that spell. How do you know you and Orval could have made it without starving if I hadn't come up there?"

"That's the truth," Orval Tanner said. "We didn't have the flour left to make a pan of gravy. I thought Henry was a goner till we seen you coming."

Henry sort of sputtered. "Were you on the payroll, Ab?"

"What payroll?"

"What the hell payroll have you been on for five or six years? Did somebody send you up there? Bull, did you tell Ab to bring that pack of grub to us?"

Bull Vaughan was sitting there on a bob-wire spool, smoking his pipe and taking it all in. He nodded. "Mr. Robertson said to tell him and I told him."

Henry had got a little miffed. He said "Well, Ab, I'm glad you did what you were told to do and what you were paid to do. That's all I say."

Skinny said, "When you get to clerking in Albuquerque, what will you sell? Ladies' shoes or what?"

"It's none of your business."

Orval Tanner had sort of the brain of a woodpecker. He had the bad habit of coming out with sounds that didn't make much sense, barking or crowing, maybe pretending to be a snooty woman with a high voice. Now he piped up, "You old nasty cowboys ain't nice!" No one paid much attention to him.

Henry said, "I'll tell you one thing: when I get married and get away from here, I won't come back. That's a dead cinch." He had said it without smiling; then, like he saw it wasn't polite, he said, "Aw, I don't know; I might come by sometime and see if the place is gone to pot." In fact he could not hardly make up his mind if he was sore or not.

Skinny said, "Boys, since this is Henry's last night in

our midst, could be we ought to shivaree him a little. Like tar and feather him maybe."

"We'll get him in town tomorrow night," Ab said. We had learned that Gloria May Adams would not arrive in town till day after tomorrow.

Skinny asked, "Well, Bull, what do you think? Something has got to be done, hasn't it?"

Bull Vaughan had a big red face and big red nose and ears. He might have been twenty-nine years old or forty-nine. He didn't look old but looked like he'd always been heavy and silent, like you couldn't budge him with a crowbar. When he looked at a new hand or a horse wrangler they might think some horrible thing worse than getting fired was going to happen to them. He seemed to get the work done without giving many orders, so he was a good ramrod. It could have been that he just couldn't think of many orders, but the effect was the same.

He took his pipe out of his mouth, scratched his head, and said, "We go into town with Henry he's got to buy us all a drink. Then he can get married."

Henry said, "Then I'll have permission, huh?"

Bull nodded solemnly. I think about then Henry decided to accept permission on the stated terms, suddenly getting the idea that Bull's proposition was an easy and safe out and he'd better grab it. Of course, he could not foresee what buying the boys a drink might lead to, with him in his present odd position of being a bridegroom-to-be.

The truth was that when Bull nodded solemnly he probably meant it and was not laughing inside. But Henry Shaw should have stopped to think that some things you settle with Bull and some you have to go elsewhere. If you feel bilious and want to lay around the bunkhouse all day, you can get permission from Bull; but if you're over twenty-one and fixing to do a strange thing that's nobody else's business, yet somehow you still need permission, you'd better check with Skinny Lambert.

We got up early next morning. The Mexican woman who did the cooking knew it was payday, and she had breakfast on in the big-house dining room an hour before daylight. We had two days off, but some of us hadn't been to town for a couple of months and saw no reason to waste time. Our horses were saddled by sunrise. Mr. Robertson set up a table on the south veranda and paid us in cash.

He told Henry how much he appreciated his years of work and how much we hated to see him go and to keep in touch. Then he said, "Mr. Vaughan"—Mr. Robertson usually called him "Vaughan," but he must have been feeling more serious than usual—"Mr. Vaughan, I want you to keep an eye on Henry and don't let the boys hurrah him too much."

To the rest of us he said, "You boys have a good time and don't get into trouble."

We mounted up. Bull Vaughan got in the lead and we headed for Almas Muertas.

This town lay in a bend of the river some ten miles from the Lazy Eight. It was a supply point for a lot of ranches but had grown to a fair-size town on account of the silver mines back in the mountains to the west, the Ignacio Mines, the Big Hope Mine, the Johnson Diggings. Also, sometimes soldiers from Fort Sumner came to the place to blow off steam.

A quarter of a mile from town we kicked our horses into a run in order to enter in style. Henry hung back. Skinny yelled at him, "Whip up! We got to let them know the Lazy Eight's in town!" Henry came on.

Almas Muertas had a wide main street with a tall wooden

windmill and horse trough right in the middle of it. We barreled through, raising dust, and went to the Lone Star Stables and Wagon Yard over toward the river. Luckily we were the first crew of any size to come in that morning and got permission from the man who ran the stables to sleep in his hay barn, as many of us as might want to. We turned our horses loose in the small pasture, then walked back up to the Silver Saloon.

I could almost see Henry's mind working. He knew he couldn't escape buying a round, but he was wondering if he could get away with ginger ale for himself and decided he couldn't. Standing at the bar we toasted him, Gloria May Adams, the happy event, the years of bliss to come, any little ones that might result.

Skinny slapped some dollars on the bar and said, "I got the next round!"

Henry said, "I hate to go, boys, but I have to be moseying on now. Got a lot of things to take care of."

"No," Skinny said. "You don't have to go yet. What's the harm in one more little drink? You bought us one; now we want to buy you one."

"But I have to buy me a good suit of clothes and everything."

Bull said, "I'm going to keep an eye on you, Henry, like I'm supposed to."

"Sure," Skinny said, "we're going to take care of you, Henry. Drink up."

Mexico Ortega offered a few toasts and we drank to the flower of the prairie, Gloria May Adams, to the beauty, the soul, and the heart of that lady. Then Mexico bought a round. I proposed that we drink to Ab Brown and the many times he had saved Henry's life, which we did. Then I bought a round.

Skinny wanted to know if Henry had his license. Henry

said he had it in his pocket but didn't want to show it. Everybody wanted to see it. Joe Lefors said he would give five dollars just to look at it.

"I better check it," Bull said.

Henry was not too eager but he handed it over. At first we looked over Bull's shoulder to see; then we passed it around. Henry was saying, "Don't get it dirty. Don't tear it. Don't get anything on it." Finally all of us and the bartender too agreed that it was in order.

Those who had not paid for drinks bought bottles to carry along and we went out and walked down the street. Bull got in front to lead us. Orval Tanner started crowing like a rooster and we made him shut up for fear the people watching us would think we were a bunch of rowdies.

In the front window of a feed store we saw a little curly white pup. We stopped and watched him. He waddled back and forth against the glass, trying to get out to us, wagging his stub of a tail for all it was worth. He was just like a ball of cotton. A cardboard sign said "Good Pup—$1.00."

"Ain't that something though," Bull said.

"That little feller needs a good home," Ab said.

Skinny said, "We'll buy him for a wedding present for the bride. Chip in, boys."

A minute later we had us a pup. Mexico put him down the front of his shirt and opened a button and carried him with his head sticking out.

When Henry found out we were headed back with our bottles to the Lone Star Stables and Wagon Yard he began to object. He said, "I really better not go. Look, this is serious to me."

"What is serious?" Skinny asked.

"Well . . . everything."

"Why, it's serious to us too," Skinny said. "Henry, your intended doesn't come in on the stage till tomorrow. Why don't you loosen up? Aren't we your old pards? Haven't we been on many a spree together? Don't you know us?"

"I know you, all right. That's the trouble. I'm afraid you'll go too far and things will get out of hand. I've got to be in good shape tomorrow, not in the calaboose."

Bull said, "If they try to throw you in the calaboose we'll fight 'em."

"Henry," Skinny said, "just loosen up. We're your friends. What you need is a drink. Give Henry another pull on that bottle."

We went to the hay barn and sat around on bales of hay drinking while the pup scampered from one of us to the other, trying to chew on our boots. For a while we talked about things that had happened through the years on the Lazy Eight. Henry seemed to relax.

About a hundred yards down the fence line the Lone Star horse pasture joined somebody's cow pasture. An old dun milk cow stood out there working on her cud. Mexico and Ab went down there, got through the fence, roped the cow, and milked Mexico's hat full. They brought it back to the pup. The container leaked, but the pup lapped at the milk and got plenty. His little stomach pooched out so much he could hardly waddle around.

It came to us that it was time to go see about buying Henry's new suit to get married in, but he didn't want us to go with him. His main objection seemed to be Orval Tanner. Orval could get carried away when everybody around him was having a good time. He not only made silly sounds but he had the habit of saying something and suddenly thinking how good it sounded, then taking it up and you'd never hear the last of it. He had got to saying,

"We got to take care of you, Henry! We're just like your mammy and pappy, Henry. Don't be concerned. Don't look sad, Henry. Your mammy and pappy are here."

Henry claimed that Orval was drunk.

We all had an argument about being sincere when you are drinking, and most of us decided you are more sincere when you are drinking than any other time.

Henry said, "You're all drunk."

Bull said, "Whiskey has no effect on me. It's just like water."

Henry did not want us to go help him buy his suit because he said he wanted to choose it himself and not have a bunch of drunks making cracks, and besides that, Orval would draw attention and probably get us thrown out of the store. Skinny swore that we would not say a word about the new suit one way or the other unless we were asked by Henry himself and if Orval didn't simmer down we would all jump on him. Skinny swore that Bull would make Orval keep quiet and not draw attention.

The pup was asleep. We took handfuls of hay and made him a good warm bed and put him in it. Then Bull got in front and led us up the street to the dry goods store.

The man had about twenty suits and several of them seemed good enough to get married in. Ab got into an argument with him about Henry's size. When Henry would try on the coat or the trousers the man would say they fit when we did not think they fit at all. The seat might be baggy or the sleeves might come right down over Henry's hands. The man seemed to look on us as a bunch of suckers, but we told him he'd better fit Henry exactly or he'd have to answer to us.

Three of us got to looking at some swanky walking canes on a rack. We decided to buy Henry one for a wedding present. Joe liked one that was varnished on the bottom, with a black hand grip and stuff that looked like pearl enlaid. It cost nearly nine dollars, so I and Mexico and Joe chipped in. We got the man over there and whispered to him and got him to wrap it up so Henry couldn't see it. We worried some that Gloria May's pup only cost one dollar while Henry's walking stick cost nearly nine, but decided that we thought the world of Henry and didn't hardly know her, so it was all right.

Henry finally bought a black suit costing twenty-four dollars with a checkered black and white and gray vest, also a pair of patent-leather shoes. Henry looked like a new man. The rest of us carried his old clothes for him.

Bull led us back to the Silver Saloon to get a new supply of bottles, then to a joint called Joe's Place to eat supper. We had chili con carne. Orval got to acting up and got messy with his chili. We made him act dignified. Everyone watched to see when Henry would get cracker crumbs on his high-class clothes, and we took turn about going to him every minute or so and dusting him off with our bandannas. Ab got too eager dusting and knocked a spoon of chili right down Henry's front. It got worse when Bull tried to help. He had tried to clean up some chili Orval spilled on the oilcloth and had got his bandanna dirty, so when he tried to wipe off Henry it did more harm than good. We all agreed that the spots would come out all right.

The people in Joe's Place were looking at us. Even the cook and his swamper looked out the kitchen door. Skinny yelled at them, "What's the matter? Didn't you ever see anybody eat chili before?"

Bull led us back to the Lone Star Stables and Wagon Yard. The pup was awake and ready to play. Ab wanted to give him some whiskey, but we stopped him.

It seemed to be a back-and-forth struggle with Henry.

He would be having a gay old time one minute, then get to worrying and saying we weren't treating him right. Joe mentioned that we might go to a whorehouse after a while, and Henry got insulted. He said we didn't have any decency about us; we were a bunch of low-life, thick-headed, sorry, dirty-minded cowhands that never had a fine thought in our heads. He tried to go out the barn door, but we stopped him and brought him back to reason with him.

Skinny said, "The trouble, Henry, is that we just can't *see* you married."

About that time we missed Bull. We found him lying in the road out in front of the livery stable. We dragged him in and propped him up against a bale of hay so he could help keep an eye on Henry.

We took up the fact that it was hard to see Henry married. Ab finally said that he didn't think *anybody* was married, that it was a dream or a rumor or such. Then someone said that Henry was not actually going to get married; he would go back to the ranch with us tomorrow night; Gloria May was only a picture and would not show up on the stage. Henry didn't like what we said and suddenly got mad about the chili on his clothes.

It struck me that it's strange how, when you drink, you are turned loose in certain ways, but a little feller seems to be sitting up there in your head watching shrewdly what you do and what other people do.

The man on night duty at the stables came and brought two lanterns for us and asked if everything was all right. We told him it was fine, that Henry was a little drunk but we would be able to handle him. The man asked for Mr. Vaughan, so we got Bull up on his feet. The man said that he only wanted to be sure that some responsible man would watch things and be careful that the lanterns were not spilled and catch the barn on fire. Bull assured him that he was not affected by liquor; it was just like water.

Henry began talking about getting some coffee and sobering up. Joe said, "That's the last thing to do. Once you start drinking cheap whiskey the only thing to do is keep on. That way you beat the hangover. If you stop you're a goner."

Henry seemed to have forgotten about the spots on his new suit, but since Bull was in good shape again we decided it was time to try to sponge Henry off. Putting liquor on our bandannas didn't seem to do much good and seemed a waste. We saw we would have to go down to the windmill. We made a bed for the pup out of Henry's old clothes and boots and left him one of the lanterns so he wouldn't get scared of the dark; then Bull led us down Main Street to the windmill and horse trough.

The town was lit up and humming. Music was coming out of a couple of places. Skinny said, "This is a wild town. They can't lure me into any of those joints. We are going to tend to our business. Go ahead, Bull. Straight ahead."

Henry balked when we got close to the horse trough. He said, "It's overflowing! That's mud all around there!"

Mexico held up the lantern. "Tiptoe, Henry," he said. "Step light."

"Go on," we said. "You can scrape the mud off, Henry. Go on ahead. We can sponge off your patent-leather shoes too."

We wet our bandannas and began dabbing at Henry. He dodged. We had to hold him by both arms.

"What are you doing?" Henry yelled. "You're going to ruin my clothes!"

"Water don't hurt clothes," Ab said. "Don't jump and jerk!"

"Hold still," Skinny said. "Listen, Henry, stop and think.

You get a spot out you got to smear it around quite a lot or it will show. Now, Henry! We're trying to do it right and you got to quit jostling. Henry! You're going to make it worse! Quit! Hold still!"

"Don't ruin my suit!" Henry yelled. "I gave twenty-four dollars for it!"

"You want to get married with chili on you?" Joe asked. "Quit fighting! Henry, give in and quit fighting!"

Henry flounced around with us trying to hold him till he got clear down on the ground. Skinny said, "Now, look at you! Hold that light over here, Mexico, where we can see. Look at you, Henry! See what you've done now! Man, you got to get married in this suit! What will Gloria May think? There you are wallowing in the mud in your new clothes! It's your fault!"

We held a council of war and decided that there was nothing to do at this stage of the game but put him in the horse trough. It was one of those made out of cypress planks, white and fuzzy from the water, held together by rusty iron straps. He splashed quite a lot, because he did not agree with us. We let him soak some and swabbed around on his clothes the best we could. He claimed we were trying to drown him. Since he was already as wet as you can get, we washed his hair; then we got him out on our shoulders, and Bull led us back toward the Lone Star Stables and Wagon Yard.

The pup was asleep and we didn't want to wake him up. We went around shushing each other. Joe and Ab went uptown to get a new supply of bottles, so we wouldn't run out during the night. Henry seemed unhappy. Skinny said to him, "Just stay on your feet and you're all right. Don't sit down in the litter or on the hay because it will stick to you. Keep moving and stay on your feet and you will dry out, Henry. You don't have any problems. You will dry spotless. A suit don't look good anyway till you get it wet once and it gets set to your body good."

For a long time Henry seemed to enjoy himself. He walked around among us, petted the pup, thanked us for the pup for Gloria May, answered all the kidding, and seemed like his old self. We sat around and gave each other advice and wisdom about marriage, religion, and other weighty matters. Suddenly Henry turned straight back toward where a lantern was hanging and you could see his screwed-up face. He looked like a cow on loco weed or like he'd been snake bit.

"Shivaree me!" he yelled. "In the name of God, why don't you shivaree me and get it over with? Whatever you're going to do with me, do it and let me loose!"

We shushed him. He had waked the pup up, but we didn't blame him too much because he seemed worked up and sincere.

Ab said, "What is the matter with you? You want to get the law on us, yelling that way? Disturbing the peace?"

Joe said, "What you need is another drink, old pardner. Here. Try to look at the bright side."

Henry yelled, "You're going to ruin my life!"

"Enrique," Mexico said, "I have ruin my life meny time, and she always come back some day. Don't be esad, *paisano*."

We gave him all the comfort we could, and Skinny said, "We are your old friends. Now I ask you: Is anybody tying you down with a piggin' string and making you stay here? Henry, we don't aim to do anything to you but take care of you. Bull, laying over there, is got his eye on you right now. Or he will open his eye in a minute and check on you. We ain't forcing you, Henry. This is a wild town. Think about those dirty miners and soldiers. What if they got hold of you? Seems like they ain't got no decent habits and appreciation. But us! You know us, Henry."

"You're going to shivaree me!" Henry said.

"No, we're not," Skinny said. "We gave that up. Is anybody here means to do anything to Henry? Not a soul. We wouldn't harm a hair on your head. Not a one. Are we holding you here? Are we making you stay with us?"

"I don't know," Henry said.

"No," Skinny said. "All we want to do is stay with you and reason with you and talk over old times, like Ab saving your life."

"We're just like your mammy and pappy," Orval said. "Don't be concerned, Henry. Think about us like your mammy and pappy."

"Well, I'm leaving, boys," Henry said. "When Bull comes to, tell him I went up to the Meacham Hotel."

We said, "We can't let you go, Henry. You'll get arrested. You're still wet. We're afraid some miner or prospector will jump you. You know how they are when they drink."

After that some of us stayed between him and the door, though I do not know, and don't guess anybody else did, what we would have done if Henry had got mad and stayed mad and fought and kept fighting to get free. He was in a bind and wasn't sure but what we had the right to do whatever we were doing, but he couldn't keep from worrying that we might do more to him than we meant to. Evidently he had hopes that if he stayed up out of the dirt his clothes would dry in time and be passable. He was no judge of clothes in his condition. Actually what probably troubled Henry more than anything else was Orval, who kept on baying like a coyote and coming out with that silly laugh. You couldn't hold him down.

Henry got to saying that he was enjoying himself and everything was all right, that there was only one thing: Us old friends had our ways, but people like Gloria May Adams had their ways, and she would not understand. This was serious and he didn't want to get in Dutch with her.

Skinny told him that was the last thing we would do— get him crossways with his intended. He said he would swear on a stack of Bibles six feet high that all we wanted was one peek at Gloria May when she came in on the stage, that we would deliver Henry over to her at that time, then skedaddle and make ourselves scarce. This promise seemed to satisfy Henry for a while.

That night we held a court trial there in the hay barn of the Lone Star Stables and Wagon Yard. The solemn judge presiding was Bull Vaughan. The constable was Orval Tanner. The criminal was Henry Shaw. The lawyer against the criminal was Skinny Lambert. Mexico Ortega defended the criminal the best he could. The charge was getting married. Among other testimony Ab Brown swore under oath that he had saved the criminal's life seven times. About the time the first light of dawn came, the trial became confused and we started trying the constable for making undignified sounds. By this time Skinny was making rulings, and he said, "Clap that man in irons!"

We never knew how Henry's trial came out, because he was discovered attempting to escape. In one end of the big barn about a half dozen box stalls had been partitioned off. He had climbed up on top of these and was going across the rafters toward a high window that was swinging open. We figured on going around to meet him when he dropped out the window, but suddenly he said, "Whew!

Hey! Get out!" He was slapping at his face. He scrambled back over the rafters toward us. "Whew!" he said. "I'm spider bit! Or a stinging scorpion or something!"

He was flailing around at the same time that he tried to climb down. We caught him. A swarm of wasps was circling over the box stalls. He had stuck his head in a wasp nest. He looked sickly white. We spread some saddle blankets on some hay bales and made him lie down. It looked like he'd been stung twice on the right eyebrow and it was swelling.

"Man alive!" he said. "Whew! Man alive! Lordy, that hurts!"

Joe Lefors had a plug of chewing tobacco. We shaved it up into a bottle that had about a cup of liquor in it and also put in a sack of smoking tobacco. With this mixture we dabbed at Henry's eyebrow, but the swelling kept on around his eye and up onto his forehead. Somebody said coal oil out of a lantern was good medicine, but others said the only thing to put on a wasp sting is blueing, such as is used in washing clothes. Bull sent Ab up to the hardware store after a bottle of blueing and told him if the store wasn't open to keep beating on doors till he got some. We gave Henry a few stiff shots of whiskey and he seemed to ease up.

Ab brought the blueing. With a bandanna Bull painted all around Henry's eye on the swelling the best he could. Evidently Bull was feeling guilty because he hadn't taken good enough care of Henry.

That morning Mexico and Orval went and hunted up the cow again and milked enough for a good breakfast for the pup. Before we knew it Bull's watch said eleven-thirty. We began to shine Henry up to meet the stage. His suit had shrunk; there was nothing to be done about that. His hair had been sticking up since we washed it the night before; we combed it some and brushed him off good. We got the pup and the walking cane, still wrapped, and went uptown to the stage station.

I remember that in the back of my mind I said something was wrong; it wouldn't work. Maybe the other boys thought about it too, but nobody said anything. People on the streets looked at us. Skinny told Orval and Ab, who were carrying bottles, to put them down inside their shirts. Mexico carried the pup in his shirt with his head sticking out. Maybe a dozen other people were there to meet the stage. It came in with a big rattling and jangling, a six-horse rig. Some others got off—then here she comes.

We all know Gloria May from the fading picture we've seen a thousand times tacked up beside Henry's bunk. She's a sort of pink girl, slim, pretty, in a blue frilly dress and wide hat. It's damned funny, but we all love her when she steps her small foot down to the dust beside the stage.

We move forward, smiling and pushing Henry and Mexico, who has the pup sticking out of his shirt.

She looks at us, from one to the other, and backs up.

We step forward and smile, pushing Henry and Mexico.

She backs away, then turns and runs. She yells, "Police! Police! Help! Police!" She runs up the middle of the street a half a block to the Meacham Hotel, all the time screaming, "Police!"

The stage attendant asks us, "What did you boys want?" We don't answer him. "You all scared that girl," he says.

Joe Lefors says, "How would you like us to take this station apart and hang it around your neck?"

We go out in the middle of the main street and hold a council of war.

"What in the world got into her?" Ab asks.

Skinny asks, "Who does she think she is?"

We can't figure out whether she has acted this way because she didn't recognize Henry or because she was just flighty.

We took Henry back to the horse trough and sponged at his face to get most of the blue off, then went back to the hay barn, because it was not clear what our next move should be. Henry had quit talking. He sat down and took the pup in his lap and wouldn't say a word or answer our questions or even take a drink.

We had two ideas, the first one brought up by Orval. He said it was our fault, that we had ruined Henry's life. Orval got on a sort of crying jag about poor Henry; then he got carried away and got to moaning about Henry leaving and we would never see him again; then he forgot what he was worked up about and started saying that he hadn't seen his own poor old mammy and pappy in years and he didn't write them letters like he should. But his idea that it was our fault caught hold a few minutes. We admitted it. Then the opposite started taking hold. Who did Gloria May Adams think she was? If she was going to marry a man for better or worse, she ought to accept him with a little blueing on his face. Was it Henry's fault he got wasp stung? We went up to her smiling and did not mean to do anything whatsoever but say "Howdy" and give her Henry and the pup. Did she say, Who are you? Where is Henry Shaw? Who is that man with a swelled-up eye and blueing on his face? No. She went loping up the street screaming "Police!"

Did she think she was too good to marry a cowhand? We wanted to know who she thought she was, not even speaking. It seemed an insult to everything we stood for.

Skinny said we should not be too hard on her. She had

probably heard tales about wild towns. She might have thought we were a bunch of rowdy miners or soldiers starting to insult a lady. What we needed to do was work up a scheme and make her see the light.

We had a lot of ideas. The main one was to take Gloria May Adams out and gently shivaree her and scare the daylights out of her. Bull said he was going to take care of her too and the scheme was all right, but we must not lay a hand on her. He was not under the influence of drinking; it was just like water to him and he would watch out for Gloria May. It seemed to us that we had to do something to show we were joking and scare the fool out of her; then she would be even with Henry.

We looked each other over carefully. Nobody had shaved since yesterday morning. They decided that Skinny and I looked the best. They told us to be like gentlemen and headed us uptown in a one-horse buggy we rented from the Lone Star Stables and Wagon Yard.

A store, Williams' Leather Goods, stood by the street away from other buildings. It was a small 'dobe place with flower beds at the side, and we saw a pile of mint growing. We tied the buggy horse to the front awning post and I stood guard, looking innocent, while Skinny picked some sprigs of mint. We chewed some. We stopped at Joe's Place and swilled down a cup of coffee. We stopped at the dry goods store and bought ourselves clean shirts, which we put on. We tied up at the Meacham Hotel, chewing some more mint, then went in and inquired for Miss Gloria May Adams. Skinny told me that he was not sure I was sober and I should not talk much.

Gloria May looked suspicious when the clerk brought her.

Skinny said, "We were sent by Mr. Henry Shaw and

Reverend Bloomsworth, ma'am. They told us to bring you."

She said, "Where is Mr. Shaw?"

"He's waiting, ma'am."

"Why didn't he meet the stage? He wrote me he would meet the stage. Who is Reverend Bloomsworth?"

"Well, ma'am, Mr. Shaw was held up. I mean he had a little trouble, but he requested us to bring you."

"Is he hurt?"

"No, ma'am. He's fine."

"Why didn't he meet the stage? Who is Reverend Bloomsworth? I never heard of him."

"He's the pastor of the United Protestant Church, ma'am. I'm the assistant song leader. This is my buggy driver, Mr. Charles Blankenship. We were sent to welcome you and take you to Mr. Henry Shaw."

"Where is Mr. Shaw?" she asked. "Why didn't he come? Where is my suitcase? I don't even have my suitcase."

We got her little tag. I walked down to the stage station and got her suitcase and brought it back. That seemed to ease her mind and make her trust us. I guess she primped a few minutes in her room; then she came out and we put her in the buggy.

She said, "It seems like a lot of mint grows here. I keep smelling it."

Skinny said, "Yes, ma'am. Reverend Bloomsworth grows it all around here."

He drove, although he had said I was the buggy driver. It was a big rawboned black horse that looked like he was born between the shafts of a buggy. The thing had a black cloth top and a small bed behind the seat to carry a light load. When we passed the Lone Star Stables and Wagon Yard, out ran Bull, Mexico, Ab, Joe, and Orval.

They began chasing us. Skinny whipped the horse into a trot. Some of them hung on to the rear of our vehicle. Bull grabbed on the side, dodged the wheels, and plunged over onto us, hitting Gloria May in the back and winding up behind the seat.

"Stop this buggy!" she says. "Take me to Mr. Shaw this instant! Where are you taking me?"

Ab is pushing the buggy part of the time, dragging part of the time, and waving a half-full bottle.

She yells, "Police! I've never been so insulted in all my life! Take me back! Police! Help! Police!"

Her hat blows off, but we don't stop. We trot out across the flat toward Panther Creek a mile and a half from town. The old horse labors under the load. Gloria May raises Cain all the way, trying to stand up and falling back on Bull, screaming. She tells us, "Mr. Shaw will thresh you within an inch of your life!"

Where the road crosses Panther Creek is not a rocky bottom and the ore wagons have beat out a mudhole there. The water isn't six inches deep, but that's where the horse decides to balk. We pile out to push. Gloria May grabs her chance to escape. She falls down and gets her dress muddy, then runs right up the creek bottom, splashing.

Skinny yells, "Wait, Miss Adams, please!"

We all take out after her. She climbs the creek bank and runs up through the brush. We keep calling to her.

"Come back, Miss Gloria May! It's a joke!"

"Please, Miss Adams! We don't mean any harm! We're fooling! We want to take you back to town!"

"Don't run, Miss Gloria May! We're not chasing you! It's a joke! We're friends of Henry's."

"You're going the wrong way, Miss Adams! Town's back this way! Please stop!"

We chase that gal an hour in the hot sunshine. The reason it takes so long is that we only want to get close enough to talk some sense into her. Cowhands are not used to much footwork. Boots are not made for it. Our liquid diet of the past two days does not help matters. It gets to be a case of catch her before she runs us to death. We finally surround her in a wild plum thicket.

We come in toward her from all sides. She stands there crying and looking at us like a cornered bobcat. When Orval sees her crying, he starts in again himself.

She says, "I think you're all crazy."

"Yes, ma'am," Bull says.

She's sunburned and has got scratches on her face and arms. To Skinny she says, "Mr. Shaw is going to whip you for telling me fibs."

"Yes, ma'am," Skinny says.

"Look at my best dress," she says. "And this is my wedding day!"

It is a good thing that glances cannot draw blood; she would kill us right there.

The horse has got the buggy out of the mudhole and come up the creek to a good patch of grass, where he's grazing. Ab goes and gets him. Gloria May doesn't want to get in the buggy.

"We'll take you straight to town," Skinny says. "I'll drive slow and easy."

"I wouldn't get in a buggy with you if you were the last man on earth," she says. "You said he was the buggy driver. I want him to drive."

I get in and take the lines. She won't let anyone help her in but manages it herself. Bull sits on the back; he looks pooped. As we start toward town nobody talks. The only sound is when Gloria May sniffs once in a while.

We haven't gone far when we see a man coming fast on horseback, raising the dust. It's Henry's big paint saddle horse. It looks like a long-barreled gun the rider has and proves to be in fact a double-barreled shotgun. *Ka-boom! Ka-boom!* it goes. We imagine we can hear slugs passing our ears.

Skinny begins shouting, "Don't shoot, Henry! You'll hit the lady! This is your old friends, Henry! Don't shoot!"

He's reloading as he comes and not slowing down.

"Run for it, boys!" Bull yells. "He'll kill us all!"

I look around and see Bull tumble out. I thrust the lines to Gloria May, scramble over the seat, and dive out the back. I pick myself up and run after the others. In a minute we stop, out of range, and look.

They're standing between the saddle horse and the buggy, him with his arms around her and patting her on the back. The patting goes on for some time; then they get in the buggy, leading the paint, and go back to Almas Muertas.

We sneaked into town about two hours later and went to the hay barn. There was the pup; the little fellow seemed to have more energy than all us seven cowhands put together. We drew straws to see who had to take the gifts up to the Meacham Hotel, and Joe and I lost. We went up and peeped in the hotel lobby. Nobody was there but the clerk. He seemed suspicious of us, but when we told him the swanky walking cane and pup were wedding presents he agreed to hold them for the happy couple.

The ride back to the ranch was long. The distance seemed to have grown from ten miles to fifty. Our bottles had long since gone dry and everybody began to moan about that cheap liquor and swearing we would never touch another drop. Sooner or later, like they say, those that dance will have to pay the fiddler.

I've wondered since then just how sharp Bull Vaughan was, if he knew what he was doing at the time or if he did it by instinct or by accident. When Skinny hollered, "Don't shoot, Henry; this is your old friends," which was the wrong thing, Bull hollered the right thing, even it it was a lie: "Run for it, boys! He'll kill us all!" That was a decent thing to yell and a good present for a bridegroom on his wedding day.

Chapter 7
The Natural Increase

I LEFT THE LAZY EIGHT for two reasons. In the first place the Scotch money people who owned part interest decided to fence the place, and I didn't care for fencing work. In the second place, it got clear that I wasn't going to save much money working there; we had too much fun in Almas Muertas. Those nuts working there would put in twelve-hour days, six days a week, draw their pay, then fling it around in town like they were feeding the chickens. They would say, "Easy come, easy go."

The desire to go home did not strike me as often as it once had. Maybe I wouldn't think of it for months. But then it would strike me deeply. Whenever I would run onto the silver bracelet with turquoise sets in my warbag, I would look at it and wish I could take it to Ma. As for saving up the good outfit and the thousand dollars before I went home, my ambition for flashy clothes and a silver-mounted bridle and such had cooled off; also, in those seldom times when the pull of southern Missouri and my folks struck me, I wondered about cutting that thousand dollars down to five hundred.

When I left the Lazy Eight in the late spring of '86 I rode east into the flat high-plains country they call the Llano Estacado and which some old Texans called the "Yarner." I hired in to a big new ranch that was starting up. They would hire anybody who could ride a horse and did hire some who couldn't even do that. They put me on a crew receiving stockers they had bought down south. They were branding XIT. I'd worked at it a week when a big emergency came up and they sent a bunch of us to set up a horse-powered pump and watering trough at a well they had dug. It seemed their cows were starving to death. I'd worked at that a week when they gathered all the hands they could and sent us up north of the Canadian River to fight grass fires. When we got the fires out, I drew my time and let them have their confused mess.

That ranch finally got straightened out and did all right. Their early troubles came from the fact that the moguls who owned it lived in New York and London and didn't know a cow from a camel. Reader, I've been with a few cow outfits, and nearly all the gripes a hand might have come from owners living a long, long ways from what they own.

When I quit the XIT it was the middle of the summer. I rode north to Beaver City in No Man's Land. That country was not part of a state or a territory either. It was also called the Neutral Strip and the Cimarron Strip. They said the land was lost by the politicians when they were drawing the lines. My horse Chili had thrown a shoe and I took him to the blacksmith shop in Beaver City. That's where I met Johnny Fox.

He was about as friendly and talkative a fellow as I'd ever seen and full of ideas. The first thing I remember ever hearing him say was to the blacksmith: "Why don't you cut you a door in the side wall and you can get a better breeze through here."

The old smithy was working on some strap iron for Johnny, bending it and punching holes. He quit his pounding and looked at the wall a minute and said, "Blamed if you ain't right. How come I didn't think of that?"

Johnny must have been about thirty years old, and he was one of these kind who never saw a stranger and never heard of a subject he didn't know something about. He helped us shoe my horse, then took me to a saloon and bought me a drink. He said he had a small herd of cattle which he intended to drive to a range farther west and he was looking for a good cowhand. Of course, I was interested.

Nothing would do him but that I must come out to his camp and have supper. "Charley," he said, "my wife Maudie loves to cook and you haven't lived till you've tasted her cooking."

I took him up. He had a light wagon in town, pulled by a team of old mares. One of them had a mule colt a few weeks old and Johnny called the little fellow Jackrabbit. It was comical to see it trot around exploring, then get scared and gallop back to get as near its mother as it could. Johnny drove the wagon and I rode Chili and we went out a couple of miles on a creek south of town.

In a grove of cottonwoods they had a tent. The most noticeable thing about the camp was ropes and cords and wires stretched between the trees and clothes hung to dry, every kind of clothes, colored and white, big and little. This was one thing I would learn about his wife, Maudie Fox—she was a big one for washing. I was surprised to find that he not only had a wife out here but a boy they called Sonny, maybe three years old, a baby girl named Junie, less than a year, and a big shaggy mongrel dog named

Tige. To say nothing of a milk cow and a dozen Domi-necker chickens.

Johnny said to his wife, "Whip us up a good mess of venison, Maudie Pie. I've been telling Charley what a great cook you are."

She was padding around on the sandy ground barefooted. She was redheaded and had a sprinkling of freckles on her nose and cheeks, the same as Sonny and the baby had. She carried the baby sort of straddling her hip with one hand around it and did her cooking with the other hand. In fact, the food she put on the small table was nothing to brag about; it was passable, but I wondered how the dickens she could do anything at all and carry that kid.

Johnny and I sat under the stars talking. He insisted that I hobble my horse and stay the night, and I figured that this was as good a place to spread my roll as any. Maudie worked a couple of hours by lantern light cleaning up after the meal and feeding the two kids and Tige.

The next morning Johnny and I rode up the creek to look at his cows. He had eighty-two head of mother cows and four bulls, longhorns, which he had come by through inheritance. He had been working for two uncles, helping raise cattle on land rented from the Cherokees farther east, and one of them had died and the outfit had broken up. Anyway, he had come out with this stock and he was determined to establish a ranch.

We saw an old rawboned cow coming through the brush with a calf behind her, and Johnny asked me, "What will she weigh?"

"I'm not any good at guessing weight," I said. "Eight hundred. Maybe a little under."

In a minute he pointed out a young cow and asked, "You think that heifer's old enough to be bred?"

I told him, "Looks to me like she'll drop a calf in about two months."

He was checking up on me to see if I knew anything about livestock and not making many bones about it. He said, "Charley, I want you to go to work for me. Starting today. I'll pay thirty a month and found. But when we get settled I'll make you a proposition a lot better than that."

I laughed and said, "What's the proposition?"

He said, "Thirty a month right now. Isn't that fair?"

In a minute I asked him, "What's shady about the deal?"

"Not a thing."

Well, it's pretty plain you can't run eighty-two head of cows and hire help. I told him, "I don't know. I sort of favor working for larger outfits." I wasn't clear in my own mind why I was suspicious, but it had something to do with the fact that Johnny Fox had a wife and little boy and baby girl and a dog and a mule colt. To say nothing of the milk cow and chickens.

"Look, Charley," he said. "What can you lose? I'm good for your wages. I'll pay you a month's wages in advance right this minute if that's what you're worried about."

I didn't take him up on that, because a man would be a fool to work if he couldn't even trust his boss for his pay, but I hired on.

Johnny and I had another trip to make to town; the place he meant to locate his cattle was a long ways from any stores. As we rode off Maudie came out of the tent and yelled, "Get me some bought soap, Johnny! Or some lye to make some! I'm running short!" He waved at her and we went on. In Beaver City he went to a couple of stores and I strung along to stock up on ammunition.

Back at camp she went through the things he had bought,

coffee, salt, rope, nails, then said, "I wish you had a thought to get me some lye, Johnny, or some bought soap. I've only got nine pieces left."

"Darn it," he said. "I forgot it. Well, that's all right. We'll run short on some things, Maudie Pie, but we'll make out. That's all right."

It took us a couple of days to break camp, load the wagon, and gather the cattle. We forded Beaver River not far from town and headed west, Maudie handling the wagon, Johnny and I driving the herd. The going was slow north of the river on account of miles of sand dunes.

Maudie had a bigger job to do than we did. That wagon was something to behold, piled ten foot high with a tent and bedding and trunks and a cookstove and washtubs and every kind of ax and shovel and pick. On the back hung the coop with the dozen Dominecker chickens, the milk cow leading along a rope behind and the mule colt cavorting around the team in front. Maudie walked beside the wagon, holding the lines in one hand and holding Junie on her hip with the other. She would let Sonny walk till he got tired, then pull up and find a place on the wagon for him to ride.

Tige stayed with us and the herd. Johnny claimed that he was going to make a cow dog out of him.

We made eight or ten miles the first day and stopped on a small creek with a hole of clear water. Maudie began to dip water and fill one of her washtubs, but Johnny told her to whip us up a good meal first; we'd all put in a hard day and needed some grub. We didn't raise the tent. We sat there and talked while we waited for her to get supper ready.

Johnny said, "Maudie Pie, I'm going to tell a little joke on you, because I know you don't mind. Charley, she's got a good pair of shoes. Good as you'd want. But they're tight on her. So she said, Well, she'd just wait till winter to break them in. Your feet don't swell so bad in the winter, you know, and shoes don't feel so tight. But there's the joke; if you've only got one pair of shoes you either got to wear them or not wear them. Maudie Pie, I see you started breaking them in today."

She blushed. "Law, I didn't know which one to put up with, that hot sand or them tight shoes."

I'd seen her going barefooted that afternoon and had sort of put it out of my mind because it's hard to believe. Evidently the tight shoes had won out over the cactus and hot sand, because she'd taken them off. She'd been walking barefooted, driving the wagon, carrying Junie, and taking care of Sonny. She struck me as the most easygoing redheaded woman you ever saw.

"If it gets too bad," Johnny said, "we'll have to let you ride my saddle horse or something. Can't have the best cook in the world coming up lame."

After supper she took about two hours feeding the kids and cleaning up the table and feeding Tige and the chickens and milking. Then she washed out a tub of clothes, strung up a line, and let them dry overnight.

We drove day after day out through the lonely country between the Beaver and the Cimarron. Johnny had explored out this way and knew where he was going. Sign of human settlement got thinner and thinner. In fact, you could see for miles across some of the prairie without even seeing a cow grazing.

One morning Johnny and I had loaded the heavier stuff, put the team to the wagon, caught and saddled our horses; then we started to leave the camp area to go out toward the slope where the cattle had bedded. Maudie was stirring in the dead fire with a poker, pushing out the black ends of wood and the few red coals.

Johnny said, "What in the world are you doing, Maudie? We got to get moving! Here it's past sunup!"

She stood up with a hand on one hip and the poker in the other hand. She was mad. I swear I thought for a second she would throw the poker at him. Then she said, "I'm going to get me some ashes, Mr. Fox, even if it holds us up a few minutes."

He said, "What for in heaven's name?"

"To make soap! I'm going to save ashes and make soap!" Then she said more calmly, "I've only got eight pieces left."

"Oh," Johnny said. "That's all right. I didn't mean to rush you, Maudie Pie. That's all right. Go ahead and get all the ashes you want."

We traveled on a couple of days; then it rained and everything on the wagon got wet, so we camped and laid over two days. Maudie said she couldn't get clothes dried good and Junie had caught the diaper rash. Also she wanted her chickens to run loose a while and stretch their legs. Johnny and I took the opportunity to hunt fresh meat. We got three antelope.

It took over two weeks to reach the place that Johnny had scouted out for a ranch headquarters. It was near a shallow lake that covered about twenty acres. Just north of the lake stood an old corral someone had built for a horse trap, catching mustangs. We parked the wagon about a quarter of a mile east of the lake by a little bluff hill, where Johnny had planned that we would cut a dugout. The location was only a few miles south of the old road to Santa Fe, but it was hardly used any more since the railroad had gone into New Mexico Territory.

Johnny and I had unloaded the heavier things from the wagon and were pitching the tent and staking it down good and ditching around it, while Maudie was taking care of the two kids and unpacking some stuff. Me and Johnny got wind of the fact that something was going on because Sonny was standing there crying and Junie was sitting on a piece of canvas crying and Maudie was standing at the end of the wagon paying no attention to them. In fact, she was crying too without making any noise. We went over there and looked. She had been taking china dishes out of a barrel and unwrapping the newspaper they were packed in. The newspaper pieces were lying there, wrinkled, but smoothed out carefully to save. Six china plates were on the wagon tailgate; four of them were broken. They were white china with little pink and blue flowers on them.

Johnny said, "That's all right, Maudie. We're not worried about that. We've got all the tin plates we need to do us. Don't worry about it."

She didn't answer him but gathered up the two good plates and the pieces. She walked a ways down to a place where some sand rocks were exposed in the soil and tossed the pieces of china away. She looked at the two good plates a minute, then threw them as hard as she could into the rocks.

That set me to thinking that she might not be so good-natured as I had thought at first. I did not hear her say a word all that evening and the next morning till she had carried a bucket of water up from the lake. Then she said, "Law, I wish we'd a located a little closer to the lake where the water would be more handy."

Johnny said, "Come next winter, you'll see why we located up here, Maudie Pie. We're going to dig right into the south side of that hill and get away from that old north wind. I don't want my family spending winter out here in a tent."

We kept the herd of cows within a mile of the lake for

two or three days, until it became plain that they accepted it as their range and wouldn't wander off. Johnny and I started digging the dugout, eight feet wide and fourteen feet back. He told me there was another reason for this job besides the north wind this winter: If you want to claim you settled a place first you've got to have some construction to show for it. We hit a couple of shelves of sandstone which made our digging slow. It looked to me like I was more of a pick-and-shovel man than a cowhand.

One day Johnny and I dropped our tools and sat down to rest a minute. We could see Maudie coming up from the lake, barefooted, one hand holding Junie on her hip, the other carrying a bucket of water.

I said, "I don't aim to stick my nose in anybody's business, but it looks like it would wear Maudie out carrying that baby around all the time that way."

"I've thought about that," he said. "And the only way I can figure it out is this: when a woman gets used to carrying a baby like that it's just as natural and easy as wearing a hat or something, Charley. I believe that's the answer to it."

She had tied three wires between the tent and the wagon for clotheslines, which she kept full all the time. She had carried flat rocks down to the edge of the lake and put them far enough out so that she could dip clean water. One rock she lifted had a rattlesnake under it. After that she kept a close eye on Sonny, who was of an age to prowl around and poke into everything. She drew a big square on the ground in front of the tent with a stick and made the little boy stay in it while she was scrubbing clothes and such.

Her shoes kept on giving her trouble. She would wear them a while trying to break them in, but they would make blisters on her feet. Then she couldn't get them on at all till the blisters healed up. One day I overheard her say something which made me see her mind a little better, or at least I thought so at the time. We were working on the dugout and I came after a shovel lying beside the tent. From inside came Maudie's voice. "You have to be a big boy, Sonny." She said something I couldn't make out; then she said, "Your daddy will make us all rich some day."

A month after I had first met Johnny Fox he handed me thirty dollars. We were fixing to dig that morning, but we sat down on the pile of dirt and talked. He said, "Charley, I'm thinking if you're going to stay around here you're going to have to accept a raise."

That was his way—sort of friendly blarney.

"What's the catch?" I said.

"Because a good hand like you shouldn't be working for thirty a month. You're worth forty."

I asked him, "Is that what you're getting?"

"I'm worth it," he said, "and I demand it, starting today."

In a minute he said, "Charley, I want you to go in partnership with me. I told you I'd offer you a deal, and I don't want you to say yes or no till I've explained it to you.

"First, look at the natural increase of a herd. We start with eighty-two. We save all the heifer calves. Now, we don't get a hundred percent calf crop, but say every year we got thirty-five percent more females than we had the year before. The increase starts slow, but it multiplies. At the end of ten years we've got a thousand head. You can take a pencil and paper sometime and work it out and it's a fact.

"But that's just the females. In a few years we drive a hundred head of good steers to Dodge City. Now, we've got to trade some bulls and buy some bulls. With the rest of the money we scout around and pick up some more young cows. You know how fast we can build up a big spread if we want to?"

"What do you live on all that time?" I asked him.

"The fat of the land. Milk, eggs, butter, garden stuff, wild meat. The fat of the land. There's still a few buffalo scattered around. Bear. Deer. Elk. If we can't find the meat we want, we got turkey or rabbit or prairie dog.

"Charley, let me tell you something else before I make you the partnership proposition. Look at that range out there. No taxes. Those people back in Beaver City talk about wanting a government; they don't know how lucky they are. No taxes. Well, who can use this land? Whoever's here first. Us! How much can we use? As much as we can spread over. When other ranchers come out here, we tell them, Welcome, but don't crowd us. We got the jump on the whole pack. This country is going to be controlled by rich ranchers some day, and we'll be the richest of all because we started first.

"Now here's the proposition, Charley: I got the cows and bulls, one wagon, one team of mares. Those mares are broke to ride in case we need them. That's two thousand dollars. I throw that in. I throw in my saddle horse and my forty a month wages starting today. You throw in your saddle horse and your forty a month. We got a thing we call the Fox and Blankenship Land and Cattle Company, Limited and Incorporated, see? Only we don't care what you call it because it's all between you and me. What part you own and what part I own comes from what we throw in. Proportionate, see? I own it all now, but because you're in on the ground floor, you keep getting more and more of a share."

Every cowhand thinks about things like natural increase and does some figuring like Johnny was doing, whether he gets serious about it or not. I was half convinced myself. I said, "You never mentioned the mule colt. You mean you're throwing him in for nothing?"

"Hell, yes," he said. "And I never mentioned a good cow dog named Tige. We won't act cheap with each other. I'm serious, Charley. What can you possibly lose except your time? If a cow-eating monster came out of his hole a year from now and ate the whole herd, what would you lose? Your time. But if that monster doesn't show up, look what you gain. If we'd done this ten years ago we'd be rich right now."

I said, "It looks like you would always be two thousand dollars ahead of me."

"That's exactly right," he said. "I'm not dishing out something for nothing. But you can make it up any time you get ready. I just paid you thirty dollars; you can throw that in if you want to. You might have some more money; you could throw that in. It's up to you. Only I think you'll come up with the money in the long run. When this ranch is worth two hundred thousand dollars and we are taking out some big profits, all you've got to do is kick a couple of thousand back in and we're even. Then it's fifty-fifty. I'm telling you that's a good deal by anybody's arithmetic."

"Who's the boss?" I asked.

"Nobody. We talk things over and decide."

"You ever figure that lake down yonder goes dry some years? I believe you can walk across it and not get your belly button wet."

"We manage, Charley. We dig tanks. We haul water. We throw the cattle on the river. We get us a well-drilling crew in here and put up windmills. We figure we can handle whatever comes up. What about it?"

I didn't answer him and he said, "Well, you're thinking, Here's old Johnny Fox and he's got a wife and two kids. I don't see what difference that makes. Think of this: You get a free cook. Maudie doesn't eat much and we're living on the fat of the land anyway. But she cooks free. And not a bad cook, right?"

"Right," I said.

"Maudie understands this future business," he said, "because I explained it to her. She's a hard-working woman and good-natured besides. I'd get her a new pair of shoes right now if I had a chance. It's her fault she got shoes too tight. You know the way women are, proud of their small feet. But I don't care; if a place you could buy shoes was around close I'd cough up the money and get her a new pair of shoes this minute. That's the way I am. I'll tell you this: You and me don't need to be cheap. The future; that's it. We'll be rich as lords. What do you say?"

I hemmed and hawed around and said why didn't we let it ride a while?

He said that was all right, but he didn't want to hold any secrets back. He was broke as far as cash money went, and I was either working for the Fox and Blankenship Land and Cattle Company, Limited and Incorporated and So On, and throwing my forty a month into the common pot, or I was kidding myself.

I told him I'd go along on that basis for the present until I made up my mind. I'd work and think and we'd see. He didn't say anything about the thirty dollars he'd just handed me, and I didn't say anything about the hundred and fifty I had stashed away.

When we'd dug out the dirt and rocks level, eight feet wide and fourteen feet back, we cut sod like big bricks to

build up the front. We had to haul it in the wagon a couple
of miles, because the grass around there was mostly too
thin to hold the dirt together. Then we hauled poles from
the Cimarron bottoms to roof the front part. On top of the
poles we put some sod and a thick layer of dirt. For a door
we hung a piece of canvas over the opening. Johnny and
Maudie and the kids moved into the new home, but I kept
my bedroll out in the open where I could get a breeze. It
was like a damp oven in that dugout. Maudie said, "Law!
I don't mind the heat so much, but the dirt keeps falling
down on us and on the clean clothes." Johnny assured
her that the roof would settle and the ceiling would not
fall down so bad later on.

She said, "I sure hope so." It was plain she didn't like dirt.
She had worn out her broom sweeping the ground around
the tent and now had made another one out of broomweeds
bound together.

The soap shortage she had solved by cooking three gallons of lard with a lot of ashes water in her wash pot. She
seemed to be satisfied with the soap, though the whole
process of washing clothes was hard, mainly because little
Sonny wanted to hang onto her leg while she was working.
It would take her a while to carry her water, lugging Junie
on her hip and waiting for Sonny to keep up. When she got
her tubs full, she would put the baby on a pallet under the
canvas shade she had built. No sooner would she start
rubbing than Sonny would start hanging onto her leg. She
would get him loose; then he would do it again. She would
take him over and draw the square with a stick and make
him stay inside, but he would forget and come back. Finally
she would paddle him. He would stand over there with
his little bare feet inside the line, crying, his nose running,
his face sunburned. By the time she got to hanging the

clothes out, he would come back and get hold of her leg and she would let him, because if he cried too long he would get Junie to crying.

She had trouble with lice and fleas getting in Sonny's hair. She washed it nearly every day and kept it cut close to his head. Also she put grease on his head.

If both of the kids got to crying at the same time Tige would come and watch them a while, then turn his nose up and start howling. Maudie would chunk him with clods or rocks and make him get out.

Every couple of days she would go out on the prairie trying to find where the Dominecker hens were laying. They ranged a half a mile from camp. Probably they would have gone plumb wild, but the biggest trees around were a few scrub oak and chaparral not over waist high, so they came back each night to roost on the wagon.

Since we lived mostly on wild meat, Johnny and I spent a lot of time hunting. We would ride over ten miles north or south to the Cimarron or Beaver or perhaps farther west into the canyon country. We talked about what a rough and empty land it was and what a likely hideout it would be for a gang of outlaws, but we hardly ever saw anyone, suspicious or not. Our nearest neighbors were a few Mexicans who lived in good adobe houses and ran flocks of sheep along the rivers. Sometimes we would hunt all day, but we tried to make it home by dark. When we rode into camp Johnny would yell, "Maudie Pie, we brought home the bacon again!"

One day he said we'd better get used to every kind of meat, so why didn't we try some prairie dogs. We rode out west where a prairie-dog town covered a hundred acres or so. Hardly a blade of grass grew there, just their bare mounds scattered around like big pimples on the soil. We found it slow getting the little critters. When you shot they would not stick a single head up again for half an hour. Also, you had to really knock one sprawling or he would escape down in a hole and you'd never get your hands on him. We spent three or four hours getting eleven of them. They seemed fat.

When we rode past the shallow lake near camp I said to Johnny that we might as well stop and clean our game since it was only the middle of the afternoon.

He said, "Naw, Maudie will. You know how women are. They like to clean their own game and that way they get it done to suit them. If she hasn't got time this evening she can do it in the morning."

When we rode up to the dugout he yelled, "Got a little surprise for you, Maudie! Boy, now we can have prairie dog and dumplings!"

We threw them in a pile on the ground.

She walked around the pile looking and all she said was, "Law! it's a batch of them, isn't it."

It turned out that they were not particularly good to eat. They were tough as boot leather and tasted like you'd expect a rat to taste, but I had to agree with Johnny that we had a good supply to fall back on if everything else failed.

We did some fishing also, in a couple of good sloughs along the Cimarron. It was fun but we didn't catch much, a few catfish and perch. Maybe we'd be gone all day and bring in our catch and by the time Maudie got them cleaned there would only be enough for one meal.

It was getting along in the fall and one day we decided to try to get some prairie chickens or sage hens. Not that we needed them so much for food, but we were determined to live off the fat of the land. Johnny carried his shotgun and left his rifle at home. I carried my Winchester, which was all I had. We rode to a valley out southwest, where there had been a good crop of grass seeds. We had come to the right place. You could see a half dozen flocks of them feeding. We tied the horses and made one sweep down the draw on foot. Johnny knocked over six and I got two. They were fat birds; two or three would make a good mess. We tied four on behind each of our saddles and headed home. It was an hour or two after noon when we came past our shallow lake and we didn't suspect anything unusual.

Suddenly: *Whoom!*

We drew up and Johnny says, "What in the world was that? Sounded like a shot."

"I thought I heard a whistling sound over our heads," I say.

"Something's going on," he says. "We better get up there and see about Maudie and Sonny and Junie."

We start on, getting our guns out of the boots.

Whoom! A slug hits Johnny's hat, knocks it off, and sails it back fifty feet. We come out of our saddles and hit the ground.

Johnny yells, "That came from up at the dugout! Some outlaws have got Maudie and Sonny and Junie!"

The horses shy back toward the lake. Johnny and I drag along on our belly and elbows, trying to do the impossible, stay down and also stick our necks up high enough to see what's going on.

"They must have come in on foot," I say. "I don't see their horses."

"Probably around behind the hill!" he yells. "Be careful shooting! We've got to drive them out, but we don't want to hit Maudie and Sonny and Junie!"

Then starts a gun duel which is uneven. We're not shooting at anything but the empty air over the dugout, and we're hiding behind clumps of bunch grass and sage not big enough to hide a terrapin.

Johnny yells at me, "Let's edge around towards their horses! Maybe they'll run for it when they see what we're doing!"

It's hot today. The ground will nearly blister your hands. We hug the dirt like two snakes and try to sink into it when a shot comes at us. We wriggle and roll and push and pant for two hours till we come to where we can see the other side of the hill. Not a single outlaw's horse is in sight. By this time I've started noticing something funny. When that *Whoom!* comes, the bullet always throws dirt on Johnny and nowhere close to me.

"We got to try to dicker with them!" he yells at me. He lays on his back and cuts a stick off a bush with his pocket knife, then takes off his undershirt and ties it to it. He waves it back and forth.

Whoom! A slug jerks his white flag clear out of his hand.

A person dashes out the door of the dugout and runs behind the wagon. It looks like a woman wearing one of Maudie's dresses. In fact I know that's who it is, and she's got Johnny's rifle in her hand.

"Is that you, Maudie Pie?" he yells. "Run for it, Maudie Pie! We're down here!"

Whoom!

"How many outlaws are up there, Maudie Pie?"

Whoom!

"Don't shoot, Maudie Pie! It's us! We're going to save you!"

Whoom!

Tige comes from somewhere up to the dugout door, sits

down on his haunches, points his nose at the sky, and begins to howl.

"My kids must be in there crying!" Johnny yells. "I can't stand this! I'm going to rush them! It's me, Maudie Pie! Don't shoot! Turn your gun on the outlaws! It's me!"

When he's run ten steps the *Whoom!* sounds and he spins around and falls back.

I know we've got a woman on our hands who is nutty as a fruitcake, but it seems like the time has come to stop hiding. I get up and run over to Johnny. He's gritting his teeth and holding his left upper arm. Blood squeezes out between his fingers. He's taken his shirt off before, and that man is dirty as a hog from head to toe with the sweat and dust. I tear off half my own shirt to bind up his arm and stop the bleeding. Luckily, he can still move his fingers all right.

I look up and there stands Maudie. She says, "Law, I'm sorry! I guess I lost my temper for a while."

We get him up under the canvas shade near the dugout. Maudie has a tub of used wash water there, and we swab him off some. He looks peaked under the dirt and doesn't say any more about outlaws.

A couple of days later I talked to him while he was lying out there on a pallet in the shade.

He said, "I got to explain something to you, Charley. It's private and delicate. Maudie found out she's expecting, see. You know? The stork. The patter of little feet. You know? Now, I'll tell you something about women that way. They may get crazy ideas. They may want to eat pickles, for instance. You can't understand it, and they can't help it. It's just their condition, see?"

I had decided to bust up the Fox and Blankenship Land and Cattle Company and was determined not to put off telling the senior partner. I'd no sooner started than Maudie came out and began arranging her washtubs, but I didn't care if she heard. It seemed partly her business to me. Of course Johnny argued and told me I was throwing away a fortune. I told him he could have the fortune. The only question about me was when I would leave. As soon as he could ride I would help him move his cattle and family farther east if he wanted me to.

Maudie stood there with the baby on one hip and her hand on the other. The next thing I knew I was arguing with two people instead of one. As the talk went on I found out that the two of them had evidently agreed to start hauling wash water from the shallow lake up to the dugout with the wagon and team, like that would solve all the problems.

I said, "Johnny, you can't keep a family out here in the winter."

Maudie said, "We'll stay in the dugout in cold weather. I don't see how Johnny's family is any of your business."

"Don't lose your temper, Maudie Pie," Johnny said.

Like a fool, I went on arguing. All I was really trying to say was that I was sure enough leaving but would stay a week or so if they wanted me to.

"Good riddance!" Maudie said. "You didn't have a thing but the shirt on your back, and Johnny took you in partners on a big ranch, and now you act this way!"

"Don't lose your temper, Maudie Pie," Johnny said.

She was standing there in the sun and her face looked nearly as red as her hair. Her green eyes seemed to be crackling at me. I remembered what a good shot she was and shut my mouth.

Two days later I packed my gear on Chili and rode away south. Reader, don't ever come between a man and his wife; you can't win. For a half an hour there during the big gun battle, after I had guessed what gunfighter we were up against, I had thought that I knew why that woman went on a rampage. Later I wasn't so sure. Johnny's explanation may have been right. Who knows? I haven't heard anything of them since that time and don't know how Johnny's idea of the natural increase worked out. If he put up with as much and worked as hard as his wife, they are probably rich by now.

I spent that winter in Tascosa, picking up a job now and then freighting supplies, bob wire, posts, windmills, anything. We had a couple of bad blizzards. With the new grass I signed on with a trail outfit moving cattle for the Matador Land and Cattle Company, and we drove two thousand head of mother cows to a range they were stocking in Dakota Territory. I rode point on that drive and acted as ramrod. The foreman was Zack Mallory.

Stopping over in Dodge City for supplies I saw a sign that really struck me. A new livery barn had been built, and painted on the front was a big running elephant. I looked at it and thought what Buck had said to me and Pete a hundred years ago: He had to go see the elephant and listen to the hoot owl prowl. I'd heard a few hoot owls and now I'd seen the elephant.

Up north Zack had a falling out with the Matador people and gave up his job. Some of us came back with him and worked about a month with him putting up hay on the Brazos River.

I sold my horse Chili to a horse buyer in the town of Jacksboro. I hated to give up that horse, but he was just getting too old to stand up to a full day's work, and I didn't have any pasture to turn him out in. I and Zack Mallory had read his teeth and decided he was seventeen, though the horse buyer in Jacksboro said eighteen. There was a cow horse. One thing, I got seventy-five bucks for him, and that's sure not any glue price. My hope was that some old cowman would get him and appreciate his cow savvy and understand how it is to get old. Chili had some good work left in him if you wouldn't push him all day. I'd ridden him five years or more and we had crossed some mountains and quite a lot of plains together. I won't ever forget him. You want to know the truth? I can't even forget old Cricket, and he was an eighteen-dollar joke. Chili was a cow horse on anybody's ranch, any place, any time. I won't ever forget him.

Before time for roundup in the fall of '87 I left Zack and his confounded hay business and signed on with a big outfit in northwest Texas, the J's, owned by Old Man Jackson.

Chapter 8

The Meanest Horses in the Country

WHEN A BUNCH OF MEN who have been working cattle a long time are sitting around shooting the bull they will finally get to talking about rough horses. They will remind each other of things they forgot years ago. Then some old boy will say, So and So outfit had the meanest horses in the country! They had this one horse. . . . Some of those stories are true. Among cowhands you get about the same percentage of liars as in the population as a whole, no more and no less. But as for knowing what outfit really had the meanest horses, that's another question. If in that bunch of men is one that has worked on the J's he will sit there and look down his nose in pity at the rest. If two of them have worked on that particular ranch, they will look at each other and shake their heads and shudder; then they may grin and go to remembering names like Whirlwind and Hong Kong and Dodger and Cotton-Eye Joe and Rusty.

I wintered on the J's and along in March it began to rain. The manager, Amos Lockhart, sent me over to Stubby's, which was the east line camp, to ride bog. Stubby had tried to farm over there at one time and had built a two-room house out of logs and mud, but his farming had broke him and he'd been working for the J's for years. They said the ranch paid him a hundred dollars for his house. It was all right for a line camp.

Stubby was a short fellow, built like a badger, and he had a name for being a great talker and kidder. When he had lost all his money and used up all his credit trying to farm, his wife had run off, so he said good riddance, and after that he always laughed a lot and made sarcastic remarks. They would let him get away with murder, but he was actually a good hand.

He gave me the welcome of a long-lost brother, and I wasn't long in seeing why. He had to cover six miles each way up and down the Beaver Fork, then clear over the divide to the Wichita River, and all the washes and draws that led into both streams. It took plenty of hunting, because if a cow is going to get bogged down, she'll do it in a low place where you can't see her. Also, she may be starved and helpless, stuck in a buffalo wallow with four inches of water, but when you snake her out, she has a way of blaming all her troubles on the first thing that moves. And here she comes on the prod, right at the man who saved her bony carcass from the buzzards. It's not exactly a job for one hand alone.

It suited me to leave headquarters at that time, since I got away with two decent horses, one named Blackie, which I figured was a gentle all-around cow horse and which I meant to hang onto as long as I worked for the outfit, one a dun named Sleeper, which was hard to saddle and hard to mount, but one which pitched a little and then settled down. I couldn't pull a cow out of a mudhole on Sleeper, but when I rode him I worked on the ground and let Stubby do the pulling. I had learned that on the J's if

you got hold of a horse with only a little devil in him you'd
better be thankful and shut up.

We rode bog for two weeks, half the time in a drizzling
rain, and pulled four or five critters out of the mud each
day. As many cows as Old Man Jackson had, he never
would have missed that many, but we made him money. I
remember Stubby shot one that couldn't stay on her feet,
then got out his knife and began to whet it. When I saw he
meant to skin that mud-caked beauty, I told him to count
me out; the Old Man would just have to get by without the
money one dirty hide would bring, for all of me. Stubby
laughed. "Blankenship," he said, "that's what I like about
you, always thinking about your employer. I'm going to
make me some rawhide chair bottoms. Get hold of that
leg and hep me."

We had two sunny days and it began to dry off. On a
Friday afternoon we rode into camp, and Billy Tuttle was
sitting there in a buckboard with a load of grub.

Stubby rode over and looked critically into the bed.
"Where in the hell's the meat?"

"One side of bacon," Billy said. "Red beans. White beans.
What did you want?"

"One side of bacon? Look at that! One sack of prunes!
You all trying to starve us? That ain't enough grub to
feed two working men!"

Billy Tuttle was a little fellow with a nose like a weasel.
He grinned like a man will when he knows something you
don't know. "One working man," he said. "Amos Lockhart says for Blankenship to come on back to headquarters this Sunday."

That held Stubby for a minute.

I asked, "What does he want with me?"

"Wants you to help with the horses."

"What horses?"

Billy grinned, then began to laugh silently. He had a way about him, if he thought you were teasing, of laughing, just shaking as he grinned, making only a slight hiss now and then.

"You tell Amos Lockhart," Stubby said, "we still got work out here."

Billy said, "I don't know about that, but I think the order came from the Old Man. He's started to worry about spring roundup."

I said, "I'm not going to tame that herd of wildcats for other cowhands to ride."

"I don't know about that," he said.

Stubby said, "You tell Amos Lockhart that Blankenship is leaving his black horse here, because I need me another horse out here."

"That'll be a cold day in July," I told him. "Listen, Billy, you tell Amos Lockhart I couldn't make it and Stubby will be in on Sunday in my place."

Billy sat there grinning and shaking.

"I don't believe he's got the nerve to tell Amos Lockhart a thing," Stubby said. "Billy, you may aim to sleep here tonight, but we can't feed you. We just ain't got the food."

We helped him carry in the grub and unsaddled and unharnessed the horses; then about dark we rustled up something to eat and pulled up our chairs around the plank table by the light of two coal-oil lanterns. Billy Tuttle ate a half a gallon of cold red beans we had. It's amazing how much some little fellows can eat. Makes you wonder where they put it.

I took the edge off my appetite and mulled it over. Finally I asked him, "Is that all he said about me coming in?"

"Yep. Come back to headquarters on Sunday." It seemed

like he considered saying more, but he was spooning it in, and talking got in the way of the serious business.

Stubby said, "I guess you know why Amos Lockhart said Sunday. He's a bigger tightwad than the Old Man. What he don't know is that we don't work around here on Saturday anyway. It takes one day to get ready to rest up on Sunday."

"Well, at least I won't have to wash any more dishes at this camp," I said.

"I believe it's your time tonight."

"I was thinking we have enough clean ones to last till I leave."

Stubby rolled himself a cigarette, lighted it, and flicked the match at the front of the cookstove. He said, "I don't see how you can set back in your riggings so easy, Blankenship. It looks plain to me that you're going to catch it."

"Why? I haven't done anything."

"They're fixing to make a bronc stomper out of you."

"Not me. I didn't hire on for anything like that."

"Can't you ride the mean ones?"

"I ride them like they come." The fact was I figured I could stay on a bad one as long as anybody. On the other hand, I had known a few older men that got their liver and gizzard scrambled together from being too confident about bronc riding when they were young.

"What wagon did you go with last fall?" Stubby asked.

"Snuffy Detweiler's."

Stubby shook his head sadly. "That's what I was afraid of. Who rode the rough string for that bunch?"

"Hell, every hand on this place rides a rough string. You're lucky to get one gentle horse."

"But think about it," he said. "Didn't they have one hand, and he had to take the outlaws?"

"That Comanche Indian boy, I guess."

"Whereabouts is he at now?" Stubby asked.

"I don't know. Gone back to the reservation, I guess."

"Yeah. How about that? I wonder did they ever hire anybody to take his place?"

"Stubby, they don't make a man do that unless he asks for it. They can't do that. I didn't hire on for anything like that."

"Don't tell me your troubles. I just want to know where we should ship the remains."

Billy Tuttle was turning his weasel nose from one of us to the other, keeping busy eating and grinning and shaking silently.

Stubby said, "I didn't even know you were scared of bad broncs."

"Listen, I had Dodger in my string last fall, and I worked him every time in his turn. I guess you might have heard of Dodger."

"Did he throw you?"

"A few times. But I worked him."

"That's what I thought. There's an eye up above watching you, Blankenship. They've figured out what you're good for. Why do you think Amos Lockhart sent for you?"

"Help wrangle the horses a little, I guess. Help shoeing. Maybe help the blacksmith make some new branding irons. How would I know?"

He went to laughing and slapping his leg. "How would you know? Ha! Ha! He! He! Ho! Ho! Ho! How would you know? Ho! Ho! Ho! Ho! Make branding irons! He! He! He! He!"

I said, "Stubby, being out in this line camp so much by yourself, you have blown your cork."

He would look at me and laugh the next day, and he was

still going after it when I rode away Sunday morning, riding Blackie and leading Sleeper. He thought because I was young they would be able to work me into doing something I didn't aim to do. I liked Stubby, but I remember thinking he was running his joy and merriment into the ground.

Headquarters was sprawled out over twenty acres with a building called the Old House in the middle. It looked like a dozen line shacks grown together. One long wall was adobe two feet thick; most of the rest was lumber, but jammed into it about the middle was a two-story log house. If you went in the back, which was the only way I ever entered, you passed through the woodshed into the dining room where the hands ate, with a kitchen off to the side; straight through the dining room was Amos Lockhart's office, and evidently the remainder of the Old House was storage space where they kept everything from chicken feed to barn paint to cow dip. The Old Man himself lived in a good-looking stone house a couple of hundred yards away with a collection of poor relations that came and went; mostly they were a crowd of dudes and not necessarily poor; only if you were kin to Old Man Jackson at all you were a poor relation.

I sneaked into the dining room for supper that Sunday afternoon, figuring I'd just as soon not get any instructions from Amos Lockhart till the next morning, but he caught me as I was leaving. He yelled, "Hey, Bud!" and came stalking out of his office door. He had got the idea my nickname was Bud.

"I see you got in all right," he said. Then he edged on out through the woodshed with me, asking stupid questions about how Old Stubby was getting along. When we got outside he stopped and shifted his cigar around in his mouth, and I figured he was about to get down to business.

Amos Lockhart was a large man. It seemed like he had to dress clean and neat to keep from looking like a bum. He had something sloppy about the way he walked, like he was double-jointed. Usually he had a cigar stuck in his mouth, and always he had a narrow-brim felt hat jammed down on his head. I guess he wore that kind of hat to show he wasn't a hand but a manager. Whether he slept in it or not I don't know, but he ate in it and once I saw him thrown so hard from a horse it would jar your eye teeth and that hat stayed on his head like it was glued on.

"Bud," he said, "guess what we got down in the picket corral?"

I said, "I thought I saw a few horses down there."

"About a dozen or so. We caught Dodger. And that roan Pepper. I've got a crew out right now bringing in all the horses."

"I reckon it's time for spring roundup before long," I said.

"Yeah. I want you to go down in the morning, Bud, and ride Dodger. That fool has got to be broke fresh every spring, but I never saw anybody that could handle him the way you can. Give Pepper a whirl too. Make sure all that bunch is rope broke. Billy Tuttle will help you. Joe Christian will be back by noon, and I'll send him to help you too."

"Something I wanted to mention, Mr. Lockhart," I said. "Of course, I didn't hire on to be a bronc rider. I don't claim to be one. I just want to make a hand. I don't mind to help with the horses a couple of days or wherever I'm needed, but I don't claim to be a bronc rider."

"That's what I told the Old Man," he said. "I says, 'That Bud Blankenship—we kept him over the winter, and he'll pitch in and help where he's needed.' But, listen, don't downgrade yourself when it comes to riding. That's what I like about a tough young feller like you, Bud; you pitch right in and do your duty."

I started to say something about being kept over the winter. Thinking about all the hay I'd handled and all the cows I'd tailed up and all the fence I'd fixed and all the miles I'd ridden in the cold wind, it didn't seem like the right way to put it. But he didn't mean it the way it sounded. He meant they "employed" me over the winter instead of "kept." It's supposed to mean they rate you high if they keep you the year around.

I guess I should have taken the bull by the horns and told him I didn't mean to cripple myself up being a bronc stomper, and not only that, but I could ride any outlaw on the place if I took a notion to, and if they didn't like my attitude I would ask for my time that minute. The only trouble is that ranch managers and such people don't give you a clear-cut case; they string you along so you can't tell when it's time to get sore and put your foot down. Amos Lockhart was a master at it.

He went on in a confidential way. "I want to talk to you about a rumor that's going around. Did you ever hear anybody say this outfit has got the meanest horses of any outfit in the country?"

I laughed a little. "Well, yes, sir, I've heard it said for a joke."

"That's what I told the Old Man." He shifted his cigar around in his mouth as if he was trying to find a place for it to set easy. "Detweiler said one of his men told that story about the meanest horses last fall, and two weeks ago I was over in Kimble City hiring some hands and a clerk in a store mentioned the same rumor. A tale like that don't do the reputation of this place any good, Bud. We got to tame these horses down a little."

"It's mostly a joke," I said.

"Sure it is. Not a word of truth in it. Every ranch has naturally got its share of pitching horses. I hope the boys that work here don't spread those tales around. You're a good judge of horses, Bud. What do you personally think? Has this outfit got good horses or not?"

"Well, of course, the ones that run loose all winter. . . . Then some talk has it. . . . Maybe some horses that are supposed to be broke when they are bought are actually outlaws other outfits couldn't handle. I'm not complaining myself. I expect to take them like they come."

"Right," he said. "You get good, strong saddle stock and they won't be all gentle little lambs. Any good horse wants to shake a few kinks out on a cool morning. You got to expect that. Well, we want to tame them down the best we can. I know the hands on this place don't mind a horse to pitch a little. The Old Man wants us to be well mounted. He's just bought thirty or forty head of first-class horses. I want you to go up to Sealey Station with me to get them on Wednesday. So you throw a saddle on that bunch down in the picket corral in the meantime and give them a little workout."

We left it that way, whatever way it was. The news that the Old Man had bought thirty or forty head of first-class horses did not ease my mind. I was thinking, You can buy thirty head or forty head or thirty-seven head, but if you say you buy thirty or forty head that's not very clear news. And what do they mean by "first-class horses"? I took it with a grain of salt.

At sunup the next morning Billy Tuttle and I rode down to the picket corral a quarter of a mile below the Old House. It was a round pen made out of mesquite poles the way the Mexicans used to make them: the butts charred so they wouldn't rot, then stood side by side in a trench, and the tops bound together with rawhide. It looked crude with the bleached, crooked posts, but it was handy, with a stout snubbing post in the middle and a short wing running out from the gate.

A dozen horses came up to the fence and studied us, looking for some feed. They'd been up three days, only getting out long enough to be driven to water, and somebody had been hauling hay to them. It was a typical bunch of J's horses. Besides Dodger and Pepper, I saw two blaze-face bays named Brat and Caesar, a big paint named Goodfellow, and a red horse named Youngun, as well as several others I'd seen before but didn't know their names.

Dodger is an overgrown flea-bit dun with black scratches in his hide. When he sees me come in the gate he immediately strolls around behind the others and acts like he's looking the other way. He knows me all right. I mean one thing to him: work, after he's spent a gay, free time kicking up his heels all winter.

I feel good. That time of year it's cool and fresh-smelling early in the morning. You feel ready to tangle with anything. I make a loop, get it straightened out to suit me, and get it all cocked and ready. Then Dodger gets interested in smelling of the ground.

I move over and wait. He moves over and looks out to the far prairies. When I'm ready he ducks his head again.

I say to Billy, "Run them around the fence. I'll see if that crowbait can smell of the ground while he's running."

When he's in the clear I get lucky and put my first loop on him. He drags me a ways while I plow up two nice garden rows with my bootheels; then I swing around the snubbing post. He pitches a few jumps, practicing, and I take up slack on him till he has to simmer down or choke himself.

We leave him there a few minutes to think about it, while

we get my saddle and bridle. Evidently he decides to bide his time, because he takes the bit and doesn't paw or kick when I throw on the saddle. All he does is hump up and lay his ears back. I whomp him on the shoulder with the flat of my hand a few times, talking to him. "Dodger, you remember me. Relax, old friend. We're going to treat each other nice, me and you. Lovey-dovey!" Billy Tuttle stands and grins like an idiot, laughing silently.

We get him out through the gate, and Billy mounts his horse and holds Dodger's bridle, while I climb on top of him.

Dodger has seen about twelve years and he's had experience getting cowboys off his back. He has a mean reputation and looks rough as a cob. Actually, he doesn't buck to jar a rider. He comes down soft-legged as a cat, but when he hits he's ready to go some place else. He's quick for a horse his size. You can't afford to get behind. You'll never catch up.

Soon as Billy lets him loose, he goes at it. I rake him with my spurs. He jumps like he's never had a man on his back before. Billy lets him clear the wing fence, then hazes him away from the rocky ground and down toward a flat that has a good stand of dry grass.

Dodger means business. I get that feeling of jouncing power and action that I haven't felt in months. Kind of surprising—you know it but don't really remember it. Jump left. Jump left. Jump right. I relax, try to be loose and quick. Jump left. Jump left. Jump right. I'm saying to myself, I've got to watch out and outguess this wild brute. Jump left. Jump right. Jump right. I lose my balance and my left stirrup. I'm clawing leather. The next time he comes up, the cantle of my saddle hits the inside of my left knee and he flips me out into empty air. I light on my shoulder with a good jar. It hurts a minute, but I don't find anything busted.

Instead of running, Dodger is trying to get rid of his saddle, so Billy catches him only a hundred yards away. It comes to me, as I'd already learned once and forgotten, that you don't want to get ahead on this horse either.

When Billy brings him to me his ears are still thinned down and closed up and flattened back. I whack him on the shoulder a few times and talk to him. "Dodger, calm down. You're not treating me right. You know I can ride you. Old friend, you're going to get me mad."

I climb back on board, and he's waiting for me, warmed up and in tune. Like they say, same song, second verse, only I aim to do more of the calling this time. He's jumping high and twisting, but every time his front feet hit bottom I rake him good. It seems like he tries on purpose to get in the rocky ground, but he can't run through Billy's nag, so he plunges down toward the grassy flat, pitching for every cent he's worth. Dodger's got a hard mouth and a neck ten times as strong as my left arm. I don't try to hold his head up. I pull and let off, pull and let off, to get him off stride. Let him try to outguess me. I yell a little. "Pitch, you devil!" He circles the flat twice and luck is with me. I stick. He stops to blow, but I kick him into a run.

I run him hard out west above the creek, about a mile and a half, then make a turn and head back. This big dun can go. Billy can't stay close to us. By the time we make it back to the picket corral, Dodger is showing sweat and obeying the rein. We unsaddle and unbridle him and put him back in the pen.

After that I rode four more horses and two of them, Pepper and Brat, threw me, Pepper twice. The second time Pepper put me down he kicked me in the hip. I couldn't walk for a minute, but when I finally got back on him he was worn down enough that I could handle him. I worked him into a foaming sweat before taking my gear off of him.

A picket corral has got advantages and disadvantages. One thing, you can't sit on the fence worth a hoot, which is just as well if you plan to get the work done; cowhands waste a lot of time sitting on fences. The trouble with this corral was the plank gate. It had caught all the heavy sitting by itself and had not merely sagged down to the ground but actually into the ground. You had to lift it and drag it to get it opened or closed. Along toward noon we saddled up the big paint Goodfellow. When I started to lead him out the gate he was jerking so it was all I could do to hold him. The other horses commenced to follow him. Billy yelled, "Wait! Whoa, there! Hold it! Wait!" trying to lift the gate and push it shut. Every time he'd get it clear of the ground another horse would bump it, trying to crowd through, and he would lose his hold. Every mother's son of those broncs got out.

I tied Goodfellow and told Billy, "Let's take them to water while they're out." We dragged the gate back against the wing and Billy mounted and took off after the eleven horses, which were kicking up their heels and heading for the wide open spaces.

I'd been told Goodfellow wouldn't pitch, but that's as far as the guarantee went. He shied sideways till I finally got set in the saddle; then he ran away. Before I found my right stirrup he was halfway up toward the Old House. Even after I got situated well enough so I had a decent chance to ride him, I couldn't slow his mad run nor do much to guide him. He circled the bunkhouse and dashed back past the picket corral and toward the creek bottoms, a mile away, like he had forty miles to go and already late. I got his neck pulled around so he was running half blind, and he ran smack dab through a bush six feet high. I never used a spade bit, but only a curb bit with a short port. It always seemed to me that if you couldn't ride, why take it out on the horse? But I began to wish now I had a bit where I could tear his head off.

After going through the bush I started throwing my weight to the side and managed to guide him toward the tank where Billy Tuttle had caught up with the horse band. Goodfellow saw the other horses drinking and headed for them like a bat out of hell. I thought he would drown us both, but he splashed into the water knee deep, stopped, and began to try to nose out enough loose rein where he could drink, just like a gentle old saddle horse. Billy had enough sense not to mention the detour I'd taken.

About that time we could barely hear the cook pounding on the cast-iron wash pot he used for a dinner bell. I was ready, but it took us an hour to get all that fine horseflesh back up into the pen again.

After dinner I rode two that I knew wouldn't pitch; then Long Joe Christian came down with a load of hay, and the Old Man himself came down with him.

The Old Man's eyes fastened immediately on the sagging gate and he called Long Joe over. "Quick as you get that hay off the wagon, start to work on this gate. Hang it a foot higher. Have Newt make you some bigger hinges."

He had a kind of dry voice and could size a thing up quickly. He stood a little shorter than the average man, a little lighter, had white hair, and usually wore a big hat. The thing about his clothes was that he wore hundred-dollar suits and always had a red flannel rag wrapped around his neck. Rumor said he had rheumatism in his neck. He wasn't as young as he once was. But that old man had followed the free grass west for thirty years, sacking up the money as he went; then he had bought a few hundred square miles of land. He had forgot more about raising cattle than many a man ever learns. An owner that way has something distant about him even when he's standing right in front of you. It's because you can't add him up.

He said to me, "You can go ahead and work these horses while Joe fixes the gate, can't you? Tie them all up to a post if you need to. Billy can go get you some stake ropes."

"Yes, sir, I think we can."

He smiled. He had false teeth. You could never tell when he was about to smile, nor what he might smile about, like he had his own private sense of humor. In that, he was different from Amos Lockhart, who never smiled, but Old Man Jackson didn't waste much time on jokes. He said, "I saw you giving Dodger a little go-round this morning."

"Yes, sir, I worked him a little."

"That's a good strong horse," he said. "Needs a little training."

The question was going through my head whether he considered that I was in charge of bronc training, but he went on talking.

"We start roundup the second week in April. We've got to get these mounts in shape. That's one thing about this outfit; we start roundup on time. I want to be sure everything is well shod. These barefooted horses that run in the bottoms all winter, Blankenship, their toenails get too long. Cocks their pasterns. I want the hoofs trimmed right. I want shoes that fit. I want them set down solid and tight. One thing I believe: You take care of your horse and he will take care of you."

It was a cinch he didn't consider me to be in charge of horse shoeing. Newt Tanner handled that.

"I just bought thirty-six good horses," he said, "to improve our saddle strings. Lockhart tells me they'll be in on the railroad Wednesday. All first-class stock. Some of them may need a little training." With that he went over and began to study the poles in the picket fence; he walked around it once, then walked back up toward the Old House.

One by one I saddled the remaining horses that hadn't been ridden and tried them out. Long Joe Christian, usually a solemn fellow, would get excited when one of them would pitch. He'd stop whatever he was doing and yell, "Ride him, Blankenship! Spur him! Look at him go! Hang on there, boy! Give him what for! Yip-eeee!"

I thought I'd give Dodger another turn that afternoon before he backslid on me, but I'd already waited too long. He pitched wild as ever and dumped me twice, in spite of Long Joe cheering me on. One time he threw me in the rocky ground but I came out with only the back of my hand skinned up. When I managed to stick and got him to running I gave him another half hour's hard run. By the time the sun hit the horizon I felt like I'd put in a day.

Next morning I couldn't hardly get out of my bunk. It felt like a stampede of goats had run over me. I had a dozen blue spots, and I couldn't hardly bend enough to get my clothes on. I thought, Well, that was a long one-day bronc riding career I had. But by the time I got up to the woodshed and got washed up and had some breakfast everything loosened up enough to where it seemed like I might be able to make another day.

The first horse I tried was Goodfellow, and he ran away with me again. The run served to get me warmed up and feeling good. Then I started in on the buckers and got thrown three times. Pepper kicked me again, a glancing blow on the right knee. It made me sick to my stomach for a minute.

Sometimes that morning I would think, I didn't hire on for anything like this and they are taking advantage of me. They can't do this to me. Why should I let these broncs bang me all up? Let Amos Lockhart ride these outlaws and see how he likes it. If the Old Man figures these horses have got to be tamed before the second week in April, let him do it himself. They can't treat me this way. They think they can but they can't. They think they can beat around the bush and I won't ever have a chance to tell them to go jump in the lake. I guess they'll think twice if I quit when they're trying to get hands together for roundup.

But then I would climb on one and he would pitch high, wide, and handsome, and it would dawn on me: I can ride him! He's doing his best, but I've got his number! Pitch, you devil! And I would hear Long Joe get all excited, yelling, "Go after him! Look at that buckeroo ride! Whoo! Eeee! Spur him, Blankenship! Spur him!" That's the way it was on Dodger when I would get by his tricks; then he would start pitching high and I would know I had him. When he would go up I would sit there on top of the world and I could see twenty miles every direction.

That afternoon a crew brought in the main horse band, something over a hundred head. I don't reckon anybody knew the exact number unless they checked the ranch books. It made quite a sight, that running conglomeration of horseflesh, every color, some still patchy and shaggy with winter hair. Range horses lose their hair early in a wet spring when the grass is good, but some of them seem to need a little work and sweat to shed it all. I recognized some of these: a wild yellow horse named Hong

Kong, Blue Baby, that I had ridden a few times, Cotton-Eye Joe, Pewee, and a wicked red roan named Whirlwind. We put some of them in the plank corral at the barns, some in the bull yard, some more down in the picket corral, and the rest down on the creek with two bell mares and a wrangler. The horse business around headquarters was picking up.

On Wednesday morning Amos Lockhart, Billy Tuttle, and I started early for Sealey Station to get the new horses that were coming in on the train. It was only seventeen miles and we figured with any luck to be back by dark. Amos Lockhart rode a long-legged gelding that set a good pace. Blackie could stay with him trotting, but Billy Tuttle's horse had to break into a lope now and then to keep up.

Sealey Station was a sprawling, dusty town on the Fort Worth and Denver line. We went to the loading pens and watered our horses. No cars were on the siding, so we went down to the station. The agent stood on the loading platform, scratching himself and yawning. Amos asked, "When's the train coming in?"

The man looked at his watch, looked up the track, and said, "Before long, Mr. Lockhart."

"You got three cars of horses due in?"

"Might be," he said. "I could look it up." He wandered into his office.

Amos Lockhart climbed onto the loading platform and clomped back and forth, chewing on his cigar.

When the agent came out he said, "I got three stock cars."

"When is the train due?"

Amos and the agent were both looking at their watches as if they were checking up on each other; both watches were as big as turkey eggs. The agent said, "Pretty soon now."

Amos stomped around a while and suddenly said, "Let's go to the restaurant, boys, and grab a bit of dinner. I think the God-damned train's late."

We went to Kate's Diner and ordered the specialty of the house, which on Wednesdays was Kate's hot hash. Also we took advantage of this being a railroad town where they had ice and ordered iced tea to offset the hash. Amos went outside a couple of times to listen for the train. Billy Tuttle took seconds on the hash, though his eyes had already turned red from eating all that pepper.

Back down at the station Amos Lockhart climbed on the platform and asked the agent, "What time is that train supposed to be due, anyway?"

The agent said, "It's due now."

"Looks to me like if it was due when we got here, it's an hour late now."

The agent didn't say anything. He was sitting in a cane-bottom chair in the doorway, eating a sandwich and looking at a copy of *Harper's Illustrated Weekly*. Amos lighted a cigar. I figure he thought it was frivolous for the man to sit there looking at a magazine when the train was late instead of standing up and worrying.

We waited and Amos fretted and I began to figure we wouldn't get the horses home before night and we'd have to camp out without even a coffeepot. About the middle of the afternoon the agent came out of his den and said, "Mr. Lockhart, there's been a wreck up the line."

"A train wreck?"

"Yes, sir."

"What about the horses? Is it that train? When are we going to get the horses?"

"Well, we won't have anything that's scheduled today, Mr. Lockhart. That's all the information at this time."

For the next hour Amos went in and out of the office and stalked around on the platform. Finally I told him, "Me and Billy might walk around town, Mr. Lockhart. I might buy me a few pair of socks I need."

"Stake out the horses first," he said. "And listen for the train. If it comes in, I don't want to have to hunt you up."

We staked the horses out close to the loading pens and we hadn't got to the nearest saloon before I learned that maybe I hadn't been as bright as I'd thought. Billy didn't have a cent on him. I'd figured to tank up on fifty cents' worth of beer and go on a little toot, but I was going to have to finance him too. We went to a small place and stood at the bar drinking. They had a gallon of pickled boiled eggs sitting there, and Billy had eaten seven of them before I realized they were costing me a nickel apiece.

I got him out of there and we went to a large saloon called Pete Kimble's Emporium. After we had a few I lost my tight attitude about money so that I didn't even know whether Billy got enough to eat or not. Some gent who was kibitzing the same poker game we were found out we worked for the J's and asked if they still had those bad horses. We admitted they had a few. He said when he worked down there four—five years ago, they had about a hundred. He claimed he had got both legs broke trying to ride J's horses, but he'd been soaking up so much booze you couldn't believe half he said. When he tried to take his pants off to show his broken legs, the bartender put him out on the street.

Later on Billy and I were walking along singing and we noticed every light in the town was out. We found the hotel, but the front door was locked. We banged. We called for service. Nobody answered. After a short council of war we decided the hotel front porch was dry and cheap and up out of the snakes and would make a good bed.

It was daylight when Amos Lockhart woke us up, talking sarcastically. He asked if I bought any socks. He thought I felt stiff and sore because I'd slept on that wood flooring; actually that cause was nothing up beside of the lumps and bruises I carried from my two-day bronc-stomping career. I didn't press the point; he was in a bad mood worrying about the train. He knew the Old Man was counting on the new horses to improve the saddle strings.

After breakfast we walked back to the station, and Amos went inside. Billy and I lounged around. Evidently a message came in on the wire, and Amos got to arguing about it with the agent. Amos's voice carried when he got mad. I heard him say, " . . . sue this God-damned railroad! Can't even haul a few horses!"

You couldn't understand the agent as well, but you could tell he wasn't backing down. It sounded like he said the railroad would sue the Jackson Ranch.

Not long after that a locomotive gave a long whistle up the line and we could see her coming. We went to the loading pens and the train bucked two cars onto the siding. Everything looked all right, except the caboose was missing.

We unloaded twenty-four horses out of the two cars, big healthy horses, some of them skinned up a little on the legs. They looked like they belonged on the J's, every color, strong, with an independent air about them. A couple of them had short pieces of frayed rope on their necks and one had a short piece on his foreleg.

Amos stuck his head inside one car and began cussing. It sounded like he was about to throw a running fit. The floor was strewed with a jumble of splintered wood and pieces of rope. "What kind of ignorant fools would make a car full of horses ride on a mess like that?" he demanded. Both cars were the same. I figured no kind of fools would have loaded the horses without cleaning the junk out of the cars. In fact, I had begun to smell a rat.

We got the two dozen horses strung out south. We would find out the details on what happened three days later when two hands from the Dipper Ranch sixty miles up the line drove in the last twelve of our new horses. Here's what happened: When they loaded the stock in Colorado they built stout plank gates for partitions in the cars, putting two horses in each temporary stall and tying each horse. The horses evidently did not enjoy the ride nor any of the arrangements, for they proceeded to smash up everything they could reach. They broke a bottom slat in the wall of one car and kicked one of those plank partitions part way out. The train passed a single stock car sitting by a two-bit loading chute. The plank partition hooked the empty car and carried it to the switch, where it derailed itself and one car of horses, turned over two more cars and the caboose, and knocked down a railroad water tank beside the tracks.

Amos, Billy, and I made a hard day driving the improvements to the J's strings to the ranch. Those horses knew they could outrun a horse that was carrying a man, and each one of them had a mind of his own. It was nearly sundown when we turned them over to the wrangler in charge of the remuda on the creek below headquarters.

Like they say, birds of a feather flock together, and this band of outlaws from up north that had wrecked a damned train fell right in with the J's horses as if they were all kissing cousins. It looked like a family reunion.

Billy Tuttle and I were lucky to have our claim in on

bunks, because the bunkhouse was getting crowded. The men from the line camps were coming in and new-hired hands were reporting. The next day what you might call the big horse circus started. By the middle of the morning dust rose up in clouds around that place. Out at the bull yard and down at the picket corral they were riding horses. Behind the barn a bunch of horses were tied to logs to try to teach them not to jerk against a rope. In the plank corral we were shoeing and branding.

Somehow, missing only two days around headquarters, I had got out of the bronc-riding business. Sid Wilcox and a Mexican named Vasquez were riding the bad ones in the bull yard, and a fellow from Utah, nicknamed Utah, was doing the same down in the picket corral. Evidently it had just happened in the natural run of events and I was satisfied to keep my mouth shut, though it was a cinch I could outride Sid Wilcox any day in the week.

We threw every new horse to shoe him or reset his old shoes. They would have to be tied down for branding anyway—the Old Man was determined to burn a small "J" on the left shoulder of every horse he owned—but these, the way they fought, had to be thrown for shoeing even. While they were down Amos Lockhart would check their teeth. He had a book in which he wrote a description, old brands, and age of every new horse. Newt Tanner did most of the shoeing and checked the fit of every shoe. He had seven crates of horseshoes sitting against the fence, two kegs of nails, a sack of coal, a forge and anvil, and a tub of water.

Stubby was one of the ropers. He liked to foreleg a horse and drop him quick, but Amos didn't want to bust them hard, so we would catch them by the neck and choke them down, then try to get them to walk into loops on the ground. One big rusty-colored horse we maneuvered around for fifteen minutes. Finally we got all the ropes on him and started to pull him over. He began to rare and pitch, got one front leg free, jerked two men down, and swung the rest of us around like kids playing pop the whip. One man ran into the forge and knocked it over, or he was slung into it. Amos and Newt got on the ropes to help us throw the horse. By the time we could get a breather and look around, there was Amos's horse book over by the spilled forge, burning like a pine knot and about to set the fence to blazing.

Amos grabbed it up, beat on it, then soused it in the tub of water. The rest of us did our laughing as silently as we could. When Amos would get worked up and sweaty, he looked like somebody you'd picked up off the ground behind a saloon. He said to Stubby, "If you ever have to rope that rusty son-of-a-bitch again, I want you to foreleg him and bust him where he'll crack the ground! It'll take me all night to copy that out into a new book!"

Another horse we got the ropes on was fighting and jerking and kicking up the dirt, and I noticed a little fellow hanging onto the rope in front of me, bobbing like a cork. Suddenly I realized he had on a hundred-dollar suit and a red flannel rag pinned around his neck. The Old Man. When we got the horse down, he looked around at me, smiled, and said, "Good healthy horses." I kept waiting for him to say that they needed a little training. He checked every detail as Newt fitted a new set of shoes.

We shoed and branded about fourteen horses that day. Well along in the afternoon we knew a kind of commotion was going on down at the picket corral. Long Joe Christian tore off down there in a wagon, flailing at the team. Shortly afterward they hauled Utah, unconscious, back up the hill and laid him on the ground in the shade of the bunkhouse. Some of us went over to see what was wrong. He'd been thrown hard and looked dead but evidently had only got the wind knocked out of him. He finally sat up and said he was all right. His eyes looked blank and crossed.

Amos Lockhart said, "He'll come around. Let him rest a while." Then he said to me, "Bud, you better go on down there and top off some of these horses. We got to tame these horses down a little and not many days to do it."

It looked like suppertime to me, but I went down to the picket corral and rode one horse that I knew wouldn't pitch.

It's a long lane that knows no turning, they say. That evening a new light was cast on the horse situation. It made some of the old hands happy, some mad, some relieved, some jealous. The news came from a new-hired man, Willie Caudle. He had long legs and an eager way of talking. Actually, he was halfway a greenhorn and worked sometimes as a bookkeeper for the county clerk, but he worked on ranches now and then when they were hard up for hands. Willie had no sooner come on the place than the word began going around that a great man named Red Paden would arrive in a day or two in a blaze of glory and our horse problems would be taken care of.

I walked into the bunkhouse with three or four other fellows. Willie Caudle was sitting on his bedroll on the floor, and I asked him, "Who is this Red Paden jasper?"

"Boys," Willie announced, "Old Man Jackson is bringing in a pro."

Someone asked, "A pro what?"

"Yeah, what's that? A whore?"

"Maybe it's a lawyer."

"Boys," Willie said, "the Old Man has hired a real first-class rider. A pro bronc buster. And, man! I want to tell you that Red Paden can ride!"

We questioned him, but he wouldn't back down an inch on the news.

Stubby said, "If he's so famous how come we never heard of him?"

"I never said he was so famous," Willie said, "only that he can ride. He'll ride any animal that's got hair on it!"

Somebody said, "I guess you think he's quite a lot better than these boys around here?"

"All I know is he can really ride! You can't hardly get old Red Paden off of a horse's back till he gets ready to leave!"

Stubby said, "He better stay away from these Jackson horses if he don't want to ruin his record. They'll kill him."

Willie Caudle must have had about forty dollars on him, and he laid every cent of it on the line before bedtime. They bet him different ways: that Red Paden wouldn't stick on Hong Kong the first time, that he wouldn't last a week with the outfit, that he would never ride Whirlwind, that he wouldn't ride Dodger twice in a row. They prevailed on Snuffy Detweiler to hold the stakes.

Next morning I went down to the picket corral. The ground was getting pretty well tromped up around there, which was good. In my education as a bronc rider I was learning, unfortunately, not only about staying in the saddle, but also about looking around for landing spots. If a man's coming straight down, water would be the best, or tall grass. If he's coming in on a slant to hit sliding, it's better to find loose dirt than to loosen the dirt with your own tender hide.

I tried to get Red Paden out of my thoughts. He might

be only a dream of Willie Caudle's overactive mind, I kept telling myself.

Utah came down that morning also, but it seemed clear that I was expected to ride the bad ones. His eyes still looked a little glassy. Billy Tuttle and Long Joe Christian had orders to help us, to move the ones we considered tamed to the remuda and bring back horses that hadn't been saddled since last fall. Keep us plenty of pitching horses handy. That wasn't hard to do; they'd been adding fresh horses and taking out only the tamest, and that corral was getting more and more concentrated with ornery horseflesh.

I had bad luck with the first one, that ugly red roan named Whirlwind. Billy is trying to hold his head and is getting jerked around and lifted off his feet. When I get my boot in the stirrup I jump for the saddle, which is a school-boy type of trick.

Like they say, I am shipwrecked before I get aboard. He's exploding like a string of firecrackers, going around and around, with me trying to hang on the side. I get a chance and lurch upward, but he twists to meet me and socks the side of the saddle horn into my chest. Crack! A rib goes. I can feel it pop like breaking a dry stick in your hands. I'm all over that crazy horse for a dozen hectic jumps but never get my seat in the saddle. Then he dumps me on my head on the off side.

While they're catching Whirlwind I tenderly probe my chest. My rib is numb and prickly. I can hear those cowhands in the bunkhouse saying, "Yeah, Blankenship gave it a try, but he didn't last till he got on the first bronc." I'm not positive I can ride this particular bearcat, but I figure I can sure give him a better run for his money than that.

Utah, Billy, and Long Joe all three get hold of him. Billy, feeling guilty about the sorry job he did before, takes off his shirt and wraps it around the nag's head, while the other two ear him down. This time I get set solid before they let him loose. He bucks hard and wicked for six or eight circles, and I can feel the action in my rib. Then he shucks me off.

The third time I ride him. The third time's the charm, they say. He runs out of steam, but instead of working him I slide down and lead him back to the corral, because I'm getting sick to my stomach. I take it easy a while, helping the other three while they do some riding.

That was the most miserable day I ever spent. An idea kept nagging at me, as if the Old Man was saying, "These boys just couldn't do the job, so I had to send for a professional, Red Paden." It aggravated the devil out of me that I kept thinking that nonsense. And the rib gave me holy hell every time I rode. A jolt that started in a bronc's stiff knees would rise straight up to my rib and stop there. But I had got my thick-headed stubbornness worked up to where I thought, I'll see this whole bunch in hell before I say anything about my rib.

Although Long Joe did little riding, he did most of the cheering. He would get carried away, and it did me good to hear him pulling for me. But for some reason, when I was up on Brat and he was pitching like a turpentined cat, it suddenly came through clear to me what Long Joe was yelling. "Go get him, Brat boy! Higher! Buck, you devil! Atta boy! Yip-eeee!" The halfwit was cheering for the horses! If that bronc had thrown me then, I'd have fed Long Joe a fist full of knuckles.

An hour or so before sundown Amos Lockhart turned over his teeth checking and record keeping to Snuffy Detweiler and came down to see how things were going at the picket corral. I saw him coming and roped out Cotton-

Eye Joe, a nag homely as a mud fence which I had found to be an easy pitcher, though very shy to handle. Amos didn't say much but just stood and watched.

Cotton-Eye Joe kept frisking around and wouldn't let me get near him with the saddle. We got a rope on a hind foot and tied it up on his neck so that he only had three feet on the ground. Utah eared him down. Billy and Long Joe got on the other side and held the saddle blanket on and tried to push him toward me. It didn't do my rib any good even to pick up the saddle. I got ready to swing it when he would hold still a second. He stumbled and jumped and tried to rare up. Then he planted one front foot square dab on my boot.

I'd been stepped on before. A horse will usually let up, thinking he's on a rock or something. But Cotton-Eye Joe was trying to catch his balance. He came down on the top of my foot, put all his weight on it, and gave her a little twist. I thought that wall-eyed elephant would never get off.

I dropped the saddle and limped back and sat down to take my boot off.

Amos Lockhart said, "I wouldn't take that boot off if you don't have to."

"Why not?"

"If it swells up on you you'll never get it back on."

Yes, I thought, you big, ugly, double-jointed bastard, if it swells up to where I can't get my boot on or off, I guess you figure I can go ahead and work. My rib felt like a hot iron and my foot felt busted and I was not in a respectful mood. I got my boot and sock off. It didn't look bad, but pressing on it I could guess I had another cracked bone somewhere down inside.

Amos helped them get the saddle on. Utah mounted up,

and Cotton-Eye Joe ran away with him. Billy chased after him. I don't know how far they went, but they were both late to supper.

I couldn't stand any pressure on my foot, so I took my pocket knife and cut small slits in my boot. The next day was Sunday. I spent the morning soaking my foot in a bucket of hot Epsom salts, trying on my boot, and enlarging the slits.

That was the day Red Paden came. Evidently he spent a while hanging around the Old Man and Amos Lockhart, but Willie Caudle gave us the news that he had arrived, along with further information about his great riding skills. Late that afternoon I got a chance to talk to him. Some of the boys were walking around looking at the horses in the different pens, giving him the grand tour.

Red Paden was redheaded, of course, and short. His legs didn't look long enough to grip a bronc good, but he looked strong. The fellow actually had muscles in his jaws. He stood straight and had a look about him like the statue of an explorer or a politician. He wore a black silk shirt with small pearl buttons and a pair of California pants. His boots had shiny brass caps on the toes. His hat was creased to a low crown, flat on top, with a chin strap made of plaited calfskin that could be tightened with a silver concho. He looked good for a night on the town, but these were his working clothes.

I don't act too forward with a stranger. Maybe it was because of my game foot; I was an honorable veteran of the J's horse wars. Anyway I limped right up to him, stuck out my hand, and told him my name.

I asked, "You're Red Paden, aren't you?"

"Yep."

Shaking hands with him was like shaking hands with a pair of blacksmith tongs.

"They say you're a pro."

He grinned. "What kind of a pro?"

That had me stumped for a minute. "That's what we been wondering. What do you do?"

"I work with horses."

"Riding and training? Like that?"

"Yep."

"I guess you've been riding a lot in rodeos or a circus or something."

"I've been in rodeos some. Small ones."

"They say you're a real professional bronc stomper."

"About average, I guess. I do my best."

He was grinning and not arguing, but I didn't seem to be able to get down to the nubbin of it with him. I knew I wasn't exactly polite to ask so many questions, but I know too that a new man coming into an outfit doesn't know who he can tell to go to hell and who he can't.

"What I mean is," I said, "we've got a lot of experienced hands around here, used to riding them as they come. They're about average or better."

"They say this is a good outfit," he said.

"It's a good outfit but we got some real tough horses. I don't mean to be a nuisance asking so many questions, but some of the boys were just curious and wondering why you were brought in."

"I reckon every ranch has some rough ones," he said. "A lot of good horses want to warm up a little and get the kinks out on a cool morning."

Words right out of the Old Man's mouth! I thought, Lord have mercy! What kind of a sucker is this? No more idea than the man in the moon what he's got into!

I asked him one more question. "If it's not being too nosey, did you hire on for a regular cowhand?" I didn't have the gall to ask him how much wages he was drawing.

He said, "Well, I'm just supposed to work with the horses, I guess."

That's all I could get out of him. I didn't know whether to feel sorry for him or ask what gave him the idea he was so great. A little later a bunch of us were washing up for supper in the woodshed and they were asking me about Paden. I told them, "I don't know what he can do or what he's supposed to do. He doesn't claim a thing."

I hadn't seen Willie Caudle. He had his face down in a pan of water, bubbling and spewing. He raised up and said, "Red Paden won't tell you, but listen to me; that old boy can ride! When I say ride, I mean *ride!* Man, you ain't seen it!"

The straw that broke the camel's back with me was when I found out that night where our hero was sleeping. The bunkhouse being full, Amos Lockhart had told him to bring his bedroll into his office. He was bunking somewhere in the Old House.

I thought about all those hundred-some-odd Jackson horses. I knew some personally that should have had a price on their head, dead or alive, but most of them I wasn't even acquainted with. I hadn't even touched with a saddle blanket any of that bunch that wrecked the Fort Worth and Denver train. I felt of my sore rib and my busted foot and thought about Utah's glassy eyes; then I thought about Red Paden's short legs. A sweet kind of dead certainty came over me, like you're looking down somebody's throat in a game of stud.

I figured I could use the money, so I went around in the bunkhouse announcing, "That dude won't last ten days on this place." Some of the boys had been impressed with the new pro rider. Sid Wilcox, who was not known as being overly bright, took me up, and we each put up an IOU for thirty dollars with Snuffy Detweiler on the question: Would the man last ten days?

Actually, the worst thing about Red Paden was that he was not cocky and smart aleck. One like that you can pin down and everybody can gang up on him. You know what you're dealing with. You can hate him with pleasure and wait, knowing that Providence is bound to provide his come-uppance. But this fellow didn't brag a lick; he had Willie Caudle to do all his bragging for him. And could he help it if the bunkhouse was overflowing and he got a bed somewhere in the bowels of the Old House? What a disgusting turn of events!

My only consolation was that I would make sixty dollars for this hard month of horse taming and roundup, my pay and Sid Wilcox's.

The next morning Amos Lockhart sent Utah over to the sheds where they were repairing and tightening up the three chuck wagons, and took Red Paden, me, Long Joe, and Billy Tuttle down to the picket corral in a buck-board, carrying our saddles and a bag of gear Paden had. Amos said, "Mr. Paden, you can give each one of these horses a saddle or two, and when you think one is in fair shape, the boys will put him out in the remuda. Bud Blankenship here has been working these horses; he can tell you as much as anybody can about them. If you need any more help or anything send Billy or Joe here after me." He left.

Someone had put my horse Sleeper in with the broncs by mistake. I'd figured on going up to the stables and leading Blackie down if I needed him, but I didn't intend to give Paden the satisfaction of breaking Sleeper when I'd ridden him all winter. I said to Paden, "I'll catch out one to use for a hazing horse if you don't mind." I happened to catch Sleeper.

When I had him saddled, Paden asked, "You want me to ride him first?"

"No, I'll try him," I said. I gave a nice riding demonstration; then Sleeper calmed down. It didn't help my rib and foot but did wonders for my feelings.

By the time I dismounted, Billy Tuttle had roped Dodger. Whether he did it on purpose or not, who knows? If you haven't ridden a tricky bronc in the past few days, you forget how sharp you have to be and how quick he can turn. You need to get ready for Dodger.

While Paden was saddling him, he asked me, "How's this one?"

"He pitches," I said. "Name's Dodger. He won't jar you, but he's quick."

"Might make a good cutting horse if he was trained," Paden said. His saddle was full stamped and fancy with silver-plated conchos. He had on spurs and also had a quirt hanging on his wrist.

I get on Sleeper and they help Paden mount Dodger. When they let him go he starts fast, and I haze him in the direction of the creek. He pitches corkscrews, switches ends, and ties knots in the air, and Paden stays on him like he's pasted on, cutting that bronc's bony rump with the quirt at every jump. He's ready for all of Dodger's tricks. I figure he must have suspected that his first horse would be a dilly. The next thing I know Paden has taken charge of Dodger. He's jerking him this way and that and whipping him, finally gets him to running. But before he can get lined out too fast, Paden turns him on a dime. Back and forth across the flat they charge like they're playing polo. Dodger is mad as a wet hen but he's doing exactly what he's told.

Paden pulls him up at the gate of the corral in a cloud of dust and climbs down. He says, in a friendly voice but businesslike, "I believe Dodger is about ready to go into the remuda. Let's tie him to the fence and I'll give him one more ride after a while."

He rides that swirling fool, Whirlwind, that broke my rib, and then he rides Pepper. On each of them he looks like he's a part of the horse, if you can imagine a part of a horse with a black silk shirt on.

Then he says, "Let's give Dodger one more little workout."

When Dodger is bridled and saddled and the rope taken off his neck, Paden says, "Step back a little, boys, and let's check to see if a cowhand could mount him without any help." Dodger has his ears keened back and he's walling his eyes. This horse has got a mind and a memory. Paden pulls the left rein up so short Dodger is looking at his own tail, and before the horse can make half a turn, he is stepping into the saddle.

I run limping around the wing to where Sleeper is tied and scramble into the saddle, but he starts shying and acting up. Meanwhile Dodger is bucking straight for the rocky ground; I figure it's not a matter of conniving as much as it is wanting to stay away from that grassy flat where he was whipped back and forth.

Paden is flailing his quirt. Dodger is not tired, but plenty scared and sore. He's bowing his back like a barrel hoop and hitting the ground stiff, teaching himself new stuff. One iron-shod hoof comes down on a flat sandstone outcrop and slips. Dodger goes halfway down. Paden grabs for the horn. Dodger jumps and turns and hits hard. Paden is off balance. Then Dodger snorts and cracks his back muscles and sails Paden ten feet high.

The horse is halfway to the Old House trying to pitch off his saddle before I catch him.

When I come back Paden is standing up, sopping with a bandanna at the side of his neck where he peeled off a few inches of hide on a rock. His hat is mashed. His shirt is dirty. I try not to take too much satisfaction in the sight, but Red Paden looks a lot more human.

I took Dodger down past the wing and Paden mounted him again. He rode him that time, and wore him down, but put him back in the corral without saying any more about his being tame enough to put in the remuda. After that we caught out Whirlwind the second time. No telling whether Paden was losing part of his confidence or getting tired or what, but he got a strap out of his warbag and put it on his right stirrup; then when he got the saddle cinched down, he brought the strap under and tied the stirrups together. He couldn't do much spurring in that getup, but he made up for it swinging his quirt. It looked to me like you got jolted worse too, with your feet tied down that way, and I wondered if maybe Paden got the muscles in his jaws from clamping his teeth tight to keep from biting his tongue. But, anyway, he didn't get thrown again that day.

The only thing that happened to him was that Pepper kicked him. It wasn't his fault. Pepper just hauled off and kicked him. He was walking past with his rope in his hand and his eye on another horse. Suddenly, *swish, wham!* It hit him in the hand he was holding the loop with and in the side, knocking him off his feet into the litter and horse apples. I don't believe he even saw which horse did it.

He got up and brushed off and acted like it didn't surprise him or bother him much, but he looked at his right thumb. Several times I noticed him feeling of his thumb, about like a person gently mashing a peach to see if it's ripe.

The next day Billy Tuttle and another hand took off in a

freight wagon with a six-mule team to haul enough grub and supplies to stock the chuck wagons. To take Billy's place at the picket corral, Amos Lockhart sent down Willie Caudle.

Red Paden showed up with a bandage on his thumb and a stick about the size of a pencil bound into it to keep it straight and still. Like they say, it stuck out like a sore thumb. The skinned place on his neck had scabbed over and looked ready to heal if nothing bothered it. Since I was still nursing my rib and foot, I felt kindly toward him, but before the morning was an hour old I began to lose the feeling because of the way Long Joe would cheer him and the way Willie Caudle would say Mr. Paden this . . . Mr. Paden that. . . . Once halfway to the creek Paden dropped his quirt and Willie ran after it like a trained pup. I was thinking, No wonder he can stick on these horses; with his stirrups fastened together he's practically tied on.

When he saddled up the big paint Goodfellow, you could guess the horse was too scared to pitch much. Paden didn't ask anything about him and I didn't say. I actually didn't keep quiet out of meanness, but because it sounds silly to talk about a horse running away with a grown man.

Goodfellow sprinted sideways about fifty yards, then lined out like a catamount was after him. I tried to follow on Sleeper and felt like I was standing still. Paden couldn't seem to understand; when he would try to turn Goodfellow, he would nearly lose his seat. You get that horse in a runaway mood and he's got no connection between his head and his feet. I came up on a rise and saw them pounding across the draw ahead. Paden was swinging his quirt. Goodfellow was looking south and running west.

They plowed into a brushy mesquite tree and came out the other side. Paden's hat was knocked back on his shoulders, hanging by its chinstrap. They circled two miles out ahead of me and came back still running. Paden was cutting him on the rump now, making him go. I saw that his black silk shirt had a big rip in the back.

When I got up to the picket corral Paden had Good-fellow trotting around almost like a cow horse. Then I saw another small item of damage. Paden had a red welt across his forehead. Well, I thought, I may be forced to admit he can ride, but he may admit he's got into a regular fandango of horses before he's through. A while before dinner he got a needle and thread out of his warbag, took his shirt off, and commenced to sew up the rip while the rest of us took seven horses to the remuda and brought back seven. One we brought was Hong Kong, an ugly devil, with a head as big as a side of bacon.

In the middle of the afternoon, the four of us stood inside the picket corral gate, resting a minute, looking at the horses. Red Paden said, "That yellow horse looks a little wild."

"That's Hong Kong," I said. "He's got a reputation."

I'd never seen him saddled but he had been pointed out to me a couple of times. The word had gone around that the last hand who drew him in his string had never stayed on him and had got in the habit of skipping him.

"What does he do?" Paden asked.

I said, "I don't know, but he's got a bad name."

"Let's give him a whirl," he says.

Some horses are spoiled and conniving and wise. We find out that Hong Kong is crazy. If he has a brain, all he's got in it is the idea that he damned sure won't go along with our plans. He snaps Long Joe's lariat. He grunts and kicks and coughs and slews around. He falls down and we pile on his neck and put on a hackamore.

Out by the wing, with two men on his head, with a hind foot tied up, a leather blind hung over his eyes, he is saddled by Paden. The rambunctious fool is jerking and staggering and snorting like he's trying to say, "No! No! No!"

Paden is cool and businesslike, taking his time. He steps smartly up, gets set, and says, "Let him loose, boys."

When his hind foot goes free and the blind comes off, Hong Kong takes two wild jumps. Then it seems like it comes home to him that he really does have that weight tied on his back that he can't stand. He bawls like a wounded jackass and rares up. I'm sitting there on Sleeper, who is pussyfooting around, worked up by the noise. Hong Kong comes straight at us, his mouth wide open and his lips drawn back, his yellow teeth shining. He snaps twice like he's going to eat us alive. His teeth hit my knee and Sleeper's shoulder, but by now Sleeper has enough sense to get out of there.

Hong Kong whirls, and it must be that he closes his eyes, because he pitches straight into the picket corral fence. He hits it with both front feet, squawling like a ruptured foghorn. He's fighting the fence and bucking at the same time. You'd think a mad Jersey bull couldn't get through that fence, but two posts break, the rawhide ties come loose, posts bend over and spread out. Through they go.

It seems like Hong Kong opens his eyes and sees he's back inside and doesn't like it any better in there than outside. He rares up and circles and sees the hole in the fence. He heads for it.

Paden has done all right up to now, but the jagged end of a post is pointing into the corral like a spear, ready to hang his leg. He gets out of one tied stirrup and swings his leg up just in time. Hong Kong comes out through the hole in one jump. Paden has his free leg along the bronc's back and is floundering over the brute's shoulders to keep his balance. He's grabbing all the saddle he can get.

Hong Kong is going away fast and furious. It seems like he remembers that bawling and fighting won't get a man off your back. He starts pitching seriously, long twisting leaps, scrambled up with short hops that jar grunts out of his chest. Paden can't get his place in the saddle.

There's a time to get off a horse. If he won't let you get set, the time is right now. Paden is making a mistake trying to ride it out instead of starting over. I see both of his feet in the air and his shoulder on that yellow devil's withers. He's sliding downward and I think that's it. But bad luck hits him. One side pocket on his California pants slips down neatly over the saddle horn. Hong Kong is exploding the dust out of the ground with his hoofs. Paden is hanging by his pants, upside down.

Of course he's lost his reins. I unlimber my rope, but Sleeper doesn't want me to build a loop. In fact, he's nervous as hell about even going in the direction of that dirty yellow horse.

Hong Kong's left knee is pounding Paden in the side of the head. It must be that the chinstrap on his hat loosens, because the next thing I know that fool bronc's got a big hoof inside the hat. Fortunately, the chinstrap breaks. Two jumps later Paden's California pants rip out and he drops. Hong Kong goes on pitching with the hat on one front foot.

Paden goes to the ground like a load of wet laundry. I head for him instead of the horse, because it looks like he needs help, but he begins to pull himself together and gets to where he looks more like a human being than a loose pile. By the time I hit the ground, he's halfway sitting up, with that bandaged thumb sticking out. He makes small movements, testing to see if everything still works, and looks around him as if he doesn't remember seeing this part of the world before.

I don't want to help him any more than he needs, because he might be easy to insult right now. I ask, "You all right?"

He says, "Yep," and grins, but has a puzzled look around his eyes. The scab has been knocked off and the place on his neck has got dirt in it.

Long Joe and Willie are coming on the run, so I go after the bronc. Hong Kong is down on the ground a quarter mile away, trying to roll, but he can't get over the hump of the saddle. Every time he flings his feet in the air, the saddle skids on the ground, and it doesn't do Red Paden's full-stamped saddle any good. When I ride up, Hong Kong flounders to his feet and runs.

About that time I heard Long Joe yelling to beat the band. The broncs had found Hong Kong's new gate in the picket corral. That concentration of ornery horseflesh was spilling out one by one. I kicked Sleeper into a run and went back but lost the race. Long Joe had a saddled mount tied at the end of the wing, but he was too late too. They all took off. We got two ropes and laced them in to patch the fence, opened the gate, and rode after our hookey players. Red Paden was wandering back up toward the picket corral, and Willie Caudle was down there looking for Paden's hat.

With the help of the two horse wranglers, Long Joe and I penned our horses again before sundown. Hong Kong was with them, naked as the day he was born. Me and Long Joe went to supper. Willie and Paden got in after dark with his saddle, the girt busted.

As the old saying goes, If at first you don't succeed, try, try again. The following day Paden had his britches sewed up and his hat creased back and his saddle fixed, and he rode Hong Kong. We took that booger away down in the open and got two hazing horses around him. He snorted and bawled while he pitched, but Paden worked him down.

That day we brought in some of the new horses. Most of them didn't have a name and wouldn't have till some cowhand got a bright idea, but the dirty brown one that had caused Amos Lockhart's record book to catch on fire had already got the name of Rusty. He and all the other members of the train-wrecking squad were now scattered and mixed with the other bands of horses so that you couldn't tell them except by their fresh brands. Rusty turned out to be rough to handle, saddle, and mount, but no great shakes as a bucker. He would go up and down, front and rear, like a kid's rocking horse. I don't guess Paden could see it, sitting on top of him, but Rusty's neck action looked strange, like he had a hinge in his neck. Paden had unlimbered his quirt, then jerked back quick on the reins. *Whack!* Rusty's head swung back and socked him in the nose.

I rode up closer to him in case he needed help. His nose looked flat as a pancake and blood ran down on his mouth and chin. It looked bad, but he stayed in the saddle and rode him down. I figured the nose wasn't as bad as it looked, or else Paden had more pride than he had sense. When he finally got down, his nose was red as a beet, his shirt front was bloody, and he was blowing through his mouth. Willie Caudle swabbed him off some, but he wouldn't let anybody touch his nose. He went on riding.

On Thursday Cotton-Eye Joe tried to rare up and fall back on Paden. He got free and pushed clear just in time, but he was down where the ground breaks away near the creek. He stumbled and fell and rolled into a mess of catclaw cactus. Little leaves of cactus stuck all over his back. Willie dismounted and began to pull them out while Paden stood real stiff and still. I caught Cotton-Eye Joe. Paden had got to where he didn't look nor act the same as he did at first. Seemed like he didn't stand like a statue, but more like a man getting ready to duck. He would still grin and act businesslike and say, "Well, let's give him a whirl," but while he grinned his eyes would be darting around at those J's horses.

On Friday afternoon a strange thing happens. I've ridden a couple of broncs, just enough to get my rib and foot throbbing again. Long Joe and Willie Caudle are both horseback. We catch Whirlwind and Paden gets on him. I lean against the wing fence and watch.

There's our pro rider's splinted thumb cocked out and his hat pulled down to his ears, dried blood on his neck. His nose looks like a rotten apple. Clothes all torn and sewed up and dirty. The parts of him you can see banged up, and God alone knows what kind of bruises and wounds he's got that's covered. This horse is going wild and high, and Red Paden is staying with him. He's not exactly relaxed; in fact, he looks desperate with his hat pulled down that way. But Whirlwind is giving all he's got and Red Paden is staying up there and swinging that quirt. I hear somebody yelling, "Ride him, Red! Give him hell! Ride him! You've got him, Red! Stick on there, boy!" It's me yelling. Considering that I've got a hard-earned month's wages put up against him, it's clear that I'm a bigger fool than Long Joe Christian.

The following Monday we started spring roundup. The Old Man had been able to foretell a month earlier that we would be ready the second week in April and that we would start on time. Like a wise man said, Wherever Mc-

Gregor sits, there's the head of the table. When the Old Man said we were ready, we saw that we were ready. Amos Lockhart agreed with him, and you didn't hear any of the hands dispute the fact, though Stubby did laugh. But even though all our horse strings were ready for spring round-up, they sent Red Paden along with wagon number one, which was Lockhart's wagon. I found myself on the same crew, ten men in all, not counting three reps from other outfits.

We pushed away out on the headwaters of Paradise Creek to get ready for our first gather on Tuesday. We camped on flat prairie ground. That morning it was damp and foggy. Soon as it got light enough where you could tell one horse from another, we began to saddle and mount up. Horses went pitching off in every direction in that fog. Amos Lockhart loped around and tried to keep up with it and see what was happening. He would say to some hand getting up off the ground, "Better pull your rig off that horse and catch another one. Leave him for Red Paden. We got to move out." As sure as a rider went down the second time, Amos would make him leave the horse for Paden, and he was supposed to give the bad one a good working that day.

Willie Caudle had drawn the job of horse wrangler. He was the only help Paden had. I can use my imagination about the fun they experienced trying to tame down those broncs out there on the bare prairie.

We brought in about four hundred head of grown stuff and started branding before dinner. Then we left a guard on the herd and came in to eat. Paden arrived limping at the wagon, with caked mud on his side. Caesar had got him down in a mudhole that morning, and Pepper had kicked him.

It went the same all week, with a rodeo around the wagon

every morning just before the sun came up. Some of the bad ones would be ridden out, salty and mean, to hunt cows, but the worst half dozen would be left for Paden. On Friday we brought in a small bunch and we were going to move camp a good distance, so we went on and worked them and came to the camp in the middle of the afternoon for a late dinner. Everybody was squatting around eating, using every little patch of shade. Amos Lockhart charged up with his horse in a lather and yelled at Billy Tuttle, "Hitch up the hoodlum wagon, Billy, and come help get Red Paden!"

They hauled Paden in an hour later. Hong Kong had knocked him off against a tree, then had bucked on top of him. His right leg was busted in two places, just above and below the knee. He looked white as a ghost. The scabs and scars and his swelled nose looked peculiar with all the blood gone out of his face. His shirt and hat were torn and one boot was missing.

They figured to take him to the doctor at Seymour, but it would be a rough trip in the hoodlum wagon, and he had to have a splint on his leg. We had a spare doubletree, which we took the iron off of and split to make two splints. Somebody tore up some canvas for bandages.

Amos Lockhart got into an argument with the cook about whiskey. He said, "Bring that bottle of whiskey you've got hid in the wagon."

The man said, "Why, Mr. Lockhart, I don't have no bottle. You know it's against J's rules."

"I know damned well you have," Amos said. "Get it out here!"

"Why, Mr. Lockhart, you know I wouldn't carry no whiskey on Jackson land."

"Dammit, man, can't you see we've got to have it? Dig it out, right now!"

Amos had a way of winning arguments with the employees. He made the cook bring the bottle and give Paden a long pull. Paden gripped the bottle in his lap and came out with a slow sigh, like he'd been waiting a year for a drink.

About six of us grabbed hold of him and stretched him out straight while the rest got the splints on his leg and bound them tight. We packed him into the little wagon with him leaning back on his warbag and soogans wadded around him. He sat there cradling the bottle, gazing at the outfit. He looked older, but his eyes weren't darting around now.

I can't say I was happy and I can't say I was sad, but I'd sure been counting the days. It hadn't been ten days since he started on the J's. It had been twelve. I thought, If Hong Kong aimed to do that to him, why in the name of all that's holy didn't he do it two days sooner?

Billy Tuttle was getting ready to go and getting orders on where to rejoin the roundup. Paden sat there and gazed. I walked up to him and shook hands and said, "Good luck, Mr. Paden." It was like shaking hands with a half sack of Bull Durham.

A pitiful grin sputtered across his face and he said, "I should wish you fellows good luck."

After that we continued to have our riding show each morning before sunup. Broncs went popping around like popcorn in every direction. The winning cowhands only had to saddle one horse. The winning horses got to lounge around in the remuda all day. Hong Kong only put in two days of work, but I worked Dodger every time in his turn except once; I would have worked him that day, but Amos Lockhart caught me lying on the ground and ordered me to catch another horse.

We finished roundup in four weeks. The first order of business back at headquarters was payday. Amos Lockhart set up shop on the long mess table in the Old House with his records and his iron-bound box full of money. I drew mine and turned around. There stood that dumb grinning Sid Wilcox with his hand out. I gave him his filthy lucre. He didn't make any smart remarks; therefore I didn't paste him in the mouth. I didn't mind so much not making any money in the last month, but I had cut up a good pair of boots in the process.

They wanted me to stay on, but the wages for a regular hand had to be cut to twenty-four dollars, because the price of beef was dropping. I told Amos I had to be drifting.

I've thought about that spring on the J's off and on since that time. The funny thing is that we never did break the horses, but we went on and made the roundup anyway. And that old goat with the hundred-dollar suits and the red flannel rag around his neck went right on sacking up the money. Sometimes I think the horses won the battles but lost the war. Then the "war" idea makes me ask: Who was on each side? How did we line up, the Old Man and Amos Lockhart, the cows, those broncs, and us cowhands? Seems like the Old Man and Amos and the cows had a business going and that business went right on; the horses and men were tools, used like wire nippers or a lariat rope.

But who can say? You don't forget an outfit like that. You mull it over, and once this idea came sneaking up to me: Maybe it was the other way around. Maybe us broncs and us cowhands had a game going and we just used the J's outfit to furnish us a place and an excuse.

You have to be camping way out on the prairie alone to think a thought like that.

Chapter 9
Home

IN THE TOWN OF MOBEETIE I bought me a young gelding named Dusty for a hundred and forty dollars. He was a four-year-old, a kind of dirty sorrel, but his shape and smooth single-foot gait and alertness sold me. I knew he would make a real cow horse because he wanted to learn and he had the get up and get. He was not spooky, but he wanted any back girt left a little loose and wanted boot heels and spurs kept out of his flanks; that seemed reasonable to me. We got along O.K.

That only left me about two hundred dollars. The thousand I had promised myself to save before I went home to southern Missouri had been cut down in my mind to five hundred. Sometimes I wondered if five hundred was reasonable. A rolling stone gathers no moss, they say.

I went to work for an outfit south of Pueblo, Colorado, on the Huerfano River in the summer of '88. At first I was a line rider, but after the work of one roundup the boss took a liking to me and put me in charge of a crew in the southern part of their range not far from the little mountain town of Walsenburg. I only had five men working for me, but I drew fifty a month and about all the bossing duties I had was to buy supplies and report in once a month up north; of course I tried to make a hand too.

One day a couple of the fellows came back to camp talking about a new place in Walsenburg called the Blue Saloon run by a woman named Lillian. It rang a bell in my mind. I didn't figure it could possibly be the same woman, but the first day I could get loose I rode into town by myself.

The joint was on the north road. You couldn't miss it because, though it was only a plank building with a false front, it was painted blue. There were no horses tied in front, but I saw a man out in back chopping wood. I tied Dusty and went in. Behind the bar stood a woman swabbing around with a cloth. She turned around.

It was Weeping Lil, big as life, not changed one whit.

She smiled real big and said, "Come right in, cowboy. What can I do for you?"

The bar, like the tables in the room, was pine lumber painted blue. I walked up to it and said, "Hello, Lil," without blinking an eye.

She quit smiling. The crow's tracks around her eyes, the peroxide-blond hair, the black eyebrows, seemed exactly the way I remembered. "Do I know you?" she asked.

"I don't know," I said, "but I sure know you."

"What do you want?"

"I want my eighty dollars."

She turned around and began dabbing with the cloth, evidently taking some time to think. She said, "Listen . . . that deal in Tombstone . . . I can explain. I had to leave town for reasons I couldn't help. I didn't get your money or your horse either." She was glancing at me and trying to act unconcerned.

I said, "I've never been in Tombstone, Lil."

"Carson City? Look, I can explain. . . . You'll die laughing when you hear what happened."

"I've never been in Carson City," I said, "and I don't mean to laugh any more at all till I get the eighty dollars I loaned you."

"Have you got an IOU signed by me?"

"I won't need one."

She turned straight toward me, miffed, but not sure of herself. "Who do you think you are, mister? Coming in here this way! I never saw you in my life! Look, have a drink and go on about your business."

It was a kind of revelation to me that she didn't recognize me, but I believed her. I did not feel at all like that kid she took that day in Dodge.

"Come on, have a drink before you leave," she said. "What'll it be?"

"Make it light on yourself," I said.

"I'll treat you to some private stock," she said. "A gent don't ordinarily get any of this unless he wears a heavy gold watch chain." She was pulling something out from under the bar.

I said, "Forget that. Give me a little of that bourbon there." I'd heard of special bottles with stuff in them that would knock you cold as a cucumber.

She gave me a big drink and a glass of warm water. "For old times' sake," she said.

I drank some and said, "You know where you business people make a mistake, Lil? Here you've got this fine new place. But you've put in too much glass stuff. Take that big mirror behind you. You line your bottles up in front of it and you make it look like you've got twice as much stock, but look at all that glass. It breaks too easy. Now, those two pictures of naked women there on the wall.

Nice. Artistic. But covered with glass. Then look at the window lights over there, and those fancy lamps hanging down. Glass. Lil, you get a bunch of rowdy cowhands in here and they could put you out of business with one brawl."

She said, "I've got a bouncer named George, and he's handy at taking care of things like that."

"That clown out back chopping wood?"

She didn't answer.

"Are you married to this George?"

"That's none of your business."

"Well, I tell you what, Lil; you call George in if you want to. I'll politely discuss your past with him. Or if he wants to get nasty I'll beat the hell out of him. Either one."

She made no move to call anybody. Maybe she was thinking about the fact that some bouncers look pretty good because all they tangle with is drunks. She said, "I'm a respectable woman. I run a respectable place of business."

Her remark didn't seem to the point, so I didn't take up the question. I said, "To come back to what we were talking about: all this glass and only one bouncer. Lil, I'm the boss of a crew of cowhands now. I'm sorry to tell you how rowdy they are. It's a shame. No responsibility. I'm afraid they would just make blue toothpicks out of this new place of yours."

"I run a respectable place of business," she said. "I've talked to the sheriff and to the justice of the peace. They know me. They know I run a respectable place of business."

"But do they know everything you've done in the past?" I was riding that idea of her past because it was certain she remembered plenty of shady deals and couldn't be sure what I might know. "As for people around town here,"

I said, "sheriffs and everybody, I buy supplies and grub and things here. To get down to brass tacks, if they run somebody out of town, I don't think it will be the ranching interests."

She was rubbing hard on the bar with her rag and trying to think of something. All she thought of was this: "I'm a respectable woman! I'm trying to . . . I'm a respectable woman now!"

It seemed like time to play my aces. I said, "Lil, you're taking it too hard. You win some and you lose some. Right? It's actually simple. I mean to have my eighty dollars, and it's no use for you to butt your head against a brick wall. But you don't have to. We were friends so I loaned you eighty dollars. We don't worry about you being respectable and make threats and all that. Your friend loaned you eighty dollars, so you finally found him and paid it back. It's really simple."

It seemed as if she liked what I had said. She bit her lip a minute, then said, "Actually, I don't remember you. I really don't."

"Dodge City."

"Dodge? I haven't been around there in eight or ten years."

"You worked in a place called the Blue Palace. One night there was a fire. After that you were sitting on the side steps of Josephine's Rooming House and I loaned you eighty dollars and you left town."

"No! Oh, no!" She stared at me like I was a ghost, but it was humorous too. "No! surely not! Blank . . . Charley? Mr. Charles Blankenship! General Delivery, Dodge City, Kansas! Oh, no! Of all the men, of all the suckers, you're the only one! Oh, no, Charley!"

The way she was acting and what she said made no

sense to me, but something had happened. From the time I'd walked up to her without blinking and her big smile had faded I'd been sitting in the saddle looking down at her; now it was some question where I was sitting.

She was laughing so hard that tears came out and streaked the shadow painted around her eyes. She put her face in her hands and put her head down on the bar. Between other sounds she said, "I sent . . . the money . . . back to you! Mr. Charles Blankenship . . . Dodge City . . . Kansas!"

She poured herself a stiff drink, downed some, then half-way choked. "You caught on too fast and didn't go to the post office!"

She was having so much fun I couldn't help laughing myself.

"I knew this woman that ran this house in Sioux Falls," she said. "I went up there. After I got to thinking and sent it, I told another girl. She couldn't keep a secret. I was the laughing stock of the whole street!" She went into a gale of laughter, then said, "What do they do with letters if nobody calls for them?"

"Somebody opens them and puts the money in his pocket," I said.

"Oh, no! Charley, you're the only one I ever let off the hook! The girls said I was silly, but I said it was too easy. I said you'd call at the post office every day till the money came!"

I poured myself a drink and told her about the marshal hitting me on the head and the judge lecturing me. We killed the first bottle and started on another. She loved my imitation of the judge in Dodge City. A dumb-looking fellow stuck his head in the door— I suppose it was George —and she told him we were old friends and gave him some orders about mopping the floor.

I told Lil she was all right. If ever any cowhands or anybody else gave her any trouble, call on me, or if they said she wasn't respectable. She didn't want me to go; we ought to have more drinks for old times' sake, but I had to go.

Dusty was ready. He was the kind of horse that had rather work hard than stand tied any length of time. After a couple of miles I pulled him down to a walk; then I stopped him and got off. I sat down under a tree, thinking deep thoughts. It was right at sunset.

Dusty jerked lightly at the reins and looked at me. I said, "Horse, do you think that woman did it to me again?"

He smelled of my boot and you could tell he wanted to go on, get the saddle and bridle off, cavort with the remuda, graze a little. He was right, but it took me a while to see it. You ought to settle things like that in your mind and leave them be. I just settled it by saying she really sent the money back, and if she was so sharp and quick and bright that she could fool me about it now, then she deserved the eighty dollars. I'd seen a few floozies in my day and I still think I settled it right. I mounted Dusty and laughed some more and we went on back to camp.

I remember those days in '88 and '89 not so much on account of the work I did or the places, but because of my feelings and thoughts. I thought about Johnny Fox. He might be foolish in ways that I wasn't, but at least he had a wife and kids and big hopes to go on. I thought about home and about hunting for my brother Buck. You grow above those things and see them in a different light, but they don't go away. I'd quit looking at the pieces of turquoise jewelry I was saving for Ma. I just left alone the clothes the thing was wrapped in, but sometimes the thought came out of nowhere: What if she got sick and I wouldn't even know it? I even went to looking for Buck again, when I would come into a joint in town where cowhands gathered or run into a strange cattle outfit. I had him pegged in a different way, but I really wanted to run into him.

I won't tell the name of the outfit I was working for south of Pueblo because it is beside the point. It happened to be the only place I was ever fired from. The free range was gone. All the land was under title, but they didn't have it fenced and you still had cattle scattered around trespassing. I got the suggestion from the owner that I should spray a few .44 slugs at the men of a certain neighbor ranch whenever they came on our land. Me and the owner had the matter out, face to face, and he fired me. That was O.K. I was earning all I made just working cattle, and I figured anybody that would take thirty-a-month cowhands for enemies on account of an owners' fuss was not thinking straight.

I moved north and worked one winter for the Tipton-Hall Livestock Company in western Nebraska. We had a youngster in that bunch that we called "Kid." We were sitting around a campfire one cold night shooting the bull and talking about cold winters. I mentioned that it gets cold even in the Globe country of Arizona and talked about cutting ice holes for cows to drink along the Powder in Wyoming. After a while Kid asked me, "Mr. Blankenship, where did you get your start?"

There was a question! A start? Mister?

I could have put him down and had some reason to do it, because a couple of hands sitting there had worked cattle a lot longer than me, but I told him that I had got on as a wrangler with a trail herd to Dodge in 1880. That didn't mean much to me or the others, but I could feel what it meant to Kid. He was a gangling boy, maybe sixteen, with fuzz on his face that would turn into beard in a couple of years. He had been probably six years old in '80.

You can't follow out every train of thought and feeling. I suppose having Kid around and sensing his idea of me made me think about the passage of time. I remember looking in a shaving mirror nailed up over a washstand to see if I had any gray hairs, which I didn't of course.

In the early summer of 1890 we drove a herd of two-year-old Tipton-Hall steers south and put them on the train to move them to a feed lot the company had in eastern Kansas. Another hand and I and a boss that was going to take charge of the feeding operation rode the cars to take care of the steers. We unloaded in Topeka and drove two days south to the company's pens. The boss wanted me to stay on there, but I drew my time and quit the outfit.

I remember that morning riding Dusty southeast. I won't say I was arguing with myself and I won't say I wasn't, but if I was the talk went sort of like this:

Charley, why is your horse going this direction?

I don't know.

Did you turn him this way?

Hard to say.

If he keeps on going this direction he'll wind up in southern Missouri.

I reckon he will.

What would he want in southern Missouri?

Maybe he knows it's good country.

Don't lie. You're going home.

Yes, I reckon I am.

What ever happened to that flashy outfit and that thousand dollars?

This outfit's nothing to be ashamed of. It's all I need to make a hand on any ranch in the country.

Well, the thousand dollars then?

I cut that down to five hundred. Remember?

Well?

All right, I've got nearly four hundred.

Man, you're rich.

I don't care. I'm going home. I'm really going home. It seems like a hundred years. I'm really going home.

In the town of Springfield I went to a store where they sold fancy gewgaws of all kinds, jewelry and painted lamps and china and vases and stationery and stuff. What I wanted was some kind of good paper or something to wrap up Ma's silver bracelet with the turquoise sets, because I didn't want to just leave it wrapped up in a pair of socks. The man had a tiny cedar chest with brass hinges. I bought it and also a small white silk handkerchief with flowers in the corner. Then I wrapped the bracelet in the handkerchief and put it in the cedar chest, where it seemed to fit real good.

On that ride to Virginia County it came to me that the difference between a long time and a short time is not weeks and months and years but what you see and do and what it does to you. It had been a hundred years in a way. I wondered if I had turned out anything like my Uncle Milt; the idea didn't bother me much. Nothing was bothering me much. A kind of refrain seemed to hang over my head as I rode along: I'm going home; I'm going home.

I rode through Sulphur Junction in the middle of the afternoon and fifteen minutes later tied Dusty to a picket fence I knew well. An old woman was piddling around in the flower bed beside the porch, standing flatfooted, bending at the hips like she always did when she was working vegetables or flowers. She had on a gingham dress and sunbonnet. It looked like she had got smaller.

I said, "Ma?"

She jerked straight up, stared at me, and yelled, "Peter!"

Reader, I'm going to spring a surprise on you in a minute, maybe two surprises. I apologize, but I'm only telling it the way it happened to me. When my ma yelled "Peter," I figured he was down around the barn somewhere and she wanted him to come and see. Actually, it was a thing that had to do with the way mothers are, which I will explain shortly.

It seemed like the picket fence had shrunk so much that I could practically step over it, but I went through the gate and hugged my ma. She felt little and bony; also, I am not ashamed to say, precious.

Pa came striding out of the house and met us on the porch. He grabbed my hand and went to shaking it like he had the job of pumping a barrel of water, all the time grinning like a possum. He still looked strong, but shorter and more humped in the shoulders.

In a minute we were standing in the front room and I said, "Have you all heard from Buck lately? I've been wondering whereabouts he is."

They had no idea what I was talking about. I said, "Ed. I mean Ed. Do you all know where he's at?"

Pa said, "Law! Charles, Ed's been working the old Jones place up on the river for four years. We see them every week or so. Ed's got two younguns."

That set me back on my boot heels. In a minute I asked, "Whereabouts is Pete? Is he down at the barn or where?"

It looked like Ma was trying not to pucker up and cry. Pa said, "Law, son, Pete's gone out west to hunt you. We ain't seen him in five years. We get a letter from him once in a while. He says he's doing right well."

There's the reason Ma yelled "Peter!" A mother has got one baby, the last one she had. I guess she thinks the same of all her kids, but if you surprise her, she's really only got one baby. Maybe, too, brothers are alike in the way they stand or hold their shoulders or something.

They brought a letter from Pete, mailed in Deadwood, South Dakota. He claimed he was only passing through. He'd been working as a cowhand and was doing real good and was meeting honest and upright people wherever he went. Now he was headed for Oregon, because he figured Duke might be out there. If he didn't find Duke there, he might try Arizona. Pete wrote that he had got a new nickname—Ace—that some of his friends called him. He hoped everybody was getting along all right at home.

To perk my ma up I told her I had a present for her and went out and got my warbag. It wasn't until I started pawing through it on the front-room floor that I thought about a present for Pa, and I gave him a pair of soft cowhide gloves I'd bought in Ogallala and never worn. I handed Ma the tiny cedar chest and whispered to Pa that it had something inside. We grinned and winked at each other while Ma exclaimed over the sweet present of a little cedar chest for several minutes before she opened it and found the real present inside.

That evening she stuffed me with fried ham and squash and cornbread and fresh radishes and green onions and goodness knows what all, enough for seven men.

That night I went to bed on one of my ma's duck-down mattresses, covered with one of the patchwork quilts she made. It was probably the best bed I'd touched in ten years, but I didn't go to sleep for a long time. That Pete! Ace! Running around out there thinking he was looking for me. Maybe the young whippersnapper was looking for himself, or maybe he was looking for a dream. I wondered where he was sleeping this night, in a bunkhouse, under a wagon, on a big flat rock. Wherever, I wished him well. I thought, I just hope he doesn't run into anybody like Weeping Lil or Bo Smith or Mr. Crankshaw. But why hope that? He would run into some like that sure as God made little apples. It takes all kinds of people to make a world, they say. It struck me, lying there, that I would not give back a single bruise I got wandering around in the West.

I already knew that I was going back. Coming home for a visit was the best thing I'd done in a long time, but the land out there was too big, too full of possibilities and opportunities, too full of interesting people, to turn my back on. Besides that, I was too good a cowhand to give up the business.

Reader, I've come to the end of the part of my life I wanted to tell you about. They say every story ought to have a moral or some good to be learned from it. Maybe so, maybe not. All I can think of is this: Human critters have a strange mingling in them, of sunshine and shadow, of goodness and meanness, of sense and nonsense. They are a mystery, but they are all we've got. Do not harden your heart, nor get too set in your mind about them.